D0669552

BEHIND CLOSED DOORS

Michael Donovan was born in Yorkshire and now lives in Cumbria. A consultant engineer by profession, his first novel *Behind Closed Doors* won the 2012 Northern Crime competition.

By the same author

Praise for
BEHIND CLOSED DOORS

'At a time when there seems more competition than ever in the crime-writing genre, Donovan's debut novel is a real winner...'
Lytham St Annes Express

'... a wonderful debut novel in a hugely competitive market ... an enthralling novel ... deliciously complex ... make(s) the readers hair stand on end. Donovan ... succeeds in breathing life into a host of warm, witty and realistic characters.'
Cuckoo Review

'Eddie Flynn is part Philip Marlowe, part Eddie Gumshoe, a likeable wisecracking guy but with a temper when roused ... humour ... violent confrontations ... well recommended.'
eurocrime

'I was gripped from beginning to end ... a great concise writing style ... fast paced action ... Donovan makes you feel as though you are uncovering the truth ... well worth reading.'
newbooksmag

"The plot twists and turns certainly kept me guessing to the end.'
reader review, librarything.com

www.michaeldonovancrime.com

BEHIND CLOSED DOORS

MICHAEL DONOVAN

HOUSE
ON THE
HILL
Publishing

First Published 2013 by Moth Publishing.
This edition published in 2017 by **House On The Hill.**

ISBN-10:   1 522738 91 6
ISBN-13:   978 1 522738 91 6

Copyright © 2013 Michael Donovan

The moral right of Michael Donovan to be identified as the author of this work
has been asserted by him in accordance with the Copyright, Designs and Patents
Act, 1988.

All rights reserved. No part of this publication may be reproduced, stored in a
retrieval system or transmitted in any form or by any means without the prior
permission of the publisher.

This book is sold subject to the condition that it shall not, by way of trade or
otherwise, be lent, re-sold, hired out, or otherwise circulated without the
publisher's prior consent in any form of binding or cover other than in which it is
published and without a similar condition including this condition being imposed
on the subsequent purchaser.

This novel is a work of fiction. Except in the case of historical fact, the names,
characters and incidents portrayed in it are the work of the author's imagination
and not to be construed as real. Any resemblance to actual persons, living or dead
is entirely coincidental.

Cover design by **House On The Hill** from Shutterstock image.

p0003

Published by Human Vertex Publications, UK.

for
Odette

siyempre

CHAPTER ONE
Are the other agencies the same?

I was sitting at my desk early one Monday staring at paperwork while I waited for motivation to kick in. Behind me the racket of the Westway rattled the window with the annoying reminder that elsewhere life was moving. Time had stalled only this side of the glass. I yielded to the greater truth. Eased back. Lifted my feet onto the desk and checked the barometer again. Down another tenth. Lousy weather brewing. I reached for my coffee with a sense of a long day looming. Then my intercom kicked into life with an explosion of static that threw the coffee the hell everywhere and jolted my heart with the alternative option of a cardiac, which would shorten the day but not in my favour.

The apparatus is an eighties-vintage Motorola I'd picked up on Camden Market at a price tag later explained by its built-in short-circuit that scrambled messages to indecipherable mush. I used it mostly for coffee and sandwich orders. The coffee was all over my desk and it was early for lunch. Something was up.

Lucy gave it a sec. then repeated my name.

'Mr Flynn, are you available?'

As if she hadn't watched me come in here twenty minutes ago with nothing more than my coffee cup and a hazy expression. I grinned: it wasn't the pointlessness of the question, it was the way Lucy could "Mr Flynn" me so you'd never imagine that the two of us had a history steamier than a Chinese laundry. The history was very old history but I guess something still sparked, because Lucy had hung on to the desire to mother me even after she'd wrecked my life by ditching me. I put it down to guilt.

My Herman Miller executive chair was reclined at an awkward angle for business. I strained my abs. Got a finger to the intercom.

'What's up, Lucy?'

'There's a Ms Bannister to see you.'

'We have an appointment?'

'No.'

That tallied. The name was unknown to me. Seemed the lady was

1

the type who liked to start her business early and without a call. Early was fine with me. Handed me an excuse to defer the paperwork. 'How are we fixed?' I said.

You'd barely notice the pause as Lucy offered to check my diary. Beneath the static I heard the sound of blank pages turning.

'You're free, Mr Flynn.'

That tallied too. My excuse was on. I told Lucy to show our guest through and tilted myself upright.

Ms Bannister came in, with Lucy right behind her to catch my reaction. But I'm good at not reacting. My blank expression held until Lucy got the message and backed out, leaving Ms Bannister standing alone. When the door closed I sat back and smiled at her, thinking what in holy hell?

She was a damn kid. Six stone of nervous energy in pink Fred Perry trainers, trying to look adult and failing somewhere round the five-foot mark. Her face, behind a spiderwork of mascara, was what you might call sultry in a few years, and was framed in a halo of streaked hair that looked like it had been through a mangler but had probably cost sixty quid in Knightsbridge. The agency gets its share of odd callers but not many kids come up our stairs. For a moment the thing threw me.

We could have stood gawping at each other all morning but then a crackle on my desk told me that someone was listening. I held up an apologetic finger and leaned across to kill the intercom. You do this by pulling out the mains lead. Then I looked up to see if I'd been dreaming.

No such luck. The kid was still there.

Her clothes had an agenda. Her square-cut jeans were slung low enough to give a peek of turquoise pants cinched into the puppy fat below her navel, and up top a wash-shrunken red cami sported a logo of shattered letters that made you look where you shouldn't. The letters said *Come to Mamma*.

Mamma was fifteen. Or twelve. I couldn't say. The only certainty was that she'd come in the wrong door. We're a detective agency. The girl needed a kindergarten. I smiled and stood.

'Hi,' I said. 'Are you lost?'

Apparently she was. For a moment the girl's nerve deserted her. She licked her lips.

2

'You're not a detective agency?' she said.

I held my smile and asked what the hell she meant.

Her eyes replied. Flicked round the office, looking dubious. The room isn't much, but if I hadn't known about the flaking windows and damp ceiling I'd not have noticed. I turned my smile up.

'Yeah, we are a detective agency. Since you ask.'

Her face stayed dubious.

'Yellow Pages said you were...' her eyebrows sought help.

I raised my own eyebrows.

'...a proper agency?' she suggested.

'Proper?'

'With detectives. Like the police?'

'We are. Ex-Metropolitan.'

She looked at me like I was kidding.

I held the smile. So we weren't the Ritz. A few things needed fixing around the place. But there was nothing that said I should be listening to a snot-nosed kid critique the operation. I opened my palms.

'This is us, young lady. We're happy with it.'

She still looked like I was kidding.

'Are the other agencies the same?' she said.

'The same?'

Her eyes took another tour, expressing what it was the other agencies might be the same as. My own eyes followed this time. I checked carefully. Maybe I'd missed something. Maybe the wallpaper had restuck itself or the ceiling patch had dried. Maybe the dead Dracaena had blossomed. But everything was normal. Kind of messy. I turned back.

'Yes, the other agencies are the same,' I said. 'But we've got the best detectives. That's why we're successful.'

'Successful?'

A guy's patience only stretches so far. Charm was suddenly becoming a chore. I was still trying to guess what the hell had brought this kid in here but the real puzzle was why I was being suckered into idle chit-chat when I'd work to do. It was time to move things along.

'What's your first name, young lady?' I said.

'Sadie.' She stepped forward and held out a hand.

I took it. It was the size of a doll's with half the grip. I held it gently and gave her my best advice.

'Sadie,' I said, 'you need to leave.'

She dropped my hand as if it was greased. Got no resistance.

I stooped for the intercom lead to call Lucy back in. Why the hell she'd let the kid through I couldn't imagine, though I had my suspicions. But the kid wasn't finished.

'Are you always this rude to clients?' she said.

I turned. 'Young lady you're not a client. But if you were I'd be very polite indeed.'

She looked at me. Shook her head.

'Jesus Christ!' she said. 'I bet you're not a real detective at all.'

I kept my mouth shut and got the Motorola reconnected. If the kid was trying to provoke me it wasn't going to work. Our discussion was over. Any transient curiosity I might have had about what had brought her in here had evaporated. All that mattered was getting her back out.

The "real detective" quip stung though. I had an idea. I rummaged for one of George Giannetti's business cards. Giannetti was a detective in the sense that Jack the Ripper was a consultant surgeon. He operated out of a sub-let basement under an adult shop near Marylebone Station and took anything that fell through the cracks. Giannetti worked both sides of the line. Good guys, bad guys, he bled them all. His office was only a dozen blocks away. Sadie could be there in half an hour and I happened to have an axe to grind with George. The girl wanted a real detective? Let her go mess up Giannetti's day! But George's card eluded me in the chaos and the girl wasn't waiting. She thought things through double quick and gave me her decision.

'Okay,' she said. 'I'll hire you.'

I quit searching. Turned. The agency had been going for six years, most of them a struggle. And finally our million-dollar client had arrived. I'd have to get Lucy to pull the champagne.

I didn't ask about the "Jesus Christ" and the "not real detectives" stuff that the girl had been spouting thirty seconds back. I guess that was just setting us up for a discount.

What I did was give her my brightest smile. Sadie smiled back. Sultry changed to pretty. Even if her nose was pointy and her lips a little thin I knew that she was her mother's pride and joy. The kid had charm. What could I say?

'Young lady,' I said, 'you're out of your tiny skull.'

The girl's smile vanished.

'What do you mean?' she asked.

'Crazy! Loco!' I did an act.

She was quiet a second.

'Is there a problem?'

'Yes, there's a problem. The problem is that our clients are adults. Commissions are expensive. Like buying a house. And we don't work for kids. *That's* the problem.'

Must be something I said. Her mascara locked into a smouldering stare and she spoke slowly so as not to lose me.

'I'm not a child,' she said. Her eyes could have shattered diamond. 'I know I have to pay. But hiring someone to snoop around is *not* like buying a house. I just need someone to check on a friend. You'll get paid. Just don't try ripping me off.'

That was reasonable. Business acumen I could respect. What I couldn't respect was the snooping bit. The agency's surveillance methods are the best in the business. And even if we're sneaky that doesn't mean we snoop. I stayed with the specifics though.

'Pay?' I said. 'How?'

She sighed, as if talking to pedantic fools dragged her day down.

'I've got a savings account. I can withdraw anytime.'

I laughed.

'Sadie,' I said, 'let's go.'

We'd wasted enough time. Babysitting kids didn't pay our rent. Consultation over. And Sadie, finally, got the message. Her face dropped. She watched me a moment then turned to leave. But even then she couldn't resist the last word.

'Suit yourself,' she threw back, 'I guess you're too busy.'

Now we were getting cheeky. I'd have to ask Shaughnessy if we were too busy. I wouldn't mention the snooping though. The guy had feelings. But the girl was still chipping away as she reached the door.

'You're not a proper detective, are you?' she said. She was standing with her hand on the door handle, baiting me. I knew it but I swallowed it anyway.

'I was a Met detective inspector,' I said, 'if that passes. Nowadays I'm private. And busy. Also – to repeat – this firm only deals with adults.'

'I'm seventeen. I am an adult.'

'Not by law. And you don't look seventeen.'

She rolled her eyes: 'Since when can an old guy tell anyone's age?'

I rolled my own. 'For your information, young lady, I'm thirty-eight, but I guess "old" to you is any boy with his own shaving kit.'

Witty. Not as witty as the way the side of her mouth lifted. The face said everything.

'Thirty-eight,' I repeated, 'is not old. And seventeen is not adult. I'm sorry Sadie, this agency doesn't work for kids.'

My words got through. She turned to the door. I volleyed a few more to help her on her way. 'If you need investigation services,' I said, 'come back with an adult.'

Wrong words again. She stepped back. Turned.

'There is an adult!' Her eyes were glittering with a new hope. 'She'll back me up!'

'Back you up about what?'

'About my friend. She's disappeared.'

Finally I saw a look in Sadie Bannister's face that passed for adult. Fear.

I dropped my smile. Sighed, aware that whatever was on this kid's mixed-up mind was of no interest to the agency. But there's an instinct all investigators share – the lure of the curious. We're like collectors rummaging through the shadowy corners of a bric-a-brac shop: we just can't resist intrigue when it pops up. I hesitated another moment then heaved one of my club chairs round to face the other and told Sadie to sit down. What was I? The Ghoul? All she needed was a quick heart-to-heart then I could feel good when I booted her out. She accepted my invitation. Came back. Sat down but kept most of her weight on her toes like she was watching for a bad move. I sat on the arm of the other chair and tried to look like I wasn't a bad-move kind of guy. Then I got involved in something I should never have touched.

CHAPTER TWO
Comedienne

'Tell me about your friend,' I said.

Sadie stayed on the edge of the chair. Her fingers linked and flexed.

'Her name's Rebecca Townsend.'

'And she's not at home?'

She shrugged. 'I don't know. Her parents won't let me see her.'

'Why not?'

'They say she's ill.'

'That's reasonable. You don't want to catch a bug.'

She shook her head. Her toes danced. 'They're lying. Becky was fine right before she disappeared. We had lunch together. Then in the afternoon she was gone.'

'Gone how?'

'Didn't answer her phone. Didn't show up next day.'

'Did you call at her house?'

'They said she was ill.'

'Bugs strike suddenly.'

'So suddenly that she couldn't even text me? Becky would text at her own funeral. And she's been gone a week now. It's like she never existed.'

'When did you last speak to her parents?'

'Yesterday. Every day. They just give me the same story about a virus. When I go round they won't let me in.'

I grinned. 'So you decided to sick a detective on them?'

The girl was cute. If I had a daughter she'd be like this. There were always people needed sicking. I clasped my hands and sat forward.

'Sadie,' I said, 'if your friend's parents say she's ill then that's probably the case. You can't ask a detective agency to investigate them. Why not believe them?'

Sadie closed her eyes like she was teaching a slightly stupid child its multiplication table.

'I told you. They're lying. Becky hasn't texted me in a *week*. Is she too ill to do that?'

Sadie was sticking with this texting thing. To teenagers, texting is breathing. If you're not doing it you're dead. The girl unlocked her hands and pushed them through her hair. The cami stretched to reveal more bare midriff. Mamma did a jig. I noticed that Sadie's navel was pierced with three gold rings. What were her parents thinking, sending her out like this? But it wasn't my problem. I felt kind of sorry for the kid but I had reports to pull together and invoices to post. I needed to lead this towards an exit.

I said: 'Whatever's happening with your friend there'll be a simple explanation. No reason to hire an investigation agency.'

'So what should I do?'

'You should leave it to her parents. Whatever the problem is they'll sort it out.'

Her eyes flashed. 'Not her father. Becky hates him.'

'I bet you hate your own parents sometimes.'

She threw out an exasperated sigh. 'Are you listening at all? Something's wrong in Becky's house. Her father's a creep. There's things going on at home she won't tell even me.'

This was getting tackier by the minute. Time to change direction. 'What do your parents say?'

'The same as you. That I shouldn't interfere.'

I opened my hands.

The girl's shoulders dropped. I don't know what fantasy had gone through her mind while she searched Yellow Pages, but there was no TV hero waiting to charge in to rescue her friend – who almost certainly didn't need rescuing in the first place. Sadie looked at me and I saw she was beginning to get a sense of things, knew she'd get the same answer at any agency in town. Perhaps not Giannetti's but I decided she didn't need Giannetti's card after all. He was exactly the guy to take her to the cleaners.

'Sometimes it's the families,' she said.

I looked at her.

'You read it in the papers. Kids abused, murdered. All along it's the parents. No one helps until it's too late. Teachers. Social workers. Police. All looking the other way.'

'Yes,' I said. 'But private investigators don't fill the gap.' Simple truth, even if saying it didn't make me feel better. 'You said there was an adult?'

'An old lady. Becky helps round her house. They're kind of friends.'

'Has this lady spoken to you?'

'Yeah. She's mad as hell at Becky's mum. Says she needs a good talking to.'

Interesting. We were well into the shadows of the bric-a-brac shop now. I dug further.

'What's this lady's name?'

'Gina Redding.'

'And why exactly is she worried?'

'Same as me. She can't get hold of Becky and her mother is fobbing her off.'

The thing sounded odd. But I knew there'd be an explanation. And whatever it was, the agency wasn't in the social services business. Specifically, we didn't work for kids. We worked for clients with a little capital to back up their concerns. That's why I was going to have to show Sadie the door. Knowing my luck, of course, she'd be back in a week throwing the newspapers in my face with her friend's picture under eighty-point headlines. I thought about it. Reconsidered. A quick chat with this lady friend wouldn't hurt. I'd persuade the woman to talk to Sadie and her parents. Then it was up to the lot of them to sort things out. I asked Sadie if she had the old lady's number.

The girl's eyes brightened and I realised that deep down she'd expected to get the brush-off. She'd just been on a fishing trip and Eagle Eye had been first on the hook. I made a note to check our Yellow Pages wording.

'You're taking the case?' she said.

I laughed. Miss Comedienne.

'Hell, no,' I said, 'we're not taking the case. It's like I told you. The agency only takes commissions from adults. What I'm going to do is talk to Mrs Redding, see if there's some advice we can give. Then the two of you will need to look for your friend without involving detective agencies.'

Sadie quit arguing. Opted for satisfied. She didn't have a number for Gina Redding but gave me an address on the south side of Hampstead Heath. She also gave me her own number which I wasn't going to need. Finally we were through. Sadie stood and followed me to the door.

'One thing,' I said.

She stopped.

'Thirties is not old. You'll be thirty yourself one day.'

That got a diamond smile.

'Sure,' she said. 'It's barely middle-aged.'

I gave her my best shit-eating grin and opened the door wide. Lucy was behind her desk waiting to hear what this was about, but payback was in order. I asked her to show our guest out and by the time she got back I was locked behind my door, chasing paperwork and leaving her hanging.

CHAPTER THREE
Drunk's shoelaces

I hunkered behind my roll-top and attacked client reports for a couple of hours then hit the button and printed the paperwork for posting out along with the invoices. With luck the invoices might induce a transfusion into our bank account. Then we could be friends with our utilities companies, maybe even pay Lucy's wages. I couldn't remember if we were two weeks behind or three. Lucy would know. She brought her paycheques to sign when she was confident they wouldn't bounce.

I filed the case folders and went out for envelopes. Found Lucy still at her desk. It was after twelve and she should have been gone but she was trapped in the office until she found out what Sadie Bannister had been in about. I rooted in the stationery cabinet and said nothing.

Lucy's got a way of watching you that gets you on your toes. Eventually you drop something or spill your drink and when you try to blame her she closes up her smart eyes and shrugs, as if fools are better tolerated than reprimanded. Lucy's got a pair of eyes that would have any male acting the fool. Without the eyes she'd be just a punk who'd slipped in a dye factory. Her eyes made her a punk you wanted to grab hold of. For us the grabbing days were over but her looks could still trip me like a drunk's shoelaces.

She quit pretending and perched herself on her desk, waiting. I stuck address labels and stamped envelopes. Stayed cool.

'What's up?' I said.

'Has your intercom stopped working Eddie, or am I going deaf?'

I gave her shocked. 'Were you trying to eavesdrop?'

'Someone has to look out for you.'

'What can I say?' I said. 'The intercom's shot. Maybe I should just bug my office so you can listen whenever you want.' I slammed the cabinet. 'Or did you already do that?'

'That's for you to find out. See how good you are.'

'You know how good I am.'

She looked at me. Her hair was so bright we could have saved on lighting. This month's colour was red.

I went back and switched off my computer. Lucy's voice followed.

'So what's the story on Miss Bannister?'

'Nothing's the story on Miss Bannister. She's seventeen. I sent her packing.'

'Took you an awful long time.'

I came out. 'She took a lot of persuading,' I said. 'I thought I was going to need a crowbar to get her out of the door. That's why I employ you, Lucy. To filter undesirables.'

'Is that what it says in my job description?'

'How do I know? I've never read your job description. Just ad-lib. Do what's needed.'

'Me neither.'

'Neither what?'

'Read a job description. And I was ad-libbing.'

'You sent her in deliberately? You ever think she might have been dangerous?'

Lucy's eyes closed up again. 'Actually, Eddie, a hornet was what came to mind.'

I wagged a finger. 'I wonder about you, Lucy. After all these years.'

'All these years? You make us sound so old.'

I looked at her. Age was a touchy subject right now. I gave her a worried frown. 'How old do I look, Luce? No one would say middle-aged, would they? Be honest.'

'Better not, Eddie. You wouldn't like it.'

I switched the frown to an iced smile. Why did Lucy and I ever split?

I asked her.

'Because if we hadn't we'd have killed each other. Or you'd have had a heart attack. At your age.'

I chilled the grin further. 'This isn't the way to get the story on little Miss Belly-Button,' I said.

'So what is the way?'

'Come have lunch. Then we can find somewhere quiet to canoodle the afternoon away, see if we can find some more interesting belly-buttons.'

Lucy's eyes stayed closed up. 'And what about your lady-love? What's she going to say about you eloping with the office girl?'

Arabel. Now there was a girl with plenty of belly-button. If I was worried about heart attacks that's where I'd start.

'You're right,' I said. 'We'll need to be finished by three.'

'I've a job to go to,' Lucy said. 'Better stick to sandwiches.'

Ever pragmatic. But a sandwich sounded good. I locked my office and we shut up shop.

~~~~~

Shaughnessy was out so I flipped the door sign as we went out. The old-fashioned IN/OUT behind the glass adds colour, even if the BACK SOMETIME SOON has as much credibility as a plumber's promise. We went down and walked to Connie's.

Connie Papachristou ran an eatery that served kebabs and sandwiches on home-baked bread two doors up. The weather was too cold for his pavement area so his customers were squeezed into eight tables jammed down the side of the counter inside. We got the last one in the back and Connie came over to give the special attention warranted by his biggest tab. Connie always put on a good face but he was getting more uneasy by the month. If the agency went broke before we'd settled he'd go under. The way I saw it, since the problem was mostly caused by his extortionate prices it was a case of what goes around comes around. Judging by his smile Connie was hoping to even things up a little today. The smile was as nice to see as it was futile.

Lucy opted for a baguette and diet Coke. I went for a Mediterranean vegetable and feta cheese monster with coffee, extra cream. When Connie brought the stuff over I filled Lucy in on our precocious visitor. The story intrigued her.

'Are you going to take a look?' she asked.

I shook my head.

'I'm going to have a chat with this Redding woman. Nothing more. Just a mercy thing.'

'For Sadie?'

'For me. The girl might come back. Remind me to write you a list of undesirables to be kept from my door.'

'You'd end up with no clients.'

Good point.

13

'So what's going on? It sounds strange.'

'Sure it's strange. But there's strange with money and strange without. We need the "with" type. Helps pay your wages.'

'You don't pay my wages. Not for four weeks.'

Always the smart answer. Four already? I moved on.

'Lots of things are strange,' I said, 'until the blindingly obvious explanation turns up.'

'So what's the blindingly obvious explanation for this missing girl?'

'Haven't a clue. And I doubt if we're going to find out. This Redding woman will think I'm nuts coming to see her on some kid's say-so. Probably won't even talk to me.'

I pulled up Directory Enquiries and they texted a number. I hit the keys. If no one answered I'd call it quits.

Life isn't like that. The call was picked up on the first ring. A woman's voice, gravelly and querulous at the same time. Not the kind of voice to be reassured by talking to a private investigator, so I identified myself only as a friend of Sadie's and repeated what she'd told me.

If Gina Redding was surprised by the cold call she hid it well. Waded right in on the topic. In three seconds flat I was hearing what I didn't want to hear. Namely that there really was some kind of problem with Rebecca Townsend. Suddenly we were jawing like old friends. Gina wanted to know what we should do. *We!* Bang went my afternoon canoodling with Lucy. I shot Lucy a grin and told Gina I'd be over. Killed the connection. Lucy threw a smug look. I ignored it.

CHAPTER FOUR
If life was that simple

Sadie's story about Rebecca's elderly friend threw up a picture of a struggling pensioner misplaced into the millionaires' ghetto bordering Hampstead Heath. When I got to Hampstead I adjusted the picture.

Gina Redding's house was more like a mansion, a faux Lutyens crouched behind high walls on the south side of the Heath. The architecture was borrowed from the Garden Suburb but scaled up by three and with an acre of landscaped grounds thrown in. The place had to be keeping a platoon of gardeners in clover. Whichever way Rebecca was helping the old lady, weed-pulling didn't come into it.

I parked on white gravel and rang the doorbell.

I was half expecting a butler but the door was opened by a stocky woman in her late seventies with eyeglasses ugly enough to be trendy – sixties throwbacks, which was probably where she'd got them. The woman popped a cigarette from her lips and blinked up at me.

I told her my name and handed her a card. She jabbed the fag back to read it.

When she took in the *Private Investigator* detail she blinked at me again and said she'd be damned if she'd ever met a private eye, then stretched her smoke-lined tonsils to cough out a fog fit to derail a steam locomotive and invited me in.

We went through a walnut-panelled hallway to a lounge the size of my apartment and sat on a sofa bigger than my car. Gina was still damning herself and looking me up and down. I apologised if my phone call had misled her about my identity – which had been the intention – but Gina waved it off. She wasn't shocked by me. It was the thought of Sadie hiring me. Proof it wasn't only me who thought the kid was crackers.

Gina's cigarette wagged like a conductor's baton as she took a lead from those forties crime films and offered me a scotch. I said it was a little early. Asked how she knew Rebecca Townsend. My diplomatic way of asking why someone with all the appearance of wealth needed a girl helping about the house. Gina chortled; sucked her cigarette.

'Rebecca doesn't help in that way. That's just how it started. She came here two years ago as part of a voluntary initiative. Helping the needy of the borough.'

I couldn't stop myself looking round the room, out through the french windows at a landscape that most people would call a park. Some needy list. Gina chortled some more. She'd got her reaction.

'Officially I *was* needy,' she said. 'I'd slipped and broken my ankle. I had my domestic covering extra hours while I was convalescing but the local authority had put me on their list of vulnerable pensioners.'

'And Rebecca turned up to help?'

'Her school was involved in a volunteer scheme. Rebecca saw how things were the moment she walked in. But she was kind enough to do some little chores and we ended up talking. She was interested in my experiences.'

'What experiences?'

'I'm a retired doctor. Worked in third-world countries for twenty-three years after I graduated. I only came back to Britain when I married. Exchanged poverty for affluence. Never really adjusted.'

The old lady looked pretty well adjusted to me. I let it go.

'Rebecca always wants to hear about India and Africa. She's everything I was. More interest in the far side of the world than the far side of London.'

'So she's been visiting you for two years?'

'We hit it off. The home help thing was a sham but I hinted that if she wanted to call again I'd appreciate her doing a little reading for me. My eyesight's my only problem. Rebecca was happy to oblige. She's been coming ever since.'

'Sounds like a nice kid.'

'She is. Always happy to read for me or just to natter. She's here twice a week, hail or shine. Absolutely dependable.'

'Until now,' I said.

Gina's eyeglasses glinted. She stubbed her cigarette.

'Something happened last Wednesday,' she said. 'Rebecca phoned to say she'd be round after classes but she didn't turn up.'

'Did you try to contact her?'

Gina shook her head. 'Not immediately. She doesn't have to explain herself to me. I was just surprised that she hadn't let me know. It was unlike her. I only called her two days later when I still hadn't heard from her, but her phone was off.'

16

'Did you try her house?'

'Immediately. I had the awful thought that she'd had an accident. I talked to her mother.'

'What did she say?'

'Well that's the strange thing.' Gina leaned forward. 'I couldn't put my finger on it, but Jean was prevaricating. First she said Rebecca was not in. Then when I mentioned about her not turning up two days earlier she became more specific and told me that she was laid up with the flu.'

'She was contradicting herself.'

'Yes. And the flu thing was nonsense. I've worked with tropical diseases half my life and there's very few viruses can lay you out in two hours. Certainly not the flu. It sounded to me like Jean was pulling the story from thin air.'

The same suspicion as Sadie's.

Gina told me the rest: she'd talked to Jean Slater three times since that day, got the same story, no change in Rebecca's condition. Brusque answers bordering on rudeness that got Gina thinking that Jean was hiding something.

'How well do you know the family?' I said.

'Hardly at all.' She gazed out over her gardens. 'What can I tell you? Rebecca's mother remarried five years ago and I don't think it was a happy change for Rebecca. I sense a barrier has come between them through Rebecca's dislike of her stepfather. It's nothing she's said outright but I've sensed the hostility. I've suspected it's part of the reason she keeps coming to me. She feels safe here. Appreciated.'

The thing was going in the direction I'd anticipated. Family troubles. Probably a tear-jerker. But the agency wasn't in the Kleenex business. I kept my eyes dry and asked about the girl's recent state of mind. Gina pulled another cigarette out, flicked her lighter.

'She's been a little down. She had a break-up with her boyfriend and I got the impression she wasn't happy about other things too, but nothing she talked about. Oh, I could kick myself for not squeezing it out of her. I feel as if I've let her down.'

I asked about Sadie.

'The Slaters have given Sadie the cold shoulder just like me,' she said. 'The two girls are the best of friends, though I get the impression Jean has never been too keen on Sadie. Wrong class and all that, which makes you wonder, considering Jean's background. But since Rebecca was taken ill Jean won't let Sadie into the house. Unforgivable.'

She looked at me.

'What do you think has happened?' she asked.

'That's difficult to say,' I said, 'I guess something's not right.'

Just not the sort of thing the agency should get involved with. So I trotted out my spiel about how it might be good for Gina and Sadie to call at the Slaters' together. The joint approach might carry more weight. More specifically, it could be done without me. But Gina wasn't buying it.

'I can't see them coming clean,' she said. 'The Slaters are taking a hard line with anyone poking their nose in. Poor Rebecca. What on earth are they hiding?'

I shook my head sadly. The sadness was mostly at Gina not buying my suggestion. Even sadder that I had other business to attend to. I repeated my advice that they go to see the Slaters together and maybe talk to Sadie's parents, and my good Samaritan act was over. I thanked Gina for her time and stood to leave.

Gina walked me to the door, sighing.

'It was good of you to call, Mr Flynn.' Her face was resolute. 'Who'd ever imagine young Sadie hiring a private investigator? I do like initiative in a young person.'

I kept quiet. Initiative is an over-rated virtue in my experience.

We got to the door. 'I hope we haven't wasted too much of your time,' Gina said.

'Not at all,' I smiled. What really mattered was how little more we could waste.

'I suppose I should ask. Has Sadie incurred any charges?'

I kept my face straight.

'None,' I said. 'Initial consultations are free. I already told Sadie she wasn't old enough to engage our services.'

Gina stopped. Got thoughtful. 'Would there be anything you *could* do?' she asked. 'Hypothetically?'

'Hypothetically?'

'To check on Rebecca. Do you do that kind of thing?'

'Not exactly. We do a little private surveillance work but it's usually on behalf of a family member. Suspicions of infidelity, that kind of thing. We wouldn't normally be brought in from outside.'

'Of course,' Gina said. 'But I'm so sure the Slaters are hiding something. It may be none of my business but it would be a tremendous relief to know that Rebecca was safe.'

I looked at her and saw where this was going. She stared right back until my mouth opened without permission.

'In theory,' I said, 'we could take a look.'

'Could you?' Gina said. 'Could you do that? I'll foot the bill, of course. I'm just so annoyed at Jean Slater.'

I thought it through. Figured we could fit in a few hours. In this business many a payday is shored up by the penny-pullers. Jobs low on prospect but fast on cash.

And the thing had an intrigue. Why would a girl vanish with the apparent connivance of her parents? More puzzling, why were the Slaters covering it so clumsily? Why the believe-it-or-get-lost approach?

It was hard to see an explanation that was simultaneously both credible and innocent. When I found the credible and innocent explanation Gina Redding would no doubt kick herself. But her cheque would be in the bank. I made a decision.

'We'll make a few enquiries,' I said. 'But we'll probably find something very ordinary. You might wish you'd not put up the fee.'

'I'm sure there'll be an entirely innocent explanation,' Gina said, 'And we'll all laugh about it. But incurring a fee is better than worrying.'

Logic I couldn't dispute.

I waited while Gina wrote out a retainer cheque which I took along with a few more details on the Slaters, and promised to be in touch. We shook hands.

'Gina,' I said, 'you're in good hands.'

'I'm entirely confident of that,' she said. 'I feel better already.'

That made one of us.

~~~~~

I drove back to Paddington, thinking over what Gina had told me.

Rebecca's stepfather was Larry Slater, co-owner of Slater-Kline, a high-street stockbroker in Islington. Business sounded good because even Gina rated the family as well-off. Apparently the Slaters had a nice house, nice cars and took nice holidays. The kind of stuff you get with nice money.

Rebecca's mother Jean was an ex-travel rep who'd worked with one of the major package tour companies. Nowadays, when they weren't holidaying, she stayed at home and focused on the more esoteric challenges of the London social scene.

By Gina's account Jean had made the transition to the higher stratum of London life a little more comfortably than Rebecca. When Jean remarried, Rebecca had been shunted into a North London girls' academy in line with her mother's new aspirations and had coasted through three years at the top of her class before dropping back to the lower stratum of the West Kilburn College after her sixteenth birthday. Whether the purpose was to team back up with her friend Sadie or to cock a snoot at her mother's pretensions, Gina didn't know. She guessed a little of both.

All in all, Gina's didn't have much. Hints of family secrets or of nothing at all. But if there was something going on maybe I could dig it out. More likely, the girl would turn up and we'd be off the case inside twenty-four hours.

If life was that simple I'd be on a beach.

CHAPTER FIVE
Acid tablets

'Business is business,' I said.

Shaughnessy was behind his desk washing a late lunch down with water from his cooler. He gave me a lopsided grin.

'Are we going to end up with this kid under our feet?'

'You'll never meet her,' I said.

I needed this to be true. My street cred had felt fragile enough when I described Sadie's assault on my office. There was no way Shaughnessy was going to meet the vixen in the flesh.

'A couple of college girls,' Shaughnessy said. 'It's gonna be a tough one.'

'Yeah.'

'We're going to have to watch our backs.'

I was watching his wall.

'So what's going on with this girl?'

'What's going on is that the she's sick in her room or grounded for bad behaviour or packed away in an abortion clinic. Something they're not talking about, but nothing illegal.'

'So tell me again. Why are we taking Gina Redding's money?'

'Because despite my confidence something smells.'

'What kind of smell?'

'A hunch kind of smell.'

'Hunch?' Shaughnessy coughed. 'I'd better write that down.'

'Like lunch,' I said. 'With an "H".'

I heard his ballpoint tapping on his notepad. There was a quiet moment before he gave me his conclusion.

'The family are lying.'

Same conclusion as me. Miss Brassy-Button had tossed us something that fitted mundane like the Mayor of London fitted diplomatic. Teenage girls don't disappear completely behind their own front doors. Not the modern girl armed with her preloaded iPhone. Jean Slater's flu story had a credibility gap a mile wide. And Gina Redding's retainer gave us the incentive at least to take a peek.

Shaughnessy snapped his notebook closed with *Hunch* or *Lunch* written down. You sensed the case building.

'How are you going to play it?'

'I'll start at the Slater house. See if anything's out of kilter.'

I was meeting a client in West Hendon at four. That would leave me a stone's throw from the Slater address at the top of Hampstead Heath. I'd detour through on the way back.

'If you need help just call.'

'I'll do that.'

'These kids...' Shaughnessy repeated.

'If it gets dicey I'll text you.'

'I'll keep the line open.' He pointed to his mobile on his desk so I knew where it was.

I left him to it and went to meet my West Hendon client.

~~~~~

I was running late but mid afternoon traffic was light on the Edgware Road. I put my foot down and got off the North Circular a little before four then followed signs to an industrial park and a haulage depot with a gate sign displaying the name HP Logistics. My client was the owner, a guy named Harold Palmer. He'd not given much over the phone other than that the work was urgent.

The depot was housed in a defunct machine-tool factory constructed of dirty yellow brick with mesh-reinforced windows. The building had been converted to a warehouse, with offices and an HGV maintenance shop at one end. Out beyond the loading bays I could see parked tractor units.

The depot was secured by twelve-foot mesh topped with razor wire and cameras, but the uniformed pensioner who hobbled out of the gatehouse notched the image down to Dad's Army. With twenty thousand square feet of transit warehouse behind the wire I figured they'd use a different crew at night. The pensioner checked a clipboard while I watched a solid guy with a razor cut and dark glasses watching me from inside the office. His shirt-sleeved garb and calm observation marked him as the security boss. The pensioner ticked my name and sent me through.

I parked in a visitors' spot and put my shoulder to a heavy metal door opening onto a flight of stairs. I climbed them into the upper reaches of the building. They topped at a door that swung outwards and threatened to knock you all the way back down. Beyond the door was a reception area fronting a sixty-by-thirty office. A dozen clerks with headsets jabbed at keyboards under spitting fluorescents in a working environment that suggested high staff turnover. The reception desk was manned by an eighteen-stone woman whose main purpose seemed to be to frighten callers back down the stairs. She continued battering her keyboard without noticing me. Either her job description said ignore visitors or she'd already marked me as a nobody, the way a good waiter clocks the lower-class diner.

When she finally looked up it was with the welcoming expression of a boar disturbed at its toilet. The look was enhanced by a fretwork of frown lines that would have made a rhino swoon.

I announced myself and Rhino ran a finger down a desk diary and told me I was six minutes late. I didn't ask if that included the two she'd had me on hold. We just skipped the small talk. She pressed a button and spoke my name, then waved me at a door and I went through to see the boss.

Harold Palmer was a big man behind a bigger desk. The flesh I could see above the surface, combined with my knowledge of icebergs, put him at close to twenty-five stone, with a face hardened by decades of clawing for market share in the trucking business. Palmer extended the company policy for warm welcomes and skipped the handshake. He just gestured towards a collection of chairs by the door. I walked back to grab one. The office space would have made a city tycoon agoraphobic, but the bare walls and metal cabinets said that Palmer hired cheap when it came to interior designers. Not a potted plant or sales chart in sight. What did get my attention were the panoramic windows that gave him a god's eye view over the maintenance bays on one angle and the warehouse on the other. The maintenance window showed two Volvo units being serviced down below. The glass was single-glazed to let the din of air tools through. Muzak for the trucking business.

My seating choice was between a couple of wooden chairs that made me wonder if a church hall was missing furniture and a frayed leather swivel that was mostly lumps but had the benefit of castors to save me from lifting. I rolled the swivel out in front of Palmer's desk and discovered its down-side when I sat. The seat was convex, slippery. Balancing took muscle and gave you the body language of Quasimodo. Just right for a little business negotiation. Palmer watched me a moment and I watched him. He seemed to be concentrating on something bad he'd eaten. At least he didn't tell me I was late. He had a receptionist for that. Finally he opened the discussion.

'I hear that Eagle Eye are discreet,' he said.

He stressed our name as if it was the known practice of all other agencies to shout their clients' business from the rooftops. But his puzzled look let me know that he wasn't convinced about his information.

I kept quiet. With that kind of opener it's best for the client to talk.

'I've some business that needs discretion,' Palmer said. 'Can I trust your agency?'

No idle chat about the challenges of the trucking business. No mention of who had put in the good word for us. Not even a polite query about which partner he was talking to. Palmer was sticking to the simple fact that this thing was giving him indigestion.

'What can I do for you, Mr Palmer?' I said.

He pulled a pack of king-size from his jacket and lit up. Seemed the guy was running the last bastion of pro-smoking policy in London. It was my second dose of the afternoon. The amount of fug I was inhaling today I'd soon need a respirator to work. Palmer took a drag, blew out a cloud.

'I've got a sensitive matter needs attention,' he said.

'How sensitive?'

'Big bucks sensitive. If you do the job right I'll pay.' He watched me from behind his cloud. 'I'll go triple your standard.'

He waited for me to be impressed. Private investigators don't come cheap, and Eagle Eye are not at the bargain-basement end of the market. That's why no one had ever offered us three times our rate before. What people usually offer, when we present our commercial rates, is an awed silence the same as in a good lawyer's office. Private clients – like Gina Redding – get sixty percent discount. The differentiation lets us cover the market.

Palmer gave me time to go over what we had. So far we had discreet and we had reliable and we had three times the going rate. The ingredients of a perfect deal. So perfect that I knew it was going to fall apart. It would unravel the second Palmer described the nature of his sensitive matter. I could see it a mile off.

Palmer heaved himself from his desk and dragged a smoke trail over to the panoramic window, did his God bit watching over his warehouse. He was proud of his view the way City types love the strip of river they get with their corner office. He sucked on his fag for thirty seconds like I wasn't there, contemplating his empire.

'We're bidding for a haulage contract,' he said finally. 'The tender closes at the end of next week.' He did a ninety and strolled along the other glass to watch his crew down in the maintenance bays. He was talking to the glass but his voice had an edge that reflected.

'The client is a clothing wholesaler relocating from Birmingham. They're opening a warehouse here in Wembley. They run their own logistics but they don't own their fleet. They wet-lease thirty units to cover their European and UK distribution.'

I asked what a wet lease was.

Palmer left his window and orbited back to his desk. He sat down and stubbed the cigarette and looked at me to figure out whether I really didn't know what wet leasing was. Then he leaned forward to educate me.

'We supply the trucks, maintenance, drivers and fuel. The client pays a retainer and a straight mileage charge. He says where we go and when, controls the schedule. It's the most efficient way for some businesses to run their logistics. More flexible than owning a fleet. Cheaper than paying ad hoc haulage.'

He stabbed a finger in the direction of the haulage world beyond the panoramic window. 'For a number of reasons we need to land that contract.'

'A number of reasons?'

'A number of reasons.'

I had it.

'How many trucks do you operate?'

'Our main business is container. We run fifty trailers.'

'So this contract would cover most of your fleet.'

'For two years.'

'That would be a good contract.'

He gave me a kind of smile.

'So what's the problem?' I said.

25

'The *problem* is that we have to win the contract.'

He stayed silent, watched me take this in. I was wondering how much of HP Logistics had been built on legitimate operations, because I recognised Palmer's type.

'What help do you need from us?' I said.

He waited a moment, deciding whether to bring me in or kick me out. Went with the risk.

'There are three firms bidding, including us. The way the client works is they contract to the second-lowest bidder. They don't want to pay high prices but it's essential to avoid the vendor who's under-bidding. He's the one who will let you down when he can't deliver.'

Made sense.

'In this particular case we believe that all three bids will meet the key operating requirements. So the selection will come down to price.'

'The second lowest.'

He nodded. 'The middle bid gets the job.'

'So ideally speaking HP Logistics would be the middle bid.'

Palmer thought about it as if it was the first time the concept had occurred. Then he sat forward and dropped his fist gently on the desk. The smile came back. I'd got it again.

'We need to be the middle bidder,' he said. 'Funny how simple life is.'

I thought it through.

'So what you need,' I extrapolated, 'are your competitors' prices before you put in your own bid.'

The smile held.

'And you want us to get that information.'

The smile broadened. Palmer raised a fist. Pointed a pistol finger. Fired off a shot.

'I need you to get that information *fast*. I want those bids on my desk this weekend.'

'So,' I said, 'we burglarise your competitors and steal the information.'

Palmer's smile chilled. I sensed disillusionment stirring. A creeping suspicion that he'd gone with the wrong risk.

'We don't steal anything,' he said. 'I just want you to copy the key figures and get them to me. So we can finalise our bid.'

I had it. A little break-in at his competitors' offices. Find out what their tender prices are. Quietly. So no one knows that the HP Logistics' bid is rigged. And for this discreet operation Palmer was offering three times the agency's going rates. There was only one fly in the ointment.

'Rigging bids is illegal,' I said.

Palmer's face transitioned to certainty. His instinct had been right. He'd gone against his gut feeling and gambled wrong. His expression was granite.

'Sometimes you have to bend the rules in this business,' he said.

I gave this some consideration then explained our policy.

'I'm sorry, we don't do illegal stuff.'

He watched me. His expression remained stony but a fuse had been lit. Suddenly he leaned forward like he was coming over the desk.

'Illegal?' he said. 'Am I hearing you right? Are you shitting me?'

We continued to lock stares while he tried to figure out just how big a blunder he'd made.

'Since when did legal come into it? All you guys play behind the rule book.'

'Not me.'

Palmer watched me a moment then threw out a laugh like a Volvo backfiring. He pointed his finger again.

'You're Flynn,' he said. 'The ex-filth. I knew it the moment you walked in. Smelled it a mile off.' He rocked back in his seat and shook his head. 'Half the private dicks in this city are Met failures,' he said, 'but not many of them have the gall to squeal about legalities. Coppers are the most bent people I know.'

'You don't know me,' I pointed out. I wasn't smiling myself. Maybe the sound of the triple-fee bubble popping had spoiled my mood. I'd known the bubble was going to pop but it didn't make it easier. At least as commissioning interviews went this was short and sweet, because I was through.

I slid off the swivel chair and wheeled it back to the wall. Palmer waited until I reached the door.

'Sure I know you,' he yelled. 'I did my homework. I made sure I knew what kind of a fuck-up I'd be hiring. And I found it was the worst kind. The high flyer who thinks he's God right up to the day they cut his strings. How does it feel now, Flynn? King of the shit heap.' I heard him getting up.

'You're as bent as any copper I ever met,' he said. 'But my information said that your agency was the best. Name your price. I'll pay it. Only don't give me pious. Pious gives me acid. I never met an ex-filth yet who didn't have his price!'

I had the door open. I should have walked out. I shouldn't have been listening to any of this. Instead, I turned and wheeled the swivel chair back.

Palmer laughed and slapped his desk. The crash shook the place.

I picked the swivel up. The thing weighed a sodding ton. It's how you get hernias. I saw Palmer's eyes pop as I heaved my shoulders and launched the chair. It went through the panoramic window as if it was paper, showering glass down onto the bays. Palmer was charging round his desk like a scalded walrus, but his tonnage was against him. By the time he'd got half way across the room I was out of the door and down the stairs.

I guess the bastard's acid tablets were going to take a hit today.

CHAPTER SIX
Life is spooky like that

My business acumen had shaved forty-five minutes off my schedule, which meant that the North Circular was still moving. Two minutes got me to Brent Cross where I turned south towards Golders Green.

The Slater home was a two-storey Spanish villa facing woods in a cul-de-sac south of the golf course. Ten-foot hedgerows guarded the roads like the avenues of a maze, testifying to the area's premium on privacy. The Slaters' house was the exception. It stood open to the road, served by a driveway that encircled a fir-shaded lawn. The driveway was deserted. The house stood lifeless.

Fibre optics were going down in the area and an abandoned ten-foot cable drum offered cover on a stub road fifty yards back. I reversed in alongside it and settled with a view of the house, tuned in LBC and listened to two hours of regurgitated headlines and traffic nightmares. Sometimes you learn just by waiting and watching. Sometimes you get nothing. In two hours only three vehicles passed me, heading for properties further in. One was a Porsche with a forty-something woman at the wheel. The others were high spec Mercs that whispered by as the light faded, shirt-sleeved execs behind their tinted windscreens.

Thick cloud drifted over and killed the light. In response, the glass above the Slaters' front door lit up. So someone was home. I gave it another thirty minutes but nothing more happened, and I'd just decided to call it a day and was reaching for the choke when another car passed. A Lexus with light metallic paint, driver invisible. It slowed and turned into the Slaters' drive and stopped in front of the garage. When the driver got out the light and distance worked against detail but I got an impression of a tall, casually-dressed guy. No business suit or briefcase. He was expected. The house door opened and a woman's figure held it while he entered. There was no embrace, no welcoming kiss. The man strode past without acknowledging the woman. Then the door closed and the show was over. Seemed affection was not the family strength – assuming these were the Slaters.

On a hunch I flipped the radio to a music station and gave it another thirty minutes. Bad hunch. The guy didn't reappear. The house looked like it was settled in for the night. The family was probably sat round EastEnders, or maybe Father was helping Rebecca with her studies whilst Mother worked at her embroidery, blissfully unaware that they had London's hottest detective sitting on their doorstep.

Life is spooky like that.

At seven thirty I gunned the engine and left them to it.

~~~~~

I reviewed what I'd achieved. Distilled it down to having avoided the rush hour. Not something to trivialise. I headed towards Cricklewood and slotted in a Gil Evans tape. Added my own rendition to the opening of Little Wing. Drops of rain hit the screen, turned heavy. I pulled in for petrol on the Edgware Road and watched the rain dance a crystal cataract beyond the fluorescents as I pumped lead replacement. The breath of the city hissed on wet tarmac. I rolled again and reached Battersea by eight twenty, and luck combined with the Frogeye's dimensions to get me a parking space outside my apartment. When I climbed the stairs I sensed more luck. An aroma of fried chicken and paprika was percolating through my door. Maybe my fairy godmother had dropped in. I hoped she'd cooled the beer.

I went in and found Arabel in the kitchen. I'd known it wasn't my fairy godmother. That old crone had left home when I was six years old and hadn't shown her sorry backside since. Luckily Arabel's backside made an adequate substitute. I walked up and got reacquainted with it to the best extent possible when the owner is holding a frying pan erupting like Vesuvius.

'Nice surprise,' I stated. Arabel pushed her rear against me in what was meant as a fend-off but had the opposite effect.

'Babe,' she yelled, 'you're gonna be wearing this chicken.'

I wasn't sure what she was offering but I backed off. She returned the pan to the gas and turned to fend me off some more. It still didn't work. When we got our lips unglued she gave me a big 'Wow'. And that smile.

Wow!

'Thought you were working,' I said.

'Doing a favour. Swapped for an early next week.' Arabel's skin was golden in the kitchen spotlights. The gold comes from mixing Anglo-Saxon and West Indian blood. I don't know what mix had produced her brown-speckled eyes. They were pure Caribbean warmth – the thing I loved most as long as I kept a weather-eye for the tropical storms. Arabel got my arms untangled from her body, changed her mind and tangled them back. Her eyes were closed. Mine stayed open, watching the pan. When Arabel realised that the saliva she was drowning in had nothing to do with her she broke the clinch and told me to go freshen up.

'Make it fast, Flynn,' she said. 'Stir-fry doesn't reheat.'

Flynn.

It's what she calls me. Nothing impersonal: Arabel just comes from a generation that likes its names backwards. I wondered about age again. I'd never considered thirties old until my encounter with Sadie Bannister this morning but when I thought about it I realised that Arabel was halfway back to Sadie's age. Made me wonder why a twenty-seven-year-old was cooking my dinner. Then I looked at Arabel and I knew why. A man has no defence against a girl like that. She wants you, she gets you.

I showered and scurried back and Arabel served the chicken on a green salad with a home-made dressing that was heavy on honey. We sat at the table overlooking the street and the food disappeared fast, washed down with Grolschs to souse the chillies. Arabel was all ears about my missing girl. She still found private investigation romantic even though her instincts must have been screaming that this was not a good profession in a guy. While she listened she attacked her chicken like she was on the run between shifts. She finished ahead of me and sat back with her beer.

'So, is there something funny going on?'

'There's always something funny going on. The longer you do this job the more you realise there's no one leads a simple life.'

'Some people must.'

'No one I met.'

'What about us?'

I gave her incredulous.

'Relatively,' she said.

'Relatively,' I agreed. 'But we're probably the only people we know who aren't trailing skeletons round in their closets.'

Arabel's eyebrows raised. 'How do you know I've got no skelingtons, babe?'

'Your skeletons would have scarpered years ago,' I said, 'to save their insurance premiums.'

'So how about you, Flynn? How do I know you've no boneyards? Since you never tell me.'

I stopped, fork in mid-air.

Good point.

'You don't,' I said.

She watched me, let the point smoulder.

'I just wonder sometimes,' she said.

'My skeletons are buried,' I said. 'Six feet under. Better leave them be.'

'Sometimes it's better to know, Flynn. Even the bad stuff.'

'That's what my clients say. Till they hear the bad stuff.'

I downed more Grolsch. The chillies gave the beer an edge, brought out the sweetness of the fermentation and sent the liquid down my throat like a spring stream. Arabel got back to the subject.

'What's your guess?' she said. 'Has the girl run away? Is she in danger? Are the family hiding something?'

'Any of those,' I said. 'Or all. Or none. Who knows?'

Her eyes opened. 'Babe! You've almost solved the case.'

'The biggest part of solving a case is knowing how to open it. Head off in the right direction and you're as good as home. You just listen and watch, tug a few lines and see which tug back.'

The trouble was that the tugging usually started with inside information. This time I was outside, looking at a family who were saying there was no problem. Maybe there wasn't. Just Sadie Bannister's overactive imagination and the fears of a lonely pensioner, leaving us to disprove a negative. Arabel asked what I'd been asking myself.

'How you gonna start?'

'I'll figure something,' I said. 'Tomorrow.'

Tomorrow would bring inspiration. I knew it.

CHAPTER SEVEN
Brightvoice

I ran three laps of the park before six. At each turn along the river needles of rain stabbed my face to remind me that this was healthy. In the investigation business it pays to keep ahead of the ageing process – or ahead of the self-destruct process, in my case. If I ever relaxed I knew that the gremlin that grinned at me from the other end of my lifestyle see-saw would come scampering across and devour me. After forty minutes I was done. I jogged back to my apartment with health oozing from every pore.

I showered, sliced wholemeal rolls and stuffed them with ham, dropped them into my old briefcase and went back up to kiss the duvet under which I'd last seen Arabel. The duvet didn't move. I grabbed my Burberry and headed out.

I crossed Battersea Bridge at seven in a burst of sunshine that lifted the morning. I cranked the radio up and beat the traffic through Chelsea and Kensington. By seven twenty I was parked in the stub road by the Slater house.

The house was dark and the Lexus hadn't moved. I tuned in Capital and listened to a mixture of hip-hop and news headlines and watched the place.

At seven thirty the two Mercs from up the lane drove out. Then a lull until the post van passed at eight fifteen. Ten minutes later an elderly woman walked up to domestic duties further in. The Slaters' front door stayed shut the whole time. No sign of Larry Slater and no sign of a girl heading for college. Rebecca Townsend was either indisposed or absent.

The show finally started at nine fifteen. Slater came out wearing a leather jacket and open-neck shirt and fired up the Lexus. He rolled by me without a glance. The casual garb intrigued me but I stayed put. I was interested in the house. I wanted to know whether Rebecca Townsend was in there.

I tuned in Radio Four and ate my sandwiches, giving Larry thirty minutes to fight through traffic. Then I pulled a number from directory enquiries and dialled his company, Slater-Kline. The call routed to a computerised pitch that alternated muzak with assurances that my call was deeply valued. After five minutes even the computer was sounding unsure. I was about to hang up when the line was picked up. A bright female voice asked how she might help me. I asked for Larry.

'He's out right now. May I help?'

'I'll perhaps catch him when he's back,' I said. 'What time will that be?'

Brightvoice told me she didn't exactly know and offered to take a message.

'An hour?' I guessed.

'I'm sorry,' Brightvoice insisted. 'Mr Slater's out on business. We're not sure when he'll be in. Did you have an appointment? We're rearranging his schedules.'

I told her I'd ring back and cut the line.

So Slater was not at the office. And schedules were being rearranged. Something had interfered with Larry's plans today.

I settled back to watch the house, wondering if I should have followed Slater. But if I'd been tailing him I'd have been fretting about the house. The endless neuroses of the private investigator.

As surveillances went this threatened to be a slow mover. Conventional surveillance is typically away from home – tailing rogue husbands and the like. Less often it involved watching for house calls whilst said husband was away. This one was different: I was entirely on the outside.

At ten fifteen I donned my Burberry, grabbed my briefcase and walked up the road and rang the Slaters' doorbell. There was no response. I leaned on the button and kept it pressed. That seemed to work. I heard footsteps and the door opened.

It was the woman from yesterday. She was tall, elegant, late thirties. Classic high cheeks, blue eyes. She would have been beautiful without the fatigue. She looked at me with a tight mouth and made no attempt to start a dialogue. All she wanted, her body language said, was to see me gone, whoever I was. Jean Slater, assuming this was her, was not in a party mood.

Her lassitude helped gloss over the rudimentary ID I held up. The card was one of an inkjet stock conjured up by our part-timer Harry Green. It was designed to look as official as possible whilst remaining sufficiently generic to fit most bills. The trick was the heavy use of acronyms and meaningless titles, supported by a few machine-readable numerals and a generic logo. Add a dorky-looking photo of yourself, encase the lot in plastic and your legitimacy will never be challenged. When police recommend that you check visitors' IDs they don't tell you that con man has the best of the lot.

Jean looked at the card then looked at me. I clipped the card onto my Burberry and informed her I was from the Local Education Authority.

'Just a routine call,' I said. 'Is this Rebecca's home?'

Jean looked surprised for a moment but then her expression closed in.

'What's this about?' she asked.

'Nothing official,' I assured her. 'May I come in?'

She thought about it but lacked the resolution to refuse me, and when she stepped back I walked in.

I held out an official hand and apologised for intruding. The handshake is another con man's trick. Confers legitimacy to even the most outrageous of cold calls. If I wasn't in investigation I'd be a top-notch insurance spiv. Jean's palm was clammy. I asked how Rebecca was.

'She's fine,' she said.

I nodded. 'You're no doubt aware of our policy of helping students when they miss class through illness? I understand Rebecca's been off a week. If she has a doctor's note she'll be eligible for home assignments.'

The spiel sounded dodgy even to me. I let Jean digest it while I looked round the entrance hall.

The hall was designed to impress visitors whose own lives were dedicated to impressing others. It was an oval two-storey space with green and gold wall fabrics and an Axminster carpet you could run a combine harvester through. The Axminster curved seamlessly up twin oak-banistered staircases that came together at the top to feed a gallery servicing the upper rooms. Everything was Ideal Home perfect. No discarded coats or bags, no cast-off shoes or domestic appliances. The only item out of place was the half-empty wine glass Jean had dumped on the Italianate telephone stand as she came to the door. Maybe the wine explained the slight thickening in her voice.

My pause left a deadly quiet. When I looked back Jean came out of her trance.

'Rebecca's convalescing from a virus,' she said. 'Sleeping most of the time. I doubt if she's up to academic work.'

'Any chance of a short chat with her? She could let me know if she'd like something preparing.'

Jean's head shake was emphatic. 'No,' she said. 'That's not possible.'

'It would take just five minutes.'

'No. Really.' Her eyes were hardening and she was staring at my ID, drawing herself up to ask questions. I backed off.

'Fine, Mrs Slater, we'll trust your judgement. Perhaps I could call in a couple of days?'

'I'm sorry.' Again the wine-assisted head shake. 'Rebecca's with her aunt in Berkshire. She'll be there at least another week. And I'm sure she'll catch up when she gets back.' She pulled up a smile that didn't quite make it. 'I'll tell her you called.'

I said that would be great and handed Jean a generic card and told her to have Rebecca call me if she did need anything, although it was unlikely she'd get me on the card's number. Jean took the card and held the door wide and her smile was suddenly so bright that you almost missed its insincerity.

She certainly missed mine.

~~~~~

I pulled off the Burberry and made a call. Arranged a meeting then fired up the Frogeye and pushed in a Claire Martin tape, cranked the volume to fill the car with her gutsy, smoky flow. Drove south.

Rebecca Townsend wasn't at the house. I got that from my senses rather than faith in Jean Slater's words. The silent building had screamed of something amiss. I pictured Jean wandering alone in there with her glass of wine. Was it something between her and Larry? Something that enticed a recuperating teenager to head for her aunt's? Or had Rebecca simply decided to up and leave? Was that what I saw in Jean's face?

But why would Rebecca scarper without informing Sadie?

Winter had switched to spring, micro-seasons breaking up the day. The sun flashed in and out of clouds, turning the wet road alternately grey and blinding. I cranked the volume further until Martin's voice rasped like sandpaper over my backing vocals. I drove south through Swiss Cottage in late-morning traffic and steered towards West Kilburn where I parked and walked up to a row of fast food shops, all lunchtime busy, opposite a sixth form college. Sadie Bannister was eating a Mars Bar sitting on a low wall fronting the college building.

Her belly was still taking the air but her upper parts were covered by a cotton jacket and she'd found a pair of jeans that fit. She still looked thirteen, but so did most of the youths milling about. When I stopped in front of her she wrapped the chocolate and set it on the wall and pulled the tab on a can. Her eyes were a little friendlier today. Like an affectionate rottweiler's. I sat beside her.

'Did you find what's happened to Becky?' she asked.

I raised my eyebrows.

'Okay.' She took a sip. 'Don't expect miracles. Well at least you're looking. Hey,' her eyes brightened, 'have you got a name or anything? You know,' she shrugged, 'to be friendly?'

She made it sound like friendly was a young-generation thing.

'Call me Eddie,' I said.

'Like Gumshoe? That guy off the old repeats?' She swung her fist under my nose. If she'd followed through it would have been like a gnat colliding with me but her drink can sloshed threateningly. I shifted away.

'Tell me about Rebecca's parents,' I said.

She shrugged. 'Nothing to tell. I never go into her house. I just know Becky doesn't get on with Larry.'

'Any particular reason?'

Again the shrug. 'Larry's a dick. He bullies her mother.'

'But nothing's ever happened between him and Rebecca?'

'Like him coming on to her?'

'It happens.'

'Ugh,' she said. 'Sicko. The guy's at least fifty. I'd throw up.'

'What about her mother? Does Rebecca get on with her?'

'So-so. Jean's a control freak. Tries to rule Becky's life. Where she goes, whom she sees, what time she gets home.'

'Do they argue?'

'All the time.'

'Would they argue enough to piss Rebecca off? Enough that she'd walk out?'

'No,' Sadie said. 'Becky's always pissed off with Jean but she's never talked about leaving. And she'd have told me if she was thinking of that. She wouldn't be like "see you later" then vanish. We get our diplomas next year so she's out of there anyway. We're renting a flat in Brentford.' She looked at me again: 'Becky hasn't run away, Mr Gumshoe.'

'Eddie,' I said. 'Does her mother have any problems?' I wondered if the drinking was under wraps.

'Dunno. She's okay, I guess. Like any mother.'

Perhaps Rebecca didn't tell Sadie everything. She was up-front about not liking her stepfather but there was no reason she'd want to shred her mother's name.

'How's Rebecca been acting lately? Happy? Sad?'

Sadie gave it some thought.

'Just the usual. Up and down. Rebecca's a crazy bitch.'

'Crazy how?'

'You know. Life's a big saga. She should be in a soap opera.'

'What kind of things make her crazy?'

'Just things.'

'Things?'

'Yeah. You know.' She lifted her can.

I turned to look squarely at her. 'No, Sadie,' I said. 'I don't know. Detectives never know things until people tell them.'

She stopped drinking and rolled her eyes.

'Becky's had some problems.'

'What problems?'

'She split with her boyfriend. It, like, got to her. And she's started hanging with this older guy. A creep. Into drugs. I told Becky to watch out but she says she just hangs.'

'The boyfriend. Was it serious?'

'Yeah. Marcus. They were real sweethearts. He's doing IT.' She tilted her head towards the college buildings.

'When did they split?'

'Couple of months ago. I thought they'd get back together but I guess it's not going to happen.'

'Why would they get back together?'

'They were into each other. Real sweet. Marcus is okay. Not my type.'

'What type is he?'

She rolled the question around. 'Bookish,' she said. 'You wouldn't think he was Becky's type but you couldn't separate them.'

'Why'd they split?'

'Some kind of fight.'

'Has Marcus got over her?'

'Dunno.'

'What about the guy she's taken up with?'

'Russell Cohen. A piece of dirt. Becky's been keeping it low profile but she's, like, all over him. He works the West End. She's down there every other night.'

'You don't like him?'

'I only met him a couple of times but he was coming on to me at every opportunity. I wouldn't let a creep like that near me.'

'What does he do?'

'Works on the door. Some dealing on the side. I went to the club with Becky once and he and his mates were trying to act cool for the sluts. Pricks, the lot of them. They'd never guess how stupid they all look.'

'You said the guy's old?'

'Twenties or something. Just needs to grow up past ten.' She pulled out a pack of cigarettes.

I smiled. 'I hear that smoking is what the girls do to act cool too,' I said.

'Right,' she said, and lit up. 'Sod that.'

Kids.

She blew a vapour trail.

'What's this got to do with Becky disappearing?'

'A split with a boyfriend? Involvement with a guy dealing drugs? Either of those could be related.'

'So how do you explain the fact that Becky was fine? No mention of Marcus or Russell or anything. Then she's, like, gone! And what's with all that phoney shit from her parents?'

I'd been asking myself the same question. Even if Jean Slater's virus story was true the family was still acting strange. I needed to find the aunt, confirm whether Rebecca was with her.

'Have you got the photo?' I asked.

Sadie rooted in her bag. Pulled out a four-by-three of the two of them on a beachfront, Sadie in a mini skirt, Rebecca in jeans, both wearing tops that economised on material. Rebecca was side-on, arms round Sadie's shoulders, pulling her in, but her face was turned to the camera and I recognised Jean Slater's looks, the same well-defined bone structure, the pretty eyes, a face rolled back twenty-five years and unclouded by problems. Sadie was attractive if you looked beyond the eyeliner and the combative stare, but Rebecca was the real beauty in the act.

I slipped the photo into my pocket hoping no one was watching. They'd have me down as a tutor.

'Do you know Rebecca's aunt?' I said.

Sadie took a drag. 'Kath. Never met her.'

'Any idea where she lives? Any second name?'

She thought about it. 'In Berkshire somewhere. I can't remember her surname. Something clerical?'

I already had Berkshire from Jean Slater but a clerical-sounding surname narrowed it down. A couple more gems like this and I'd be camped on her doorstep. I changed tack.

'When exactly did you last talk to Rebecca?'

'That day. At lunch. We sat right here.'

'Did she say anything special?'

'Only that she wouldn't be seeing me after class. She was going round to Gina's.'

'And did she show up in class that afternoon?'

Sadie shrugged. 'Dunno. We've different classes, Wednesday.'

'Does she ever miss class?'

Again a shrug. 'Same as any of us. No one goes all the time.'

A refuse truck pulled up and started tipping bins. The racket drowned us out.

I yelled at Sadie to let me know if she remembered anything else and said I'd be in touch.

She stubbed her cigarette. 'You agree though,' she yelled back. 'Something's happened? You're going to find her?'

I smiled. 'Sure,' I said. 'We're on the case.'

If my smile reassured Sadie she didn't show it. She stood and grabbed her Mars Bar and disappeared into the building.

I watched her go in then stood and walked away.

CHAPTER EIGHT
Personal injury and sax

I drove back to the office, which is the top floor of an Edwardian house backing onto the Great Western lines a mile out from Paddington Station. The area is mostly residential with a scattering of shops and cafés, but a nest of accountants and solicitors had invaded Chase Street, a cul-de-sac that curves and dead-ends along the railway, and the eventual arrival of a private investigation agency at Number Twenty-Six added nicely to the bouquet.

The building's lower floors were occupied by Rook and Lye, a law firm that mutated in the nineties from property conveyancing to the more lucrative world of personal injury. They'd cut loose their estate clients, taken full-page ads in Yellow Pages and bought slots on local radio, after which they redesignated their ground floor as a 'clinic' and never looked back.

If Bob Rook and Gerry Lye were uncomfortable sharing a roost with another image-challenged profession they never mentioned it. In terms of image, ambulance chasers and private detectives sit on the same pot. Where we differ is client numbers.

I was halfway up the stairs when Bob Rook ejected himself from their first floor offices and came rolling down like the runaway boulder in *Indiana Jones*. I flattened myself against the wall to let him pass. It was either that or learn about the personal injury business from the sharp end. If Bob recognised me he made no sign. After six years he was still keeping up the pretence that he hadn't noticed the flock of private investigators in his attic.

The day we'd opened for business six years back it was his partner Gerry who'd come up to suggest we relocate our nameplate and bell push on the opposite wall of the lobby where it wouldn't clash with their own. Nameplates are stacked together for a reason, namely that it makes life simpler for the visitor. Also, the wiring was set up that way. Gerry showed good will by offering to stand the entire cost of the alteration. I talked it over with Shaughnessy and we decided the plate was fine where it was. Luckily the matter was sorted amicably when Rook and Lye moved their own brassware to the opposite wall where it's never looked quite right and may explain why Bob Rook hasn't spoken to us since. When we meet on the stairs Bob's trick is to boost his twenty stones to planetoid mode and roar past. If we want to live, we get out of the way. If we get out of the way we don't need to talk.

Bob crashed by with no sign of recognition and disappeared into his clinic. When the building stopped shaking I continued up.

~~~~~

Shaughnessy was behind his desk chewing a stick of celery, and Lucy was packing to leave. She asked about Rebecca. When I hinted that I'd picked up a couple of things she hung around to get the story.

I made her wait while I poured coffee. The machine's light was on but the hot-plate was dead. I'd mentioned this only a week ago but Lucy had countered by asking for money, which settled the matter. I poured a cold cup and shovelled in sugar and took it through to Shaughnessy's office along with a baguette from Connie's.

Lucy perched on Shaughnessy's desk and I crashed in one of the leather and chrome easy chairs that he'd put in to let clients know which partner had the class. I put my feet up on the other chair to confirm it.

'How's the building trade?' I said. Shaughnessy and Harry Green had been watching a contract foreman whose company was seeing too many thefts from the building sites he worked.

'Booming,' Shaughnessy said. He watched me push my face into the baguette. Waited until I came up for air.

'Need extra eyes?' I asked.

'None,' he said. 'It's a wrap.'

'You've got the guy?'

Shaughnessy's mouth slanted.

'We watched him lock up the site yesterday. The routine included stashing five grand's worth of electrical gear in the back of a Transit and cutting the store locks to make it look like a break-in.'

'You follow the goods?'

'First thing this morning.' Shaughnessy dipped his celery in a tub of humus and chewed. 'The guy offloaded the loot at a dodgy DIY place in Ilford. We snapped the whole deal. Site to store-counter.'

43

'Material evidence?'

Shaughnessy leaned back. Strained and lifted. Tossed something onto his desk. The object landed with a crash that sent Lucy yelping like a scalded puppy, which was his intention. Shaughnessy's a sucker for dramatic gestures – ask them downstairs. Lucy swore and looked at the thing as if it might bite.

It was a hundred metre reel of electrical cable. Heavy duty. Had to weigh at least thirty pounds.

'You took it from them?'

'Cash. Over the counter.'

'Receipt?'

'I look like a fool?'

'Not you,' I said. 'You don't look like an electrician either.'

'They weren't looking too closely,' Shaughnessy said. 'I walked into the shop while they were still stacking the shelf. Told them it was just the gear I was looking for. What could they say? Come back when we've advertised on Crimewatch?'

'A wrap,' I concurred.

'The report will be in tomorrow.'

'Anything else?' I was stalling Lucy, who was only hanging around for the news on the girl. Lucy looked at Shaughnessy.

'We got a call,' Shaughnessy said.

'New business?'

'Ex-business.'

He waited for Lucy to elaborate. She took the cue and got back onto his desk. Switched to schoolmarm.

'Eddie,' she said, 'you need a diplomacy course.'

I agreed. 'I applied once but the admin clerk threw me out when I mentioned her halitosis.'

'Well someone's pretty pissed off with you.' Lucy wiggled her backside, happy to be back on the familiar ground of my screw-ups.

Shaughnessy leaned forward. 'I got in just before Lucy's ears burned off,' he said.

'One of those,' I said. We get these calls. Hazard of the trade. The utilities companies are the worst.

'This was the tricky type. The type with lawsuits.'

'Who've we been dealing with that knows about law? We going upmarket?'

44

'Not unless you consider HP Logistics upmarket.'

I gave it some thought. 'What did they want?'

'Damages. For vandalised equipment.'

'A lousy office chair. Let 'em sue.'

'That and a lousy truck,' Shaughnessy said. 'A Volvo FH tractor. HP were keen to read Lucy the list price. Eighty-six thousand on the road.'

'Road tax included?'

'Excluded.'

I pursed my lips. 'And the chair on top.'

'And the window.'

'A pane of glass.'

'Thirty-feet of toughened plate,' Lucy said.

I conceded. 'It was a big window,' I said. 'But we'll challenge the toughened bit. The chair went through it like Perspex.'

'I take it the consultation didn't go well,' Shaughnessy said.

'We didn't land the job, is my belief.'

'Personality clash?'

I finished my baguette. Swilled it down with cold coffee. 'The guy wanted us to burglarise a competitor to set up a rigged bid.'

Shaughnessy looked thoughtful. 'Did you give him our rates?'

'He'd already trebled them before I said anything.'

'And you threw a chair through his window? What were you pushing for? Share options?'

'I wanted to hit him,' I said

'Might have been cheaper.'

'Yeah. But thirty foot of glass is a strong temptation.'

'We're going to be bankrupt by the time you've handled all your temptations, Eddie,' Lucy said.

I grinned. 'You think I should phone him back? Say we'll take the job?'

'On triple fees?' said Shaughnessy. 'Might be worth thinking about.'

I finished the coffee. Looked at him.

~~~~~

We decided to let the HP thing ride itself out. I brought them up to date on the missing girl, which didn't take long. I'd six hours left of

Gina Redding's commission. After that she'd have to decide whether to throw more money in or call it quits. What I needed to do in the six hours was locate Jean Slater's sister and check whether the girl was with her. I wanted to take at least that back to Gina.

Berkshire's a big place. I needed to figure out how to track the sister down. Until a brainstorm hit I had other jobs. Lucy headed out and I retired to my office to work my desk for two hours, catching up on other business. People have an image of the private detective's job. All glamour and action. Most of the time you're better off cleaning windows. By three-thirty the desk work had thrown up neither glamour nor action and I quit and headed home.

Arabel had texted. She had a late. I had the evening to myself.

The frustration of not knowing whether the Rebecca Townsend thing was real was chasing round in my head and threatening to drive me crazy. The solution was to quit thinking. I went up to the rear attic where I practice my painting therapy. It's a therapy with a cash bonus. The random fads of city culture had conspired to create a demand for my paintings around the markets and tourist spots. I sell occasional cityscapes and a few portraits in half-impressionist style – something like Augustus John but less unkind. Acrylics on canvas, hardboard in my cheapskate moments.

The attic had the original skylights which leaked when it rained but gave the room an inspiring light when the sky was clear. The present weather was running more to leak but the light was good enough for an hour or so. My current masterpiece was a portrait of Arabel. She has the perfect face with just the right blemishes to make what I see sublime but my fixation on capturing perfection was cramping my style. Fixate too hard and you're as likely to bring out the blemishes, make an ogre of an angel. Ask John. I took a breath and approached the canvass and forgot about lost girls for a while. When the hues began to go flat under my brush I called it quits.

I showered, crossed town, ate in Camden then drove back to Paddington and parked behind Chase Street. Then I walked the quarter mile to the Podium, a spit and sawdust bar that played live jazz until two a.m. Weekdays were open house for new talent gigging to supplement day jobs and student loans. There was often more noise than talent, but always energy.

It was still early for the live sets. I grabbed a beer and found a quiet corner. My phone rang. I tapped the screen and got a background of hip-hop and yelling.

'Mr Gumshoe!'

'Sadie. Nice to hear from you.'

'I've got something!' Sadie's voice was shrill above the hubbub. A little too animated.

'Are you drinking, Sadie?' I said. 'Is seventeen legal?'

'Yeah,' she said, 'tonight it's legal.' Another voice broke through, yelling something unintelligible. Sadie yelled back to shut the hell up. 'Every night's legal,' she repeated. 'It's what students do. Chill out, Mr Detective! You gonna arrest me?'

I looked round. The Podium's noise level was barely high enough to blanket my phone. I remembered what I'd said to Shaughnessy. No kids under our feet. Now it was calls.

'What's up, Sadie?' I said.

'I've got her address!'

'Whose address?'

'Becky's aunt!'

I snapped to attention.

'I found a postcard Becky sent when she was staying with her last year. The address is right there!'

'Read it out, young lady.'

'Got your pencil out, Mr Detective?'

'My pencil's always out, Sadie.'

That got a giggle. I let it go. Transcribed a Hungerford address onto a beer mat.

'That's great. What about the name?'

'I already told you. Something clerical.'

Guess I was looking for miracles. But the address was enough.

'That helps,' I said. 'That's good.'

Another burst of laughter crackled out of my phone. Sadie's voice came back.

'Hey, Mr Detective, how about coming down here? My friends wanna meet you.'

'Some other time, Sadie.' I killed the line.

Not this side of hell.

An ensemble was warming up. I grabbed another beer and settled in. My phone rang again. Arabel. She asked how I was doing. A duel between drums and sax gave her the answer. She promised to call in tomorrow. I told her to take care and took my drink over to join a table where a regular crew were camped out. We touched glasses and relaxed into the flow of the first set. The ensemble lacked balance and swayed unpredictably between funk and down-low dirty and I knew that in twelve months they'd have broken up and recycled but for the moment the raw energy swept us along. The oldest of the musicians was twenty.

The late set finished at twelve thirty but the diehards stayed at the table and the bar stayed busy and it was two fifteen before I hit the road and told myself, as I always did, that I was going to ease up on the Podium. I'd been saying this for six years.

I walked back to Chase Street. The building's lower floors were dark. No midnight oils in personal injury. When I opened our door upstairs a freezing draught rushed out and hugged me. The offices were colder than the stairwell. Maybe we should move our furniture out here. But then our landlord would want a rise.

CHAPTER NINE
Someone you should be watching

I woke on the couch feeling like I was locked in ice. The office lease included heating but the landlord's interpretation ran only as far as a responsibility to deliver occasional metallic rappings and thuds from the feeder pipes. The radiators themselves never got above freezing. I unfolded myself and worked through ten minutes of callisthenics to restore feeling then fetched the electric fire and placed it dangerously close in the tiny bathroom whilst I shaved and freshened up.

Back in my office I retrieved the beer mat from my jacket and checked that the address Sadie had given me was legible. It was. I had the route to Rebecca's aunt.

I fired up the coffee machine and spooned in a mountain of Colombian then carted the electric fire back to my office to score some desk time on my other jobs, which risked getting behind in the excitement of the missing girl. Abandoning regular business for business that might evaporate at any moment wasn't going to work. Out in reception the filter machine kept me company with intermittent stutters and coughs.

After twenty minutes the machine hit a crescendo. I went to see. Found the thing backfiring steam into the water tub and the coffee dry in the filter. I switched the machine off and tipped the hot water out of the reservoir into my mug, spooned in instant and heaped it with Marvel and a couple of sugars, carried it back to my desk. The brew was undrinkable. I got up and tipped the mess into the bathroom sink. Rinsed my mug. Ten more productive minutes in the life of a private investigator.

Shaughnessy arrived at eight. He had a steaming cup from Connie's that filled the place with an aroma that had me biting the desk. I filled him in on our missing girl and my planned trip to her aunt's. Shaughnessy blew his drink cool.

'So we'll either find her safe or we'll know for sure that the family's telling fibs.'

'And if it's fibs we'll need to decide whether it's something we should be involved with.'

'That's Gina Redding's call,' Shaughnessy said.
I agreed. Went back to my day job.

~~~~~

At ten I decided that the traffic would be tolerable and more scutt-work wouldn't. I rolled the desk top down. Went out and picked up a coffee and roll at Connie's. Paid cash at the counter without him clocking me. He'd have wanted arrears. I ate the roll on the way round to the back of the building, sipped the coffee while the Frogeye warmed on full choke.

I called in at my apartment for a change of clothes then headed west out of London, chasing heavy jets. I made Hungerford by eleven thirty and got directions on the main street and drove to a grass verge two and a half miles outside the town where I settled in to watch a terrace of eight cottages. Sadie's address pointed to the second from the end. I didn't have a name and I didn't have a plan but what's life without spontaneity?

An upstairs window was open but there was no sign of life. I was tempted to bluff my way in to see if I could pick up a sense of whether Rebecca was in there, but if I failed I'd be locked out. Better to see if her aunt came out. It's easier to bluff someone when you catch them off their turf.

You'd almost mistake the day for early summer. The gales had died and the sun was out and the grassy bank beside the Frogeye was a carpet of foxglove. I slid the window forward and listened to birdsong until a woman appeared from the cottage and unlocked a Ford Ka parked by the gate. She was in her early thirties, a younger version of Jean Slater. A little taller, same high cheeks and attractive eyes. The real difference was the lack of wear and tear. You saw the sisters' faces and you saw different lives. The Ka did a three-point turn and headed towards Hungerford. I fired up and followed.

In the centre of the town I played cat and mouse whilst Rebecca's aunt ran in and out of shops. Spotted my chance when she drove under the railway and swung into a Tesco's. I followed her in and parked a dozen slots away and watched her walk into the store.

She came back out twenty minutes later, burdened with carriers. Her unwieldy load meant that she was insufficiently agile to avoid me when I stepped from between two cars pushing shopping trolley into her path.

She hit the trolley and staggered, hanging onto her shopping, while I floundered through an act I've copied from the types who are always looking the other way when they crash into you at airports and railway stations. Rebecca's aunt gave me an exasperated look but before she could step round me I switched to lockjaw, like I didn't believe what I was seeing.

'Jean!' I yelled.

She looked at me in astonishment but I was already making a big 'O' with my mouth, as if I'd just realised my mistake. I held up a hand and threw apologies and this seemed to end the affair for her. She gave me an indulgent smile and moved towards her car, saying things inside that I didn't want to hear. I gave her ten yards then dragged my trolley after her.

'Excuse me!'

She turned back. Wary.

'Have you a sister?' I said. 'Jean?'

She did have a sister, Jean. Cautious shifted to curious.

I cast another tantaliser. 'Hampstead?'

Her eyes widened.

'Jean Slater!' I said. 'I knew it.'

I finally got a smile. It was mostly astonishment but we were communicating.

'She's my sister,' she confirmed. She tilted her head. 'Have we met?'

I smiled back. Grin-opolis.

'I'd remember that for sure. I'm a friend of Larry and Jean's.' I held out my hand, dropped it self-consciously when she struggled to free herself from her shopping. Gave her more flustered.

Her smile held. She recognised harmless when she saw it.

'You really had me there,' I grinned. 'I could have sworn you were Jean—'

—the sister who was nearly a decade older.

It was the kind of gaffe women notice, and helped to confirm my harmlessness. I back-pedalled: 'You must be Jean's young sister,' I corrected. From gaffe to suave. Not *younger* sister. *Young* did it better. Another difference women notice. Jean's sister noticed. She laughed and gave me the standard denials about youth, but right then she'd have invited me home for tea. We both shook our heads at how small the world was. Luckily Jean's sister had never heard of the Second Rule of the investigation business which is that the world is very big. If it ever seems small it's because you're being crowded by someone you should be watching. The Second Rule complements the First Rule, which says there's no such thing as coincidence. Where a layman sees coincidence the investigator sees connections. Where a layman sees a small world the investigator sees trouble looming.

When we got over our small world chuckles I threw in my pitch.

'So how are Larry and Jean?'

Rebecca's aunt gave me a that's-life grin. 'They're just fine,' she said.

I looked thoughtful, like I was squeezing my memory.

'Kathy!' I said. 'You must be Kathy.'

The power of my recall stunned her. She nodded. 'Kathy Pope,' she said.

Pope.

Something clerical!

That Sadie.

'I'm gonna ring them,' I promised. 'They'll never believe we've met.'

Kathy smiled her Rule Two ignorance. 'It's an incredibly small world!' she agreed.

'Wait till I tell Jean!' I was nodding like a car-window dog. Then I gave her just-another-thought and asked how Rebecca was. I watched her face. Her smile strengthened. On this subject she was effusive.

'Rebecca's fine. She's coming to stay at Easter. I just wish I had her more often.' Her face was a vision of warmth. Not the look of someone nursing a convalescing niece. If Rebecca was recuperating in Kathy Pope's house it was news to her.

Kathy's groceries were thawing. We wrapped it up and said we'd see each other at the Slaters' some time. I yelled again that Jean would be knocked out about this.

She'd be knocked out all right.

If I told her.

I took the M4 back to London, chewing over what I had. What I had was a quick solution that had just popped. Someone was telling porkies.

And if Rebecca Townsend was not at her aunt's where the hell was she?

CHAPTER TEN
Fog

Back at Paddington the office was deserted. I flipped the sign and went to sit behind my desk to think things through.

First thing: I needed a chat with Larry Slater before I went back to Gina Redding. Get a little colour, even if no clarity.

His firm's name had a big-city ring but an address in high street Islington, the City shadow-land where fortunes are made on a more personal scale but with equal dependability. Slater's luxury home testified to the efficient sluicing of money through the fibre optics that burrowed their way up to the borough. They say the streets of London are paved with gold, but your best bet nowadays is in the tunnels beneath.

I keyed the Slater-Kline number again.

The call was answered this time by a human. Maybe their computer's day off. A different woman, less bright and breezy but ready with the same message. Larry was tied up. No information on when he'd be untied. An assurance that he'd call me back at the very soonest. Her words had the sincerity of a car dealer's Christmas card. I rang off.

Seemed a more proactive approach was called for. If Slater was actually at his office my best bet might be to pick him up as he left work, take a look at his movements, fish for any sense of what was rocking his boat. Maybe even talk to him.

It was still early. I had a couple of hours. I got back to an ongoing investigation of a rogue pharmaceutical executive suspected of selling inside information to a short trader. My call list included the dial-out record from the guy's office, supplied by his company, and from his mobile, supplied by the agency. Eighty contacts in total. I'd tracked twenty through company books and reverse directories. Sixty to go. Time rushes with that kind of stuff. When I looked at the clock for only the tenth time it was four fifteen. Time to pick up Slater.

The weather had turned again and a looming storm brought early dusk. Thirty minutes of red lights on Euston Road got me to Islington where I cruised past a sixty-foot window sporting the

Slater-Kline name, just up from the Angel. I found an access road a couple of blocks away whose double yellows were concealed under rubbish sacks. I backed in. If a service truck came out it would have to drive over the Frogeye.

I walked back down the main street through a freezing drizzle and looked into the Slater-Kline window. A brightly-lit office, a dozen desks scattered informally, each equipped with the latest in low footprint plasma monitors and ergonomic wireless keyboards, two or three clients sitting at agents' desks. Bigger clients with juicy portfolios would be taken through to private rooms at the back. I walked round and discovered an alley running behind the buildings and Larry Slater's Lexus waiting in a chained-off parking area. The angle of the parking bays prohibited turning. Slater would exit at the far end.

I retrieved the Frogeye and parked under a loading gate thirty yards from the alley, then walked over and stood for half an hour as the rain came on, watching the Slater-Kline parking spots free up as the senior staff shut up shop. By six p.m. only the Lexus was left. I wondered at a guy putting in the hours with family problems waiting at home.

The rain intensified. The alley behind Slater-Kline faded into a mist of spray. In those old films the private eyes stand under street lamps, kept dry by their lined trilbys and ankle macs. The old-timers would have rolled their eyes at my bare head and leather jacket. But that's progress. I did the modern thing. Stood and got wet.

Luckily the patron saint of detectives was watching over me. Slater came out barely five minutes into the deluge. I sprinted for the Frogeye and by the time the Lexus had pulled onto the street I was rolling.

Slater headed south then west on Pentonville. I kept my distance, focusing through the spray and windscreen fog.

We navigated Euston in endless stop-starts before the traffic cleared at Eversholt and the Lexus accelerated into the underpass and out onto Marylebone. Slater was not heading home. He took the flyover and we got up to fifty along the Westway as if we were heading for open road. Everyone knew different. All our speed did was rush us towards the tail end of the Hanger Lane log jam.

The rain slackened. The city rippled in a multicoloured blaze below us, poised on the edge of night. Then the rain kicked back and kaleidoscoped the whole thing. The Frogeye's wipers began to struggle. I'd just started to wonder if Slater was set for a long journey when the Lexus edged onto the off-ramp and rolled down to the West Cross roundabout. I braked to maintain distance, kept my indicator off. When the Lexus turned I followed it down into Holland Park, to a street behind the park lined with white-stuccoed Victorian mansions converted to luxury apartments. I followed him in. Up-market cars were parked nose-to-tail but Slater found a spot half way down and pulled in. I squeezed into a tiny space fifty yards back. My lights were off before I stopped rolling.

For a couple of minutes nothing happened. Was Slater waiting for someone to come out? Then the Lexus' door opened and he stepped out and walked along the pavement towards me and climbed the steps to a door with the number 93 displayed in flowery white script on a black base. He pressed the top floor bell. No response. He pressed again, turned to stare up and down the street while he counted off the seconds. Then a final attempt – a good, long push. Still no result. He came back down and walked to his car. I started the engine.

The Lexus stayed put. I killed the ignition and waited. The rain eased and the street stayed quiet. I pushed in a Roy Eldridge tape and set the volume to give me background without distraction while I waited for Slater to act. Ten minutes turned to twenty, then half an hour. The Lexus stayed silent and dark. I pictured Slater, watching No. 93 in his mirror.

An hour went by. The rain came back and blurred the windscreen and I had to switch on the ignition a couple of times to give the wipers a sweep.

Whatever I'd expected this was not it. I was supposed to be looking at something happening inside the Slater house. Instead I was watching a vigil miles away. I tried to guess how this street might be connected to Rebecca. Was Slater looking for her? What would a college kid be doing in this area? Plenty of things came to mind, all of them speculation.

The last of Gina Redding's hours ran out. We were in the free-bonus phase now and all I was getting was fog.

The Eldridge tape ended. I slotted in another, a crackly Gasser to counterpoint the slow-moving minutes. It was getting cold. Maybe Lexi had electric heaters. I checked my watch and saw that we'd been here an hour and twenty. When I looked up Slater was out of his car and walking back to No. 93. Same routine: three pushes of the bell, scanning up and down the street while he waited. Same result. His head gave a frustrated shake and he walked back to his car and drove off. I let him go. Whatever this detour had been about it started and ended here. The droop in Slater's shoulders as he came down the steps had told me that. I hoisted myself out of the Frogeye and walked up. No. 93's bell plate said that the top apartment was inhabited by someone called Brown. No initial. No title. The name narrowed things down nicely, whatever I was narrowing down. Which might be something entirely unconnected with the missing – or not-missing – girl.

But whoever Brown was, he or she was significant enough to keep Slater sat around in the cold for an hour and twenty minutes like a felon casing a target when a simple phone call could have done the job.

Something was going on. Slater was desperate to talk to someone.

CHAPTER ELEVEN
Happy families

I called at Gina Redding's first thing next day and gave her what we'd found, which was that Jean Slater was lying about her daughter and that her husband was up to something that was maybe connected. I don't believe in coincidences. When you're looking at one funny going-on and stumble across another there's always a link.

'He might be searching for Rebecca,' I said. 'Maybe she's eloped with some rich guy. There's no shortage of candidates in Holland Park.'

Gina shook her head. 'Rebecca didn't run off. She wouldn't mislead her friends like that.'

'Intentions change.'

'But she'd have called Sadie at least. If she'd run off, why aren't the Slaters interrogating her?'

Which was my own question. 'If Rebecca had run away,' I said, 'Sadie would be the one who'd know something.'

Gina blew a jet of smoke. 'But instead of talking to her they're locking her out.'

'So they know that Sadie knows nothing. Which means they know Rebecca's not run away.'

The old lady stubbed her fag. Unwrapped a new pack. 'So someone has taken her.'

'It's beginning to look that way. We just need to figure why the Slaters haven't gone to the police. Kidnap for ransom might keep them quiet but the Slaters don't stand out from the crowd as an obvious target. There are richer pickings round town. Unless financial extortion wasn't the purpose.'

Gina lit her cigarette and we watched a pair of swifts squabbling in the garden.

'The Slaters may have something the abductors need,' I said. 'Larry's line of work suggests possibilities. But we may be wide of the mark. It's still possible this is all in the family.'

'You think Larry and Jean have harmed her?' Gina was right back with her first suspicion.

'The question is, do we take this further? If we dig we'll find out. But we'll be fighting the family all the way. It's going to be expensive.'

Gina took a drag. Watched the garden.

'Do whatever you need,' she said. 'Let's get Rebecca back safe. I'll handle the bill.'

'Fine,' I said. 'Give us three or four days. We'll find her.'

Gina nodded, but she was thinking the same as me. Three or four days on top of a week was a long time. We'd find Rebecca, but that didn't mean she'd be okay.

~~~~~

I headed to the Slater house to take a look at Jean Slater's day. The early morning drink yesterday didn't point to anything particularly productive in her schedule, and if Jean just stayed cooped up I'd waste another half day. But it was the best shot I had before bringing Shaughnessy in and starting the heavy digging.

In the event a better option presented itself. As I turned into the lane I had to pull the Frogeye hard into the verge to avoid becoming roadkill under the wheels of a four-by-four coming out. My mind was on avoiding the agricultural-size Michelins, but I caught a peripheral glance of Jean Slater's face up behind the windscreen. Going somewhere fast. Seemed she'd not started so early on the lubrication today, unless I was luckier than I knew.

Decision time. It would be good to see where Jean was going but the opportunity of an empty house was too good to pass. Empty if Larry Slater or Rebecca were not there, of course. I went with opportunity. Regained the tarmac and drove on up to the Slaters' and turned in to park outside their front door. There was no sign of the Lexus.

I rang the bell. Better safe, et cetera.

No answer.

I reached into the Frogeye's boot and grabbed a couple of tools and slipped them under my jacket, then walked along the front of the building. The villa was abutted by white stuccoed walls but an unlocked gate let me through into impeccable gardens behind. Had to be regular staff tending them. I hoped today was their day off. I went round the building and found a conservatory that added nothing to the Spanish architecture. An add-on at the stage of needing either major refurbishment or demolition. Its main feature was a door that needed only hand pressure to ease the lock's tongue from the frame. I went in and walked along the back of the main house. Three doors opened into the building. Two were secure. The third was the kitchen door and was unlocked. If they put up an ENTRANCE sign it would save a burglar time. The house was alarmed but something told me that Jean Slater hadn't stopped to set the panel. I stepped into the kitchen to test my theory and walked through to an alcove in the hallway.

No alarm bell. Deadly quiet.

I took the nearer staircase up to the gallery which served doors on all four sides. I started clockwise from the east. Found two guest rooms then a master bedroom at the front of the house. The room was the size of a tennis court with walk-in dressers and a double-sized en suite. Jean and Larry's room. Bed unmade, walk-in closets open, lid askew on a laundry basket. Seemed Jean was not a neat freak. She probably had a domestic, although there'd been no sign of any when I was here on Tuesday. I searched the room fast on the off chance that there might be something significant. Found nothing. If the Slaters had anything to hide it wouldn't be here. I went out. The west side of the house had two more guest rooms, both unused and sterile, then a door at the rear of the building opened into a bright and untidy bedroom crowded with soft furnishings and wall posters.

Rebecca's room.

Two rooms knocked into one, like at the front. The ultimate teenage den. Six full-height windows looked out over the gardens and illuminated walls decorated in cheerful pastels matching the curtains and bedspread. The bed was made up but clothes and shoes were scattered about and a desk was cluttered with student stuff – notebooks, scrap paper, card files, work assignments. No computer: Rebecca probably kept her laptop or tablet with her.

I covered the room, corner to corner, in forty-five minutes. Found nothing amongst her paperwork or clothes, nothing under the mattress, no love-letters hidden in her underwear drawer. I only found what mattered by chance, when my foot caught a piece of loose flooring while I was riffling jackets in a walk-in closet. I squatted to coax up a short floorboard and spotted three slim exercise books hidden beneath. Rebecca's diaries.

I took them over to the desk. The pages were a mass of tiny handwriting packaged into short cryptic entries going back three years. I started with the current one. The entries were a teenage girl's standard concoction of drama and daydreams but it didn't take long to spot something that might be significant, Rebecca's reaction to the split with her boyfriend. Seemed the separation had cut deep.

Three months back things were fine. Rebecca and boyfriend Marcus were solid. The diary entries were scattered with Marcus' name. Sweetheart stuff. Rebecca's cryptic shorthand might have protected her secrets a generation back but nowadays everyone texts the same code ten times a day.

Eight weeks back the entries had changed in tone and length. The sweethearts had had a fall-out. A storm had closed in fast. The diary skipped specifics, avoided stuff that was too painful, but after the storm had been and gone Rebecca poured out her misery in barely-coded pain that skittered between guilt and blame. Three short sentences said it all:

He dsnt lv me.
Hate him. All my fault!!

The subsequent pages logged Marcus' phone calls but didn't say whether Rebecca picked any up, which I guess she didn't. Seemed she preferred to wallow in the misery of logging the boy's attempts. The importance of his trying was clear but I got the impression that reconciliation was locked in a bear hug with something destructive inside Rebecca. I turned a page and a torn photo fell out. Two halves. I held them together and found a chest and head view of a good-looking boy in a black t-shirt, college buildings behind him, squinting into the sun with a loopy grin.

The photo was large enough to be shreddable twenty ways. The single tear screamed restraint. Said that Rebecca's heart wasn't in it. I slipped the photo back and read another week's worth of misery, a mixture of self-castigation and stubbornness. Did Rebecca show any of this outside her room? Probably not. Something told me this wasn't a house for shared problems.

A couple of weeks later the entries had reverted to one-liners. Seemed the split was permanent. Then the first hint of Rebecca's new attachment. The code would have been tricky if I didn't already know the characters:

Kiks club. Rsl got me in. Pssd. Slept @ his.

and

Skipped class. PM w Rsl, smoked, let him.

Smoked what? Let Russell what?

Whatever it was it seemed that Rebecca was doing more than just hanging out with the guy. The entries stayed short and cryptic, but what was there was clear enough. Stuff like *2e's* and

Rsl on stuff, insistd i try – no wy – bstd got heavy, ran out.
Bstd!
Calld me latr, 4gottn!!
Pikin me up 2mor. Bstd!

I was getting the picture and Russell stayed right in it. If you were looking for signs of a slide it was there. But nothing pointed to the reason Rebecca had vanished. Unless she simply didn't come back from one of Russell's little parties. Ten days ago the diary just stopped.

I skipped back a couple of years for anything that might give me a picture of how things were inside the family. Spotted stuff that didn't look good. In amongst Marcus and teenaged angst Rebecca poured out her feelings about her mother and Larry. The stuff on her mother was mostly complaints about her interferences, her indecisiveness, her unwillingness to stand up for her daughter. But Rebecca's hostility towards Larry Slater needed no interpretation.

What did Jean ever c in this prik?
Money!!!!!

and

Bstd yelled @me ryt in front of Jean & she said nothin.
So I said it 4 her!! Letch almst hit me.
But he knows thers a line. He only has 2 cross it then
his secrets out & its goodbye Happy Famlys

Happy families. How do they get like that? And what secret was she talking about? She didn't say but I could take a guess.

I trawled for more, one ear open for the sound of anyone returning. Found nothing. Decided I was living on borrowed time.

I slotted the books back under the floorboard and searched the bathroom quickly, digging through the clutter of cosmetics and girl stuff for anything that shouldn't be there – maybe an indiscreet cache of "e" or "stuff" from one of her evenings with Russell. Nothing again.

The phone rang downstairs.

I froze like a guilty schoolboy. Waited while the ringing continued long and loud in the empty house. When voicemail kicked in I finished up and went down.

I had what I'd been looking for. The picture was pretty much what Sadie and Gina had hinted – the unhappy home, Rebecca's break-up with her boyfriend, the new guy Russell. The tension at home stood out a mile and it wasn't hard to figure what the thing was between Rebecca and her stepfather. It looked like Rebecca had been holding "Letch" at bay for a long time. I adjusted my assumptions. Wondered again whether Rebecca's disappearance might not be self-imposed. A home where you're not safe is no home.

I took a last instalment on my borrowed time to give the ground floor the once-over. Covered four rooms lightning-fast, hoping for a break – maybe a ransom note saying *Leave one million pounds in a locker at Paddington Station* – but the only extortion I found was the stack of utilities bills amongst the unopened mail. The mail dated from nine days back. Seemed the Slaters had had other priorities since then.

I picked up the phone and ran the voicemail. A woman named Meg wanted Jean to let her know when she should start back cleaning. So the Slaters had put their domestic on hold. Did they not want anyone in the house right now? I picked up Meg's number and let myself out.

CHAPTER TWELVE
Not the same girl

I phoned a number Sadie had given me. Marcus Moxham, Rebecca's ex. The call was picked up through a hubbub that sounded like a college cafeteria, a deep voice, difficult to reconcile with a youth under twenty or the nerdy photo in Rebecca's diary. Sadie had warned Marcus that I'd be talking to him. He sounded bemused at the thought of her calling in the detectives, but I heard concern in his voice. He was at the college, taking early lunch. We agreed to meet in fifteen.

I spotted him, a lanky kid in faded denim and suede ankle boots, seated on a bollard outside the college. When I walked up he stood with the uneasy smile afforded equally to private detectives and trainee dentists. Detectives – police and private – are evidence of a world that people prefer not to see, tainted by association. Marcus' grin stayed strained as we shook hands and I asked him when he'd last seen Rebecca.

'I see her here off and on,' he said. 'Last time was maybe a couple of weeks ago.' His voice was matter of fact but he was watching the street. This was a heavy subject.

'Did she mention any problems?'

'We didn't talk.'

'The two of you are finished?' I was waiting for him to look at me but he continued to watch the street. Gave the world an aw-shucks grin.

'Looks that way.'

'I heard you were serious.'

'We were. But it fell apart. Things got in the way.'

'What things?'

He finally looked at me.

'Rebecca had issues. She could be hard to take when she was in her moods.'

'Is that why you split? Her moodiness?' I recalled the diary: Rebecca blaming herself. But Marcus shook his head.

'No,' he said. 'I could put up with the difficult side.'

'So what happened?'

He took his time; went back to watching the street; thought it through; decided, finally, that it was none of my business. He came to the more immediate matter.

'What's going on?' he asked. 'Sadie's hysterical.' He forced another grin. 'I can't believe she called in a private eye.'

'Me neither. I guess she's told you that Rebecca's dropped out of sight.'

Marcus nodded. 'She told me. I don't know if I'd go calling in the cops though.'

'Why's that?'

Marcus shrugged again. 'You never know with Rebecca. She's unpredictable. Maybe just lying low. Problems at home. Late with her coursework. I wouldn't automatically assume that something has happened.'

'Has she disappeared before?'

'A couple of times. She'll lay low for a few days when she's pissed off. Hit the town, stay out nights, crash at friends of friends. Her mother always got onto my back thinking she was with me and I had to go along with it. But Rebecca's never dropped right out.' He looked at me again. 'Is she in some kind of trouble? '

My turn to watch the street. I said: 'Yeah. I think she's in trouble.'

The words coming from me and not from Sadie made the thing real. The boy's face dropped. Split up or not, Rebecca still meant a lot to Marcus Moxham.

'I'm trying to get a feel for what state of mind Rebecca was in recently,' I said. 'Did you pick up anything?'

He shook his head. 'Like I said, we've not spoken. I've seen her around but if there was a problem she didn't tell me. We've pretty much gone our own ways.'

'She'd shown no sign of wanting to get back together?'

'None at all. I called after we split but she never answered. Didn't call back. Whenever we meet she just rushes by. She's been kinda cold, actually, after what we'd had. Like I'm just history.'

It was none of my business but Marcus' account contrasted with what I'd read in Rebecca's diary. I wondered what drove a girl to bury her feelings and let a bad act play out until something that mattered was trashed. Marcus seemed like a good guy.

He still hadn't mentioned Rebecca's new friend Russell Cohen. I guess the idea of his ex- turning down-market for a replacement must have cut. Somewhere in his head, though, was a better picture of Rebecca than he was giving me. I threw Cohen's name in to stir things up. Marcus paused. Tried to find something neutral.

'I heard stuff. Don't know the guy.'

'What did you hear?'

He shrugged. 'Nothing good. Rebecca's a fool getting involved with that type but I don't know if there's anything between them.' He said the words but his eyes told a different story. Marcus saw Russell as Rebecca's new boyfriend.

'What do you know about him?' I repeated.

'He's a shithead. Works the doors down the West End. Deals drugs. Small time, but he thinks he's a mobster. It's hard to understand Rebecca. The dropout scene isn't hers.'

'She's been seeing this guy for a few weeks?'

'I heard she's been hanging out, yeah.'

Another discrepancy with Rebecca's diary. The diary didn't sound like just hanging out. To me it seemed Rebecca was dipping her toe deep into the doggie-doo.

An antique Beetle U-turned into the kerb and a scruffy youth wearing aviator shades yelled out of the window and hit the horn. Marcus held his hand up, shrugged his jacket tighter.

'You gotta understand something,' he said. 'Rebecca's a great girl. She's just a little fragile. Everyone talks about her moods, how crazy she can be, but do you know what I think of...' His guard was down. I kept my mouth shut.

'I think of what Rebecca loves most in the world: peace.'

'Peace?'

Didn't sound quite the same girl.

'We used to meet in Regents Park. There's a café in there by the colleges. Whoever got there first bought the drinks. If it was Rebecca she'd usually be outside, feeding the squirrels. Or in with the oldies, watching the world go by. You'd think she was watching the most wonderful thing in the world, the old people talking, the squirrels chasing around. You see someone that way and you know what's important to them.'

He realised he was giving a speech. Shut his mouth. Turned to walk across to the Beetle.

'Just find her,' he said. 'Make sure she's safe. It's something I could never do.'

He jumped into the car and it roared away.

~~~~~

I sat in the Frogeye and dialled the number I'd picked up from the Slaters' voicemail. Recognised the voice above the drone of a hoover. A lilt of Caribbean ancestry. I asked to speak to Meg.

'That's me, hon,' the voice said.

I introduced myself as an acquaintance of the Slaters and asked for details of Meg's domestic services. The hoover quit.

'That's nice of Jean to give me a recommendation,' she said. 'I'm busy but I can always fit you in.'

I stayed vague. Details about moving house, possible future dates. Nothing specific to mess up her diary with false bookings. Meg replied that she'd be available whenever I was ready and I tossed some bait.

'Jean says you do a great job,' I said.

That got a yelp.

'Here's me *wishing*,' she said. 'But I ain't touched their house in nearly a fortnight. Ever since Jean said they were getting some work done and didn't need me in. Left a hole in my schedule. I just wish she'd tell me when they're gonna be through.'

'Yeah. Those plumbers are unpredictable.'

'Plumbers? You heard right, hon? It's the electrics they's repairin'.'

'Sure,' I said. 'But you know how they need to earth the electrical supply to the pipes. That means resetting the pipes the right depth in the ground.' Mr Know-It-All. Sometimes known as Mr BS. But the BS works.

'Lord,' Meg yelled, 'I bet the whole house is topsy-turvy. I hope they ain't expectin' me to get it all tidy in a half-day! Honey, you just give me a call when you're ready for me.'

'Yeah. If I need some cleaning, too.'

Meg laughed and cut the line.

I fired up the Frogeye.

So the Slaters didn't want their domestic in the house right now.

Perhaps whatever was happening with Rebecca had complications that would be difficult to hide from someone inside their front door. The question was what kind of complications were we talking about?

Time for a face-to-face with Slater.

CHAPTER THIRTEEN
Tell him Jerry Pine is here

I detoured back to Paddington and caught Shaughnessy at his desk. Brought him up to date on what I had on my missing girl, which wasn't what I'd wanted. What I'd wanted was to be off the case. Instead, we had a girl who'd been missing a week and every sign that someone had taken her. What we had was urgency.

We needed to take a serious look. Starting with the question of which of the things going on around Rebecca – her bust-up with her boyfriend, the Cohen character, the issue with her stepfather and his fixation with the Holland Park apartment – were relevant, if any.

Shaughnessy agreed to come in for a few days. He'd start by talking to a DPP contact to see if they'd heard of Cohen, then take a closer look at Jean Slater. I'd take Larry.

Shaughnessy picked up his phone. I headed out to Islington.

I parked on a meter and walked down to the Slater-Kline business. Waiting for Slater's call-back wasn't going to work. Time for a face-to-face. See what the guy said for himself.

I went into the shop and walked to the nearest desk where a thirty-something woman in ovoid Day-Glo spectacles and a pinstripe suit sharp enough to raise legal action from Gillette was packing a bag. She asked how she could help in a way that made it clear it had better be of the fast kind. It was closing time and she was revving for a getaway. I asked to see Larry Slater.

She asked if I had an appointment. I hadn't. She told me that in that case she didn't think it would be possible.

I assured her I only needed a couple of minutes, hinting that Larry and I were old business buddies, used to operating on the fly. Fly operations didn't work for Ms Gillette. She turned her smile to full wattage and explained that she was personally authorised to assist all Larry's investment clients. I declined her offer, said I needed to see Slater face-to-face. She locked smiles and repeated her offer. Last and final.

We could have gone on all evening. Gillette probably got overtime. I apologised again and said that I *really* wanted to see Larry.

Personally and right now. While I was talking I was checking the place out. The office was modern – all pine furniture and pine wall cladding. The open plan room went back thirty feet to an array of pine filing cabinets and pine fire doors off to each side. The door on the left was propped open. A clerk came through it, closing up a bag; ready for the off. The door on the right was shut. Access to private meeting rooms and the bosses' offices upstairs. When I looked back, Ms Gillette's smile was set so hard it was cracking her makeup as she put finality into her voice and repeated that Slater was unavailable.

I smiled right back and asked if she had any idea who I was.

Luckily, she didn't, which explained the uncertainty that replaced her fend-off smile. She threw a glance at a male colleague and shook her head.

'I'm sorry Mr…?'

'…Pine,' I said. 'Tell Larry that Jerry Pine is here.'

My tone put her off-balance. Her voice took on something that might have been genuine regret. 'I'm truly sorry, Mr Pine, but Larry is totally tied up. Unexpected business. He's cancelled his appointments through to next Tuesday. But I'll let him know you called. I know he'll want to speak to you at the earliest opportunity.'

Appointments cancelled. Unexpected business. My bet said that the unexpected stuff had nothing to do with stocks and shares. Ms Gillette's face told me that she'd been turning clients away all week and was up to her eyebrows with it. Her spectacles glinted under the fluorescents. She was going to be late getting out. She made a decision. 'Let me call his partner Mr Kline. I'm sure you know him.' She reached for her phone.

'Don't bother,' I said. 'Larry handles my business and Mr Kline knows it. Tell Larry to call me when he has a moment. Maybe we can discuss where I do my future business.'

I walked out.

I'd not managed my face-to-face with Slater but I'd got something I needed.

~~~~~

I walked round the back of the block. Slater's parking slot was empty, ⌐hich explained why he was not available to see his old pal Piney.

Didn't explain why Ms Gillette hadn't just told me he was out and saved our confrontation. Unless she'd not been sure where he was. I got the sense that Slater was sowing chaos this week.

I called Shaughnessy. He'd finished his telephone research and was outside the Slater house. He gave me what he'd found on Russell Cohen.

'The boy's a bad apple. List of convictions as long as your arm. Twenty-eight years old. Nine inside. Young offender plus two stints in adult, both GBH. Out the first time after eighteen months, the second after three and a half years. The first was a lucky break. Cohen got into a fight and his opponent took a half-dozen slashes across the face with a Stanley knife. The story is that one cut came within a quarter inch of the guy's carotid. That's a quarter inch away from our boy going down for life. Some people are just lucky.'

'Cohen? Or the guy he slashed?'

'With Cohen's take on life I guess the other guy's luck doesn't come into it.'

'So whom did he slash?'

'Officially the incident was a random scrap. Unofficially the victim was a punter who got behind in his debts. The word is that Cohen has had a sideline dealing since before his juvie. Nothing they've pinned on him. He's just a name that crops up. The guy's strictly small time but nasty with it. According to the DPP the two GBHs are the tip of the iceberg, cover a whole list of incidents that didn't get to court. Victims who declined to testify and so on.'

'What did he go down for the second time?'

Shaughnessy laughed cheerlessly. 'You'll love this: he beat up his girlfriend and threw her out of a window. She fell two storeys and spent eighteen months in rehab. Still wouldn't shop him. Cohen only went down because a witness disputed the girl's claim that she'd fallen accidentally. Heard the girl screaming long before her acrobatics. In the end the jury went for the word of an independent witness against that of a victim with a shattered pelvis and a story about a banana skin.' Shaughnessy sighed. 'How much punishment do these women have to take before they realise that whatever they're afraid of can't be any worse than what's actually happening?'

'Psychology. Better the devil you know than a really pissed-off devil you know.'

'This violent streak. It's not a good thing to be hearing.'

'Nothing sounds good about Rebecca being involved with the guy. What's Cohen up to right now?'

'I talked to Steve at Hammersmith Magistrates' Court. Cohen's probation office is Balham. They have him officially on the dole, waiting for the City headhunters to show up. Word is he's ticking over nicely with the drugs thing. Work's a few casual door jobs.'

He gave me an address in Streatham. It was a council flat in a working class area. Whatever deals Cohen was into weren't making him rich.

Shaughnessy said he'd hang on at the Slaters' house, see who came and went. Tomorrow we'd go for the direct approach. Confront the Slaters and suggest that they bring us in on their problem or have it go public. If Rebecca was involved with someone like Cohen it needed sorting fast.

I dialled Sadie to see if she had anything on Cohen's door jobs. The call connected and her voice screamed into my ear above a racket. I held the phone away.

'I knew it would be that creep!' she yelled, 'I knew he'd got her!'

It's impressive the way people are always ahead of us. What can they see that detectives can't? Maybe the agency should recruit a few doorstep gossips and teenagers. Save legwork. I repeated my question.

'He works up the West End,' she told me. 'A place called Kicks.'

'He there every night?'

'Most. He starts around eight. That's when Becky's always gone there.'

'Okay. I'll talk to him.'

'Tell him that if he's hurt her you're going to tear him apart.'

'Sure,' I said. 'Unless he's bigger than me.'

'He's not so big. Just a mean prick.'

'Watch your language, young lady.'

'Forget my language. You just get that bastard. I hate guys like that.'

'So do I.'

'Hey, Eddie?'

'What?'

'It's a jacket and tie place. Thought you should know.'

I killed the line. The phone stayed silent for five seconds then lit up again and Arabel's voice came over the airwaves.

'Thought you were never getting off the blower,' she said.

'Just client stuff.'

'I'm just checking you've not forgotten that your girl has an appetite.'

My girl had lots of appetites. I deduced that this one was a reference to our dinner-date. We were eating out before she went on shift.

'I'm on my way, Bel.'

She made me an offer: 'If you got here early we could have a little hors d'oeuvre.'

The invitation was tempting but if we started down that road we'd never eat. Didn't seem fair to send the girl to work hungry. I turned down the offer and said I'd see her in an hour. The happy way she accepted told me she knew her priorities too. I had a thought.

'You remember if I have a suit and tie?' I said.

'We going somewhere posh or are you getting kinky?'

'Answer the question.'

'A suit? I think I saw something once. You'll have to fight the moths though.'

'That's what I thought.'

'So what's with the dressing-up?'

'Nothing's with the dressing up. Just a passing thought. We're eating Italian.'

'Suits me. Gives me my carbs for eleven hours' slog.'

I put incredulous into my voice. 'You need calories for *night shift?*'

'Babe,' she said, 'don't ever get brought to my hospital.' She cut the line. I jumped into the car and drove home.

CHAPTER FOURTEEN
If Carpet Man gets annoyed...

I decided against the suit. Arrived at Arabel's flat off Roman Road at ten past seven. Our Italian restaurant was a small place five minute walk away, not yet trendy but with the right buzz and with food you couldn't better in Rome. We ordered seafood platters and played footsie under the table while we waited. The fooling about was instigated by Arabel, to make sure I regretted her being on night shift as much as she did. In the verbal part of the conversation she asked about my missing girl. Picked up on the Cohen character. The image of a vulnerable girl tripping on the wild side had a particular resonance for her.

'You think Cohen has got her into trouble?'

'I'm going to ask him. The problem is that we've come into this a week late.'

'You mean she could already be hurt?'

'I can't rule it out, though it doesn't fit with the Slaters keeping quiet. If they thought Rebecca had been harmed they'd not be hiding anything. So she may be okay for the moment.'

'Maybe she's run off with the guy.'

The platters arrived, each the size of a small table. Our allowance for a trip back to Arabel's for her to change began to look marginal. We attacked our plates for five minutes before I came up for air.

'I don't think she's run away,' I said.

'So maybe Cohen's holding her. Maybe extorting the family.'

'Dodgy boyfriend turns predator. It's a possibility.'

We quit talking again and concentrated on the food, followed it with double espressos that would keep Arabel on adrenaline for her shift and me hovering above my bed till morning. Forty minutes after we started we walked back to her flat, and six minutes later I escorted a lady of the medical profession to my car. I opened the door for her to squeeze in. The operation takes dexterity if you're over five feet. In the case of females the squeezing is incompatible with keeping hemlines where they should be. Even NHS hemlines. It paid to play gentleman. Something about the awkwardness of the legs and the particular curves that formed as Arabel folded herself in could fairly distract a man. A girl might even suspect that you drove a car like the Frogeye to achieve that result. But Arabel was good at the game. Any difficulties were deliberate. She messed about until she figured I was truly regretting her being on shift then flapped her hand for the door.

'Come on, babe. Are we staying here all night?'

I took the question as rhetorical; slammed the door and folded myself into the other seat; drove round to the hospital and got a last showing of limbs as she climbed out. Then I headed back onto the Mile End Road and followed the traffic to the West End.

~~~~~

Kicks nightclub had a red neon sign over a smoked-glass entrance in a narrow street north of Chinatown. It was Thursday night and still early for the club scene. I watched the place for a while. Saw one couple go in and a group of girls stop to chat with the doorman before deciding to get drunk somewhere cheaper. The doorman was a gorilla in a mid-calf trench coat and dickey-bow. He watched the street with his hands in his pockets, looking for signs of enemy action. I wondered if this was Cohen.

Only one way to find out.

I walked down and stopped in front of him. The guy gave me the doorman's universal expression of boredom that lets you know that you're looking at a shark behind the respectable veneer. The genie is corked but it's your call. The guy was white, six-three, eighteen-plus stone.

'I'm looking for Russell,' I said.

'What's up?' the guy asked.

I didn't ask him if he was Cohen. If he was then he already knew I didn't know him.

'Tell him I want a word.'

He looked me over. Decided I wasn't worth it.

'He's busy. See him tomorrow.'

He moved his attention back to the street. I could either stand there or piss off.

I said: 'I need to see him tonight. Okay if I drop inside?'

I stepped forward but Dickey-Bow shifted casually and the door was suddenly blocked and didn't look like it was going to get unblocked unless I had a tow truck.

'Ties only, mate,' he said. He was still watching the street, ignoring me the way a rhino ignores a flea. I wondered what it would take to shift him out of the doorway. I didn't have a tow truck.

I looked down the street myself. Gave it a few moments for him to register that I hadn't disappeared. Then I turned back and fixed him with a stare I got from the movies. If it scared him he didn't show it. He just looked left and right like every night was this boring. I jabbed my finger at the doors. His attention drifted back.

'Ask your friend to step out. Tell him Mr E wants a word. Unless he'd like me to bring some friends round.'

That's E for Eddie. Lucky I wasn't called Xavier. Hard to get someone to take you seriously when you tell them Mr X is waiting.

I watched Dickey-Bow trying to work out whether Mr E was someone Cohen should be worried about. But the hint that the club might get a visit struck a chord. A visit didn't sound good, even to someone who likes a rumble. He transferred his attention back to me and his eyes let me know how hard he was working to hold it in.

'Are you the rozzers?' he said.

I put on an incredulous face. Looked round for the audience and said: 'Who's your optician, pal?' then shook my head and pursed my lips like I was deciding whether it was simpler just to walk away and call back later with the boys. Dickey-Bow finally opted for caution.

'Stay there,' he said. He went in through the smoked glass. I turned to face the street again so that Cohen couldn't ID me – or not-ID me – unless he came out onto the pavement. The ruse worked. When I turned back there were three of them, like a bad publicity shot for The Blues Brothers.

Next to Dickey-Bow was a black guy in shades. He was the same height but three feet wider. He'd either had his trench coat cut at a carpet factory or had mugged Demis Roussos. Rebecca's boyfriend had to be the last of the line-up. Russell Cohen was half the size of the others but with an attitude that made up for missing body mass. Cohen was five-ten and fourteen stone max but my guess was that it all counted. His hair was a white fuzz capping a puffy, mean face. He sported the same shades as Carpet Man, wrapping an expression of contrived blandness. With this guy, the first you would know about trouble was when you connected with his ten-pound fist. His body stance though told me that the visit from Mr E had him on edge. He was trying to figure if he'd brought trouble to the club.

The three of them stared at me the way they'd watch a punter with frays in his jeans.

'What's your game?' Cohen asked. 'Who the hell's Mr E?'

'I'm Mr E,' I said. 'Eddie Flynn. You Russell?'

'Who wants to know?'

I guess they keep the questions simple at the doormen's examination boards. I let the query go.

'I'm looking for Rebecca Townsend. I hear she's pally with you.'

'Never heard of her.'

His answer slipped out so fast that I knew he wanted it to sound false. Wanted me to contradict.

Detectives are the contradicting type. 'We can do this the easy way,' I said, 'or the hard way.' I wasn't sure if it was Willis or De Niro had said that. If Cohen was a film buff he'd know. 'Either way, I need to know where the girl is.'

Dickey-Bow and Carpet Man flashed each other glances. Cohen just watched me with the focus he'd apply to a fly on a turd.

'I think,' he said finally, 'that you're a geezer needs to piss off.'

His voice was calm. Still waters.

Despite the cool act I could see something tugging inside him. Maybe he didn't know what this was about, but he didn't sense anything good brewing. What I sensed was the beginnings of movement from the two stooges at his side.

Cohen decided he had enough backup. He stuck with his proposal.

'Sod off now, mate,' he repeated, 'before you get a smack.'

'Russell,' I said, 'it would take more than you.'

Russell gave me incredulous and looked sideways to check if his buddies had dematerialised. They hadn't. That must have boosted his confidence. He didn't run for cover.

'I'm looking for Rebecca Townsend,' I repeated. 'If she's with you it's better we talk now.'

Cohen shook his head more emphatically, playing to his buddies. 'What would be better,' he said, 'is for your plates to start shuffling down that old pavement. Before me and my friends get annoyed.'

The sight of Cohen getting annoyed would be interesting. The sight of Dickey-Bow and Carpet-Man getting annoyed would probably be fatal. And Dickey-Bow's face had a look that said I might not need to wait too long for the experience. I'd exhausted my novelty value. Dickey-Bow leaned forward to explain the deal.

'You've got five seconds,' he said. 'If I come off these steps Russell's gonna be the least of your worries.'

I didn't move. Russell and I had a thing going. Messages passing between us. Before I knew it the five seconds were up and Dickey-Bow and Carpet Man were coming down the steps. Cohen watched and smirked. Some people you just can't frighten. The two hulks rolling towards me were definitely frightening and looked about as stoppable as road rollers. There's only one way to beat road rollers. Speed.

I nodded to Cohen and turned away. The gorillas could still have jumped me but I was backing off and top rule in the door business is don't get blood on your suit before the punters are all in. I walked away in one piece.

I headed back to where I'd left the Frogeye on double yellows, musing at how detection is ninety per cent frustration and ten per cent results. That would be fine if the results weren't so often negative.

I'd got nothing for my detour except the certainty that if Rebecca was mixed up with Cohen she was in trouble.

The question was whether Cohen was involved in this thing at all, or whether I should be looking elsewhere.

A real puzzle for Mr E.

CHAPTER FIFTEEN
The door kept quiet

Seven a.m. The Slater house. Windows all dark. Larry's Lexus parked in its usual place. No sign of life.

There was a slap on the Frogeye's soft top and Shaughnessy folded himself in with the effort of an arthritic contortionist.

'One day, Eddie, you'll get a car that doesn't put my back out,' he said.

He'd been saying this for six years. Just part of the routine.

'If I want to drive a tank I'll join the army,' I said. I'd been saying this for six years, too.

Shaughnessy leered. 'Just a normal car would be fine. One where you don't need to consult a yoga manual.'

'You've just gotta get the technique.'

'Like with a straightjacket.'

'Houdini could get out of a jacket in sixty seconds with his hands chained,' I pointed out.

'Yeah, and look what happened to him. Dead in a fish tank at fifty! And I bet the bastard couldn't have got out of this tin can if you greased him with warm lard.'

Shaughnessy had watched the movies. History, Hollywood-style. I didn't correct him.

'You taking the first one out?' he asked.

'Yeah. Probably Larry. I'll leave Jean to you. If she stays home you can follow her round the house on the Yamaha.'

'Got it. And if Larry drives past us before I can escape from this sardine tin you can drop me off at the nearest motorway services.'

Shaughnessy and I had opened the agency when I came out of the Met six years earlier. The guy had nearly twenty years on me and had seen a different side of life by way of the special forces. He never talked about his old job and I never talked about mine. Shaughnessy was older but fitter. He could beat me in and out of the Frogeye any day. It just made him feel good to gripe.

I flicked on the news and we listened to climate change and politics for fifty minutes. Then just on eight Larry Slater came out and walked over to the Lexus. Despite his gripes Shaughnessy was out of the car before Slater had keyed his remote.

Slater fired up the Lexus and I followed him out into the rush hour. One plus about the Frogeye that Shaughnessy had neglected was that it eluded rear-view mirrors better than any other vehicle on the road. When we merged into the Hampstead traffic I was only three cars back but invisible. If Slater had been a professional the tail wouldn't have worked, but Larry was just another guy. I could have sat in his back seat and he wouldn't have noticed.

We drove through Camden and edged into the log jam on the Euston Road. Looked like we were heading for his office. Maybe he'd put in a regular nine-to-five, but if he came out early I'd be ready.

I was right about the destination. I watched Slater drive in then parked on a meter a hundred yards from the business and went to stand on my corner. Was there three hours. I'd just reloaded the parking meter at noon when Larry rolled back out onto the street. I sprinted to the Frogeye and went after him; jigged through the traffic to make up lost ground; caught the Lexus just as it turned back onto the Euston Road and stayed on its tail all the way back to Hampstead. By twelve thirty I was back at the Slaters'.

Two minutes later Shaughnessy slid into the car. I gave him the update. Shaughnessy confirmed that Jean Slater hadn't budged. A productive morning all round.

Decision time. I told Shaughnessy to hang on here and call me if anything moved. I had a house call to make.

~~~~~

I crossed the river and worked over to Streatham and a street in a run-down area wedged between converging railway lines. The address was a flaking four-storey council bunker with a facade of french windows and false balconies weeping rust stains, an architectural graffito shouldering the Victorian terrace beside it like a shady character in a bus queue. I squeezed the Frogeye into an empty slot and walked across.

The bunker's communal door was open. Seemed security locks and ~se phones hadn't reached this far down the council list. Inside, the stairwell smelt of something unpleasant. I trotted up to the third floor before my nose could figure what it was; arrived at a door with bare wires protruding from where the bell push should have been. Maybe you grabbed the wires and made your own noise. I played safe and knocked. Gave it an official crispness.

Nothing. I made a fist and beat on the wood in a way that was less easily ignored. That got a voice from inside with an inflexion that said I'd better have a good reason to be there when the door opened. When the door did open, Russell Cohen appeared like a nightmare on dress-down day.

The suit and shades had gone. Black Levis crimped a Guns 'n Roses t-shirt over a belly that was beginning to show curvature. Without the suit you could see Cohen weighed thirteen stones max. and without the shades you got the full force of one of those stares that make people look the other way, the ones powered by a lifetime's bad attitude. Cohen was twenty-six but looked fifty.

When he clocked who I was he turned round to play out a little pantomime he'd perfected for dealing with idiots outside club doors. The act comprised staring at his own front door as if it shouldered the blame for whoever appeared outside it. The door kept quiet. Cohen turned back to me.

'What's your friggin' game?' he said.

A racing channel was playing inside the flat, from where a distant cousin of the stairwell stink emanated, a cocktail of unwashed laundry, booze and TV dinners. A little spliff thrown in.

'You remember me?' I said.

'Mr Friggin' E.'

Memory Man. I grinned. Friendly-like.

'What are you?' he asked. 'Some kind of fruit?'

'Just a guy needing some answers.'

Cohen stared at me. 'I think,' he said, 'that you're a guy who needs to piss off.'

I dropped the grin. 'Stay cool, Russell. I've just a few questions.'

Cohen gave me a couple of seconds then moved up close. The movement was slow, easy. One moment he was in his doorway, the next he was in my face with eyes opened wide to emphasise a proposition.

'I'll count to ten, matey,' he said. 'You need to be gone before I get there.'

Bluff. There was no way Cohen could count to ten. 'I need some answers about Rebecca Townsend,' I said. 'When I get them I'm out of your face.'

'One,' Cohen said.

Like I said, bluff. Who can't count to one?

'Two.'

We were eyeball to eyeball as Cohen continued to show off. So maybe he could count to ten. While I marvelled at his mathematical skills the clock ticked. We got to six, then seven and when Cohen hit eight his head tilted back just enough to tell me where this was going. A light came on in his eyes. He wanted me to be there at ten.

We didn't make it.

At nine, his head moved back like a spring-loaded wrecking ball. He was focusing a headbutt on my nose whilst trying to figure the next number, and the multi-tasking did for him. Before he hit double digits I'd stepped back and kicked his knee hard. His headbutt flailed thin air as the shock of the knee doubled him over. I reached round his neck, two-handed, and pulled down with all my weight, and his face met my knee with a painful smack. He bounced up like he was on springs and I lifted my foot, sole out, and propelled him backwards into his flat. He crashed over a phone table down the hallway and the thing collapsed. Glass shattered and Cohen sat down in the mess. He started to come up but my foot caught him between his legs and that seemed to get through. He rolled over and yelled blue murder and shifted his attention elsewhere. I took advantage of the lull and closed the front door. When I turned back Cohen was struggling up to lean against the wall, gripping his thighs.

I walked into his lounge. Sparse furnishings, but what was there was expensive. A sixty-inch plasma screen on the wall had a bunch of horses going neck and neck, and a soft leather sofa was half covered by an open copy of the *Racing Post* with a smart phone flickering atop it. Cohen busy investing his ill-earned dough. I picked up the remote and muted the TV, wondering how many months wages would get me that kind of wall decoration. Figured I was stuck with emulsion for the moment.

Cohen came in cursing and I turned to face him. Waited for his
ᵈˢ to dry up.

'The story is that you've been showing Rebecca Townsend the good life,' I said. 'Or what passes for you as the good life.'

Cohen was dripping blood. He gave me a look that said I'd better not turn my back anytime soon but stayed his distance.

'We've got a problem,' I said. 'Rebecca's disappeared and no one knows why or where she is. I need to know whether you're involved.'

I tossed the TV remote between my hands to remind Cohen that there was more furniture to break. Intimidation was the only thing people like Cohen understood. 'What's going on between the two of you?' I said.

'Nonna your business,' he said.

I sighed.

Something inside Cohen's skull held him back for the moment, but with his type enlightenment is a long way from fear. Retreads like Cohen don't come with fear built in. They rely on stupidity. You could pound a nutter like Cohen all day and all you'd get would be complaints from the neighbours.

I tipped a mess of empty cans and takeout cartons off a coffee table and lifted it. The thing weighed a ton, although it wasn't in the same league as HP Logistics' swivel chairs. I approached the plasma screen and hefted the table. I didn't know how much these screens cost but I'd seen one in Harrods a couple of years back at ten thou'. Then again, Harrods are dear. Cohen probably got a deal. The kit was still worth enough for a serious insurance claim, though, assuming Cohen had insurance.

'Stop,' he yelled. 'Whazza matter with you?'

I lowered the table.

'Let's start again,' I said. 'How long have you been seeing Rebecca?'

Cohen shook his head. 'How should I know? Month or two.'

'That's precise,' I said. 'Sounds like a meaningful relationship.'

'Meaningful, shit. She's a stupid kid hanging around for action. She wants it she gets it. It's all the same to me.'

'What kind of action? Drugs? Sex? Or are we talking philosophy discussions?'

'What's your gripe? I've not even seen the bitch for two weeks.'

'I'm trying to find out what's happened to her. Starting with what's happening between you and her.'

The head shake again, like an itching bull. 'I told you. We hang out.

She likes a bit of rough.'

'Rough like tramping a little? Or rough like getting slapped around? Or do you just mean rough like hanging with a turd?'

Cohen didn't take the bait. 'Rebecca never got a single smack off me,' he said. 'And she didn't do nothing she didn't want. The best thing you can do with that kind is grab what's offered. Give it what it wants.'

It.

Cohen was going to have a problem when he decided to settle down. Getting those "it"s into the marriage vows would take finesse.

'How often have you been seeing Rebecca?'

'This day and that. Whenever she cuts class.'

'You got her on anything?'

Cohen sneered.

'That uptight bitch would be scared shitless if you showed her the real stuff,' he said. 'So maybe we have a little smoke. Maybe we don't. What's all this about? Why's everyone pissing their pants?'

'When did you last see her?'

'Told you. Coupla weeks.'

'Not since?'

'Nah.'

'Are you shitting me, Russell?'

Cohen let his sneer answer for him.

'Have you done something to her?'

He held his sneer. Still not standing straight and already getting brave.

'Have you or your slimy pals hurt her? Because I'm going to find out.'

'What are you going to find out? You're full of shit.'

Braver by the minute. I could understand Cohen forgetting the threat to his plasma screen but I had to wonder about a guy who could forget the ache between his legs.

I backtracked. 'When precisely did you see her?' I said.

He stayed quiet. For a moment I thought he'd clammed up, but then he worked it out.

'Week last Tuesday.'

The day before Rebecca went missing.

'Where?'

'At the club. She was in for a coupla hours. Went off around ten.'

'Was she with anyone?'

The sneer again. 'She'd come to see me,' he said. 'The bitch was on heat for me. She comes round the club to get herself tipsy-topsy and thinks she's living the wild life.'

'Being with you doesn't stop her leaving with someone else,' I said.

'Yes it does.'

Possessive. For a guy who couldn't care less.

'So you've not seen her since that night?'

'Nah.'

Whatever little credibility I gave to Cohen's words I got the sense that he didn't know anything. He was sticking to his story like chewing gum on angora.

'Did Rebecca say anything about trouble at home? Plans to leave town?'

'Nah.'

'Any word out about her? People talking?'

'Nah.'

Cohen's disinterest was getting emphatic. I sensed him working himself up for a second round. Time to quit. If the Slaters pointed at Cohen I'd be back. Right now my stomach had absorbed all it could of the place.

I gave Cohen a wide berth and went out, skipped down the stairs to get to breathable air. Out on the street the Frogeye was still in one piece and the sun was shining. The day seemed momentarily good. I'd just got the engine fired up when my phone rang.

Shaughnessy.

Things were happening.

CHAPTER SIXTEEN
Serious wannabe

Slater was on the move. Shaughnessy was following his Lexus south through the city. I steered out of Streatham and fought traffic towards Wandsworth. If Slater was headed out of town I'd take over.

Shaughnessy's hands-free commentary steered me north of the river to where they were snarled in roadworks at Hammersmith. I closed the gap and by the time Shaughnessy reported them turning beneath the flyover I was already moving up the eastern ramp. I put my foot down and spotted the Lexus merging into the traffic up ahead, heading out towards the M4.

I called the hit and Shaughnessy broke off to resume his stakeout at the house. I pushed in an Eartha Kitt tape and cranked the volume. I had a full tank and good music. Wherever Slater was headed I was with him. I didn't see out-of-town trips being the norm in a stockbroker's day. Maybe this excursion was part of whatever was shredding his diary.

The Lexus took the Orbital anti- and cut onto the M3 and we cruised south-west. The sun flared in the Frogeye's windscreen. Keeping Slater in sight took concentration. We hit the M27, continued south and fifty minutes later drove into Poole. On the far side of the town we crossed the harbour bridge and the Lexus turned inland and pulled into a marina called Cobb's Quay. I held back in the parking area and watched Slater pull up nose to tail with a red Toyota SUV out by the jetties. I swung in behind a beached cruiser and walked down. Enough hardware was bobbing out on the water to start a navy. Motor cruisers and yachts in all directions. This wasn't billionaires' row – there was nothing over fifty feet in sight – but it was serious wannabe.

A man in a flannel sports jacket jumped from the SUV. He shook Slater's hand then the pair walked down a jetty and onto the bow of a motor cruiser and disappeared below. I walked out after them and clocked the vessel's name. The *Lode Star*. A sleek forty-footer in brilliant white with a fully enclosed wheelhouse topped by a radar ⌐itter and raked VHF. As nice a place as any for a little discreet business.

I returned to dry land and sat on a bollard with the sun on my face. A Channel breeze ruffled the water and kept masts dancing. As stakeouts went it beat lurking in the bushes outside the Slater house. As stakeouts went it was brief: after ten minutes the two men reappeared. They quit the boat and moved back up the jetty. I walked back to the Frogeye. By the time I got there they were at their cars. Another brief handshake and the meeting was over.

I pressed the starter. Choices: stay with Slater or follow the Toyota? Chances were that Slater would be heading back to Town. I called Shaughnessy. All quiet at the Slater house. He agreed to ride out and pick Slater up as he drove back in. I let the Lexus go and followed the Toyota towards the sea. Traffic was nil. Keeping the vehicle in sight was like following a tank across a desert. We crossed back over the bridge into an area of narrow streets and tourist shops where the Toyota turned down a side street between an antique shop and mountain bike outlet. I flicked the indicator but took my time making the turn to let the vehicle get clear. Saw that it had stopped fifty yards down. I watched the driver jump out and walk in through a doorway. I cancelled the turn and rolled on, parked in a slot and walked back round. The side street was residential, terraced cottages with doors set on the street, just a handful of small businesses mixed in – a greengrocers, a furniture store and a run-down café. The Toyota was parked outside the café which had a side door with stairs servicing upstairs offices. A business plate read DK MARINE. I crossed to a ginnel and hung around in the shadows for a while to see if the guy came back out. He didn't. I walked round the block to avoid a second pass in front of the building and recovered the Frogeye. I had a vessel name, a licence plate and a business address in addition to all the fresh air.

I called it a day. Drove back to London.

~~~~~

I reached Battersea at seven. Arabel had left a message reminding me that we were shopping tomorrow. She'd be off duty at seven a.m., ready to hit Covent Garden. I started to call, warn her I might not make it. Cancelled before the number connected. I had a busy weekend but I figured I shouldn't let the girl down more than three times in a month. In my line of work you could grow a habit of letting people down. Arabel put up with it mostly but I'd cancelled a few things lately. I needed credits to shore up my next let-down.

I grilled a tuna steak and ate it with a jacket potato and steamed veg then called Shaughnessy and drove out over the river.

There was a live set scheduled at the Podium so entry was a fiver. I told Barney I'd not be staying and he waved me through *gratis*. The place was still empty. I relaxed with a pint of Pride and piped jazz. At eight thirty Shaughnessy came in and brought another beer for me and a mineral water for himself. Shaughnessy's tipple never varied much. Sometimes it was plain mineral water, sometimes carbonated. It was hard to spot today's variety in the Podium's light.

He brought me up to date. Jean Slater hadn't shown her face all day. Shaughnessy had sneaked round the rear of the property a couple of times. The first time he'd spotted her taking out the rubbish and the next she was just a shadow behind her window. His trip out to pick up Larry Slater had been the highlight of his day.

I gave him the details of Slater's nautical excursion. Speculated on whether the yacht rendezvous was connected with whatever was happening to his stepdaughter. The First Rule of the Detective Game said yes. No coincidences.

'Something's thrown a spanner into Slater's schedule,' Shaughnessy agreed. 'Chasing to the coast for a ten-minute chat isn't routine.'

'The guy go anywhere interesting when he came back in?'

Shaughnessy took a swig and planted his bottle. Bubbles rose. Carbonated.

He'd picked Slater up as he crossed the M25 and tailed him through rush-hour traffic right back to Holland Park where he watched the same routine as two nights ago. Slater had rung the doorbell. Got nothing. Sat in his car for an hour and a half. Headed home. Seemed our mysterious Brown was still absent.

'This person is part of it,' Shaughnessy said.

I agreed. 'Holland Park has me wondering whether Rebecca's become involved with someone there. Someone linked to her disappearance.'

'Maybe not an extortion racket,' Shaughnessy said. 'If the girl's been ~pped for money the stake-out wouldn't fit: Slater would know

88

Rebecca wasn't findable. So, something else.'

He came back to another alternative. 'How did Cohen pan out?'

'He didn't know or care. As far as he's concerned, Rebecca's history. He's not part of it.'

'So what's next?'

What's next was footwork. We needed to clarify a few things then confront the Slaters. Put pressure on them to bring us in on their problem. We agreed the plan and Shaughnessy went home to take care of responsibilities I didn't have. I gave him a fiver to pass to Barney. Might as well stay for the live set. If I went home I'd brood about the girl, imagining the worst.

CHAPTER SEVENTEEN
Amex

Arabel and I breakfasted in Covent Garden then spent the morning in the boutiques. Arabel has a figure that carries expensive clothing frighteningly well. Shopping with her can leave the car in hock. Mercifully, the girl has to sleep sometime. We called it quits early afternoon just before my card went onto life-support. She hit the sack and I drove back to Battersea; made a hands-free to Shaughnessy on the way to see what was happening at the Slater house. Shaughnessy wasn't at the house: he'd tailed Larry to Holland Park and yet another vigil outside the apartment. He'd pulled in Harry Green to cover the house rather than call me in. His soft spot for Arabel. Shaughnessy seemed to think the girl was good for me, which I could have told him. He'd also figured that the best chance of me keeping her was to shield her from the chronic unreliability that goes with the private investigator's lifestyle, mine in particular. Sean had the notion that the occasional morning draining my wallet would prove to Arabel that I was reliable. Arabel knew better.

'Want me to take over?' I said.

'Negative. I'm comfy.'

'Let me know if anything breaks. Otherwise, tonight.'

'Tonight.'

I called Harry. He reported that Jean was sitting tight inside the house.

'I hear this girl's been gone ten days,' he said. 'That doesn't sound good.'

'Nor to me. But if she's still in one piece we'll get her.'

Harry said nothing.

~~~~~

I killed the rest of the afternoon in the attic working my painting hobby. Quit when the sky clouded and took the light. A storm was ⁻n its way.

ᵗˡᵉd Shaughnessy and Harry for updates. Slater had ended his vigil and returned home and Shaughnessy had quit for the day. Harry was still watching the house. I asked him to hang on for two hours and warn me if Slater moved.

I changed into dark clothes and a shooting jacket with a modified vest that was useful for holding stuff, then drove across the river in heavy rain; reached Islington and cruised the alley behind the Slater-Kline business. The parking slots were all empty. I parked a couple of streets away and jogged down to a coffee bar opposite the shop. Grabbed a window seat and watched. The main office was brightly lit but nothing moved inside. The upper windows were dark.

The rain eased. I finished my drink and walked round to the back of the buildings where a fire escape scaled the rear wall. Yesterday's visit had shown me that the main office was well protected, but my guess was that the upper floors would have minimal security. I climbed the escape and jemmied a washroom window on the first platform and was inside in thirty seconds. I went through into the corridor. No security sensors in sight. I checked downstairs; squinted through the fire doors. An array of motion detectors and mini-CCTVs protected the main office but what I was looking for was on this side. Back upstairs I located Slater's office. The door was locked but the lock was meant to deter casual wandering, not a professional assault. I released the lock and went in. The room was bright from the street lights but I needed more. I flipped on Slater's desk lamp. Anyone passing would see a business partner putting in the hours.

The office had shelves stacked with company reports and trading magazines, and two locked filing cabinets that probably held stuff on Slater's personal clients. I was looking for something that didn't belong, something that might give a clue about what was going on at home: notes, telephone numbers, maybe a ransom demand. It was a long shot but Slater was spending time at work despite the family problem. Maybe he'd stashed something here.

A solid mahogany desk backed on to the window. Its leather worktop was bare except for a low-footprint PC, telephone and thinly populated in/out trays. The desk had a kind of old-world feel that solicitors go for: Slater's attempt a status symbol. I sat behind it. Three pull-out drawers ers left, a file drawer and stationery tray on the right. The were locked but the locks were for decoration. I opened with sixteen-gauge wire.

The top left drawer was sweep-up from when Slater last cleared his desk. Current customer portfolios with graphics tracking gains and losses. I skimmed Slater's cryptic market assessments and action lists, saw nothing unusual. A few printouts were dated within the last few days so something like normal business had been going on.

The next drawer down held writing pads and a couple of market weeklies. Nothing of interest. The bottom drawer was twice the depth of the others and Slater used it as a dump for old material. I pulled the contents out and set them in order on the desk, although I wasn't sure there was any order. Last year's company reports, market summaries going back two or three years, torn-out magazine pages with marked-up articles, similarly outdated. Then something interesting.

Pushed beneath the lowest layer of market magazines were some sheets that didn't belong: two Amex statements and two mobile phone bills. All recent: February and March. Odd stuff to keep at the office. Even odder pushed under a weight of fossilised junk.

I cleared space and took a look.

Slater used his phone freely. The statements were three pages each. All voice calls. Most were timed during office hours. The ones outside this were typically thirty seconds, the calls you make to tell your wife you're on your way home or to make a restaurant reservation. The daytime calls were up to fifty minutes – Slater exercising the yuppie option to talk business on his personal phone while the landline sat obsolete. Nothing stood out, but there had to be something in the list that made Slater keen to bury it at the bottom of that drawer. And the fact that he'd chosen the office to conceal the bills suggested that the person he was hiding stuff from was his wife. I took out my phone and snapped the details. Then I checked the Amex sheets and hit the jackpot.

Slater used the card sparingly, so what was there stood out. And what was there was stuff he probably didn't want showing on his normal bank statements.

The bill for February had a zero opening balance then a single transaction: Slater paid a company called Blueglades fifteen hundred pounds.

The March statement showed and adding six more transactions. Two clearing the fifteen hundred re payments to Blueglades in mid- and late-March for fifteen hundred and three thousand pounds. And coincident with these were two hefty payments to a hotel called the Royal Trafalgar in Brighton where Slater had settled an eight hundred and then sixteen hundred pound bill. A final couple of charges were for restaurants in the Brighton area on the same dates. From the size of the bills Slater was either feeding a football team or the restaurants were outrageously expensive. I guessed the latter.

Interesting.

The payments had a resonance. Hinted at some kind of extracurricular activity that Slater wanted hidden from eyes at home. An affair? What was Blueglades?

I checked the phone bill again. Correlated dates. Picked up a cluster of calls to a single mobile number matching the February and March Blueglades payments. Maybe the number of whomever Slater was extracurricularising with.

It was the kind of stuff we dig up all the time. The information would be hot if I was here to investigate Slater and not his stepdaughter.

I photo'd the Amex sheets then reinterred the bills in the drawer and locked up.

I moved to the right hand side. The file drawer held ten card files of open business. I went through them. Client files circulating from the main office. Nothing interesting.

I decided to pass on the main filing cabinets. They'd take me ten minutes to open and I doubted that I'd get anything new. The stuff Slater wanted hidden was those phone and Amex bills. I sat back in his chair and tried to picture it but the picture stayed fuzzy.

It was nine p.m. I exited Slater's office and let myself back out through the washroom window. No way to re-lock the window but no one would notice. No one would be looking.

I recovered the Frogeye and called Shaughnessy. He was ready to roll.

CHAPTER EIGHTEEN
Ghost's breath

We watched from across the street while I filled Shaughnessy in on what I'd found at Slater-Kline.

'We're looking at a mistress or a hooker,' Shaughnessy concluded. 'But what's the connection with Rebecca's disappearance?'

'Maybe nothing. Coincidence.'

Shaughnessy looked at me like I'd abandoned religion.

I shrugged. 'Gotta happen sometime.'

Shaughnessy kept looking.

'On the other hand,' I said, 'Slater watching this place day and night is stretching things.'

We were outside the Holland Park apartment. Lights showed on the two lower floors but the top was dark yet again. Seemed Brown wasn't home much.

We crossed the street and climbed the steps. The outer door let us into a vestibule with three post boxes. Junk mail was bursting from the top one. The inner door had a keypad and electric latch. Shaughnessy went to work on it while I pressed the bell. No point breaking in if someone was home. A single brief push. Nothing to stir up the tenants below.

No response.

Shaughnessy beat the lock and we went in. A light came on automatically and illuminated hallway décor that matched the affluence of the street. Plush carpeting and varnished woodwork, framed prints. Not bad for a communal space. The carpet muffled our footsteps as we walked up.

On the top floor I released the apartment door and reached for the light switch to light up an inner hallway. Inside, a stale taste suggested that windows had not been opened in a while. And something else: the place had an abandoned feel, beyond the temporary emptiness of a week's vacation.

And what owner leaves house plants to die? Shaughnessy and I both spotted the dracaena on an ornamental table under a skylight. The plant's leaves were yellowed on collapsed stems. I waited for

94

Shaughnessy to comment. Dead plants were too commonplace in my life for reliable judgement.

'The heating's accelerated the drying,' Shaughnessy said. 'These things wilt after three days without water. I'd say there's been no-one here for a week.'

A week had a particular resonance in relation to our missing girl. Made me wonder if we had another unaccounted-for person.

We split up. I took the front. Opened a door onto a lounge. A dimmer switch brought gold tessellated wall-lamps to life. I drew the curtains and turned the dimmer up, revealing Italian furniture and walls hung in expensive gold and green fabrics. An ornate fireplace supported a sixty-by-forty gilded mirror that might have graced the original drawing room downstairs.

Adjacent was a kitchen, also facing the street. Venetian blinds that wouldn't hide the light. I took the risk. Threw the switch. The kitchen was compact but expensively kitted out. High-tech appliances. Marble worktops, all clear and clean. Just a few dishes stacked on the draining board. A small corkboard beside the door was covered in notes and Post-It stickers.

Back in the hallway another door opened onto a sense of soft furnishings. I drew the curtains and hit the light switch and saw a woman's bedroom, as lavishly kitted out as the lounge. Bright colours splashing over browns and creams. Free-standing teak furniture. A queen-size bed, dresser spread with girl things, bedside table topped by an ornate lamp featuring an entwined couple holding aloft the fixture. Under the lamp were two framed photographs. One was a faded shot of a middle-aged couple posing in a garden. The woman had short-cropped hair framing an attractive face that watched the camera with an affectionate smile. The man was tall, dark-complexioned. Smile strained. The second photo featured two girls in t-shirts and shorts, one standing behind the other with her arms round her companion's waist. Both shared a beauty that stole the breath. Carefree smiles and crescent eyes. Identical long black hair and natural long lashes. Sisters. Maybe twins. Their features suggested that they were the daughters of the older couple, and instinct told me that one of the two was Brown.

I met Shaughnessy back in the hallway.

'Three rooms back there,' he said. 'Spare bedroom, used as an office. Ironing and airing room. Bathroom.'

We started at the front. Shaughnessy took the kitchen. I worked through the lounge and a picture started to emerge. I pulled out a cabinet drawer cluttered with photo albums and old letters, postcards, foreign travel memorabilia. The albums had photos of the middle-aged couple, a decade or two younger with two young girls beside them. The girls' beauty blossomed in the later albums – or at least one of theirs did. After mid- or late-teens there were no pictures of them together. Was the bedroom photo the last? The one who appeared in the later albums was snapped in a variety of desirable locations, sometimes in a group but mostly with male companions. She was in her late teens, early twenties. The guys were three decades older. A final album captured the woman as a fully-bloomed beauty in her mid-twenties, mixing with different crowds at different locations but always looking somehow alone. In amongst the albums was a scattering of loose photos, including passport head and shoulders of the woman, who had to be Brown. I slipped one into my pocket.

I moved on. Brown had wide music taste. Soul and reggae, CD stacks brimming with Motown and Marley, a stack of hip hop albums in generic covers, pirated versions bought up Camden or Petticoat Lane. The entertainment system was a top flight Yamaha suite with four-foot Ikon speakers. The woman was no pauper.

Shaughnessy came in.

'Someone left in a hurry,' he said. 'The sell-by dates in the fridge say the owner shopped a week ago. Left the stuff to rot.'

I asked about the corkboard.

'Nothing,' Shaughnessy said, 'unless we're looking at a dry cleaning conspiracy.'

I pulled out the photo album with the snaps of the dark-haired beauty. 'Our absentee tenant,' I deduced.

Shaughnessy pursed his lips.

'She's not someone you'd easily lose,' he said.

'All we need is an ID.'

Shaughnessy walked through to the back while I picked up the phone. There were six recorded messages. I expected to hear Larry Slater's voice, but the first five were females. One identified herself as Julie and had left a breezy greeting a week back, asking for someone called "Sis" to call her back. The other caller left four messages, starting a week back and ending two days ago. In the first message the caller identified herself only as "me" and asked someone called Tina to ring. A mobile number was logged.

The second and third messages were more urgent.

'It's Sammy,' the caller said, 'What's happening, Tina? Why's your phone off? I need to sort with the agents. Call me.'

Sammy's final message was more assertive.

'Tina, where are you? Ring me, girl.'

I noted Sammy's number and went on to the last message.

Bingo!

A voice almost breaking in its urgency.

'Tina! It's Larry! For God's sake talk to me.' A short pause then a final plea: 'For pity's sake, Tina, what are you doing? *Call me!'* The message clicked off.

The desperation was clear. Mirrored Slater's long vigils in the street outside. I sensed things centring. The apartment's silence thickened.

Tina Brown.

I replaced the phone and went to take a look at the bedroom.

Tina's wardrobe matched her looks. Sexy stuff – short skirts by the inch-load, low-cut dresses, designer jeans that looked like Tom Thumb's sister wouldn't squeeze into them. Probably looked spectacular packaging Tina Brown's curves.

Her lingerie drawer would give a sergeant major the blushes, might even gain Arabel's respect. A riot of silk and lace, thongs cut so tiny the labels stood out like banners. Underwear designed to kill, or at least disable. I kept my mind on the task. I wasn't looking for lingerie. I was looking for the stuff Tina might have hidden beneath it, misled by the woman's universal misconception that the lingerie drawer is a safe place to hide secrets. I got nothing. Moved on to a dressing table covered in expensive cosmetics, so much of it that I had to think of gifts. If this woman didn't get gifts there was no hope for the rest of the female species.

The bed was tidily made and patted over. Decorated with half a dozen throw-cushions. I searched in and under the bed and in less likely spots – on top of the wardrobe, underneath the wardrobe, underneath rugs – but nothing turned up. I went out.

Shaughnessy was having more luck in the office room. That was where Tina stashed her bills and that's where he confirmed her ID.

'Passport, driver's licence, birth certificate. Date of birth seventeenth of August, nineteen eighty. Driver's licence seven years old. Face matches the photo album.'

'Any sign who's paying the bills?' I asked. The oldest connection.

'All in her name. The lady's self-sufficient. Rents this place at two-five a month. Shorthold contract signed four years back. The girl's a high earner. And take a look at this.' Shaughnessy handed me a pen from the back of the desk.

The pen was a click-top ball point, slender and solid. Black with a gold band. The sort presented as up-market promotional giveaways. This one had a name in gold lettering along its length.

Royal Trafalgar.

The name on Larry Slater's Amex bill.

Bingo again.

Beautiful woman. Rich guy. Mysterious hotel bills. Slater staking out the place. Something was going on between Slater and Tina Brown that Jean Slater for sure didn't know about. Was the woman Slater's mistress?

If so, what had taken her out of town? Had she ditched Slater for a bigger fish? But I hadn't noticed any holes in her wardrobe to suggest she'd packed a suitcase, and you don't get far without your passport.

So why was this woman top of Slater's agenda the week his stepdaughter was missing? What was that desperation in his voice? My First Law was screaming the obvious: Tina Brown was connected, maybe even central.

We tidied up. Switched off lights and opened the curtains. In the front lounge the street light washed back in to restore the apartment's deathly stillness. I walked out with a sense of oppression tingling my neck like a ghost's breath. We secured the door and went down.

We'd got what we'd come for. Brown was ID'd. But who was she? And where was she?

CHAPTER NINETEEN
Everyone wants a piece of you

I breakfasted on wholemeal toast and Buckaroo coffee loaded with cream and sugar then headed out.

The city was buzzing with the hint of spring. I drove through Sunday traffic, dodging cagouled tourists crossing against the lights; played Wyn Marsalis loud with the Frogeye's windows open; let his *Levee* stuff swirl round me as I jinked lanes, hit greens and no tourists, and made Hampstead in twenty minutes.

When I pulled into the Slaters' driveway I saw that Larry's Lexus was missing. Mark that as a plus. I jumped out and rang the door bell and Jean Slater appeared. The five days since I'd seen her hadn't done her any favours. Today she looked too weary even to question the appearance of an education official on a Sunday morning.

I greeted her with a harmless smile, which must have worked because she stepped back instinctively. I took it as an invitation, and by the time her senses caught up I was in the house.

'We need to talk,' I said.

Jean started to come alert.

'About what?'

Something was seeping into her consciousness. Something about education officials and Sunday mornings not mixing.

'I think you know what.'

Jean looked at me like I'd spat on her shoes.

'Mr Anderton, why are you here?'

I put her right. Gave her my real name and one of my real cards. When she read it she jumped like she'd touched a bare wire. She was alert now for sure.

'A private detective? What on earth is this?'

I gestured into the house. 'Let's sit down.'

'No!' Her voice gained strength. Anger cracked her lassitude. 'How dare you come here under false pretences?'

'We're only trying to help, Jean.'

'We don't want your help. Please leave!' She pulled the door wide. 'My husband will be back any moment.'

Private investigation. It's like being a Jehovah's Witness. Everyone wants a piece of you. But like a good Witness I stood my ground.

'Rebecca's in trouble. You know it. I know it. You need to talk to us before it's too late.'

Jean's eyes stayed angry but there was something else there too that you might mistake for distress.

'Five minutes,' I said. 'Hear me out.'

I saw a battle raging. Then suddenly Jean closed the door and walked stiffly ahead of me into the lounge. I followed. Jean sat but didn't invite me so I invited myself. She didn't speak so I said it for her.

'Someone's taken Rebecca.'

She opened her mouth, on the verge of denial. Changed tack.

'Who sent you?' she asked.

'Sadie and Gina Redding.'

Jean shook her head in exasperation.

'Mr Flynn,' she said, 'this is a private matter. Rebecca's friends aren't helping. Just tell them that.'

'Eight days,' I said. 'That's an awful long time.'

Jean tried to stare me out but it didn't work because her eyes just gave up suddenly, of their own accord, subsided into a beaten look. Fatigue, helplessness. The woman was terrified.

'Start at the beginning,' I said. 'When did they contact you?'

I heard footsteps.

'When did who contact us?' A man's voice. No hint of trepidation in this one. Jean looked over my shoulder and drew herself in.

I stood to face Larry Slater. He was looking at me with the expression of someone who's eaten a cheeseburger too many. He glared at his wife then glared at me again. I took the initiative and held out my hand and introduced myself.

Slater ignored both. Turned back to his wife.

'Who the hell is this?' he asked.

I repeated my introduction. 'I'm working for Rebecca's friends,' I told him.

'Which friends? What the hell's going on?'

'You tell me. Start with what's happened to your daughter.'

Slater shook his head. Open-mouthed. Phoney through and through. 'Our daughter's none of your damned business,' he said.

'That's all you need to know.'

'We know Rebecca's been abducted. I was just explaining to your wife that we can help.'

'Abducted? You're out of your mind!'

I looked at Jean. She looked at her husband. 'Larry—' she began.

'Stop!' he barked. 'Have you said anything to this guy?'

'Of course not.' Jean's face hardened.

But in another minute she would have. One lousy minute. That's the investigation business: all the minutes you never get.

And right now Larry Slater was calling time. He jabbed a thumb. 'Leave,' he said.

'Think about it, Larry,' I said.

'Think, hell. You've got ten seconds before I call the police.'

I stayed put. Figured he was bluffing. 'You don't want the police here any more than me,' I said. 'But with me there's less paperwork.'

But Slater showed me his bluff by pulling out his phone. Gave me a good view as he punched the keys. Next he was going to bluff a report of an intruder in his house and a squad car was going to turn up to bluff my arrest. I had business waiting. Business that would be tricky from the holding cells of the local nick. Time to retreat.

I nodded to Jean, pointed to the card in her hand. 'Any time,' I said.

I walked out. Neither of them came after me. See yourself out, Eddie. Another tradition of the investigation trade.

I jumped into the car and headed back to town.

CHAPTER TWENTY
Ronay would have wanted the tab clearing

I had thirty minutes to kill. I detoured through Paddington and parked on Chase Street. Connie's was doing roaring business. Connie himself was behind the counter the same as every other day. He gave me a yell that expressed his pleasure at seeing his planet-size debt staying close. He had this dream that I'd just walk in one day and pay it off. Connie's a funny guy.

The day was brightening by the hour. Birdsong and children's voices echoed in the street. I sat at the bar with the sun on my back and ordered a salad-and-bacon baguette and coffee, then paid homage to the perfection of the moment by handing over cash. The joy on Connie's face was a treat to see. He rewarded me with a radiant smile that he interrupted only to hold my twenty up to the light. Then he brought my sandwich personally and set it down like he was Egon Ronay. Ronay would have wanted the tab clearing, though.

'Why you work today, Eddie?' he said. 'Such a beautiful day.'

'Same as you. Love of the job.'

He let out a laugh that would have tripped the Frogeye's alarm if it had one.

'My work is my love,' he agreed. 'What else I'm going to do Sunday morning? Stay home, fight the wife?'

'Don't kid me, Connie. You're crazy about your wife.'

He tried to throw it back but the noisier Connie got the less I believed him, and with reason. Connie's wife was a Latina with looks that had grown men howling at the moon.

I chewed my baguette and sipped the coffee. Wonderful, as always. The half-hour killed, I drove into Holland Park and found an empty space opposite No. 93; parked and slid the window open.

The street had come to life. Cars, bicycles, couples walking to bistros, oldies taking miniature dogs to the park. Five minutes after I arrived there was movement at No. 93. An old guy came out of the front door and disappeared up the street. One of the lower floor residents. After that nothing happened for an hour. I was beginning to wonder if my arrangement had flopped. But you learn patience in this game. I'd been on stakeouts in worse places and for far longer. I listened to a tape and tapped the beat on the door panel.

It got past two and the old guy rolled back. Disappeared inside. Pricey cars glided past. Couples returned from lunch. I checked my watch. The hand had crawled past two thirty. Then a red Porsche Boxster backed into a spot five cars behind me and a woman got out. I watched her in my rear-view as she walked up the street. When she got to No. 93 she climbed the steps and pressed the top bell. By the time she pressed it a second time I was beside her.

She sensed me coming and turned to stand aside but I stopped.

'Sammy?'

The woman's eyes focused on me, trying to recall from where she knew me. She was in her late twenties, slim and lithe with astonishing green eyes and gold-blonde gossamer hair. Tina Brown's voicemail friend.

I told Sammy my name and apologised for my sudden appearance.

'Mind if we talk?' I said.

My introduction hadn't clarified much. Sammy backed away, puzzled.

'Are you a friend of Julie's?' She was referring to Tina Brown's sister, the other voicemail messenger.

'In a business sense,' I extemporised.

Sammy would have continued backing off but the railing was pressing into her backside. 'Julie didn't mention you. She just told me she was worried about Tina.' She looked nervously up the street. 'Is something wrong?'

Three hours ago Sammy had received a concerned call from Tina's sister saying she hadn't been able to contact her in a week and needed someone nearby to check her out. The only number she had was Sammy's. Whether Tina's sister had actually been trying to get in touch, bar the single voicemail, I didn't know. The call Sammy had received was from Lucy May – receptionist, secretary, accountant and impersonator.

Sammy's call-back number on Tina Brown's voicemail had been an unlisted pay-as-you-go. Difficult to trace. One way to track down a PAYG is to get them to come to you.

I held out an agency card. 'We've been asked to make sure Tina's okay,' I said.

Sammy stared at the card. Now she looked really scared.

'Why shouldn't she be okay?' she said.

'We hear she's dropped out of sight. Apparently it's never happened before.' Which I hoped Sammy was also thinking. We needed to get on the same side. Sammy tilted her head, not sure she wanted to be on anyone's side, but she couldn't deny her concern.

'Yes, I'm worried,' she said. 'I don't know where she is.'

'I hear you and she are close.' A safe guess.

'We are,' Sammy confirmed. 'But I don't know what's happened to her. She's just dropped out of sight. Hasn't returned a single call all week.'

Rule One triumphant. If there'd been half a chance that Holland Park and Rebecca Townsend were unrelated, that chance had just evaporated like spit on a stovetop in the spooky similarity between Sammy's words and those of Sadie Bannister when she ambushed me in my office.

'Julie didn't tell me your full name, Sammy.'

'Samantha Vincent. Are you saying something's happened to Tina?'

'I'm saying we're concerned. We need to find her. Maybe you can help.'

'How?'

'Background. Tina's lifestyle. The stuff she hides from her sister. You could help me with that.'

Sammy shook her head. 'I can't pass Tina's private affairs on to her sister.'

'Sammy, if Tina's in trouble there may be more important issues than secrets.'

'I'm just not sure what Tina would want me to tell you.'

Sammy was still in denial, still wanting Tina's disappearance to be routine. But Tina Brown's connection to Larry Slater and his missing stepdaughter said it wasn't routine. I needed whatever Sammy had.

'How about coffee,' I said. I had a hunch about Tina and I needed Sammy Vincent to confirm it.

Sammy looked up at the house; gave Tina a last chance to show her face. I didn't look up. I knew she wasn't there. Sammy finally accepted that fact too.

'Let's have the coffee,' she said. 'And you can explain what's going on, Mr Flynn.'

'My name's Eddie,' I said. 'And I think I can put you in the picture.'

At least one of those statements was true.

CHAPTER TWENTY-ONE
They say money isn't everything

We walked up to a Coffee Republic on the main road and found a couple of chairs in the back away from prying ears; ordered coffees.

'Pardon a sensitive question,' I said, 'but I assume you and Tina are in the same line of business.'

I looked up from dunking my biscotto and found Sammy watching me.

'Tina being an escort,' I said.

Beautiful girl, single lifestyle, expensive tastes, no sign of regular payslips, no sign of relationship, given to trysts at high-class hotels. The description could have fit a millionaire's mistress but Slater wasn't in that league. The explanation that worked was that Tina made her money as a top-of-the-line escort, servicing serious wealth, which would describe Slater quite nicely.

My hunch that Sammy was in the same business occurred when I saw the Boxster and the same stratospheric looks, the haughtiness that years-long reinforcement of beauty-as-divine-provider brings. Call me male chauvinist. Sure I'm chauvinist: it's a tool of the trade.

'You'd better tell me exactly who you are,' Sammy said, 'and why you're prying into Tina's life.'

'Like it says on the card, I'm a private detective. And I'm looking into her affairs because she's disappeared. I need to know if her line of work is a factor.'

Sammy's head instinctively shook to deny the possibility. In her line of business I guess there's a tendency to stay with denial.

'Tina may be involved with someone she can't handle,' I suggested. 'Time might be critical. I need to know about her recent activities. Maybe get a pointer as to where she may have gone.'

Sammy turned things over, figuring out whether she had any option but to trust me. Saw there wasn't.

'I've been leaving messages all week,' she admitted. 'On her home and mobile.'

'How long since she's answered any calls?'

'A week.'

'How often do you usually talk to her?'

'Most days. We'd arranged a night on the town last weekend but when I didn't hear from her I assumed a job had come up, a weekend client.'

'Could she be spending the week with this client?'

She shook her head. 'She'd have let me know. We keep each other informed if we're going out of town. Security.'

'How does she contact her clients? Is Blueglades her agency?'

'There's no agency. Tina takes card payments. Blueglades is her merchant name. Tina places her own ads and takes her own bookings. Most of her work is repeat.'

'Who else know about her bookings?'

'No-one, but she takes precautions. Limits herself to quality hotels for first-time clients. Safe locations where the clients are reputable.'

Sammy was confusing quality with reputable but I let it go. Meeting at high-tariff hotels took out ninety-nine percent of Tina's risk, but like disease and rats, crime breeds in the cracks.

'Does she visit clients away from hotels?'

'With repeat work. She's flexible for people she knows.'

'She have many regulars?'

Sammy shrugged. 'The same as me. Eight or ten. Guys we see once or twice a month. But we make sure we know them well before we take trips with them. Some clients you see fifty times and you still want a safe location.'

'Judgement.'

'Yes. We develop good judgement.'

We. Sammy and Tina exchanging notes – thinking they know each other's work, thinking that makes them safe. But working alone in that profession leaves a girl exposed no matter how good her judgement. I did the sums. Twenty escorts a month at a grand or two per night and no middle man. The earning potential for beauties like Tina and Sammy was sky high. I guess the risk seemed worth it.

'How long have you known Tina?'

'Six years. We worked for the same agency.'

'And how long has Tina been in the business?'

Sammy's laugh was lined with bitterness. 'The same as all of us,' she said. 'Since we were kids. Since we first got preferential treatment at home or in the street. I had a twenty-eight-year-old boyfriend and a five carat diamond ring on my finger when I was sixteen. Got picked up from school in a Porsche. You tell me when it starts. I only know when it ends. I'm retiring at thirty. Tina too.'

Maybe.

Shaughnessy and I had found nothing that looked like a client list in Tina's apartment. My guess was that she kept the details on her phone. I asked Sammy if she knew anything about the men Tina saw.

'Only the two or three we've shared,' she said. 'None in the past couple of years.'

'You must talk about clients sometimes,' I said.

'A few first names. Nothing else.'

'Any recent names stick out? Anyone she was uneasy with?'

Sammy gave me a look. The same one she'd used as a sixteen-year-old. She hadn't touched her coffee.

'You think that's what we gossip about?' she said.

I shook my head. 'Gossip doesn't interest me. But I need any names Tina's mentioned. Any places. Clients who stand out.'

'It's almost like you're looking for dirt. Are you sure you're not with the papers?'

'I'm trying to find out what's happening to Tina,' I said, 'on the off chance we can get her back safe.'

The melodrama got through. Sammy closed her eyes for a couple of seconds.

'What are you not telling me?' she said.

'I've told you everything I can. Specifically, the possibility that Tina's in trouble. There's nothing else.'

'Why hasn't her sister called the police?'

'There'd be nothing for them to act on. By the time any evidence comes up it might be too late. We want to find Tina while she's still okay.'

Sammy blinked.

'Give me any clients you know,' I said.

She closed her eyes again briefly.

'There's only a few. One of Tina's clients used to be David Lancaster.'

'The MP?' I raised my eyebrows.

'Yeah. The one screaming last year for the Home Secretary to resign when it came out about him hiding a gay affair. Tina told me he used to like it up against the car window with the world passing.'

'Is she still seeing him?'

'I don't know. One guy she *is* still seeing is Sir Alec somebody, ex-chairman of the CBI, big donor to the Conservative party. They spend weekends together – travel round Europe. He taught her to ski.'

I knew which Sir Somebody she meant. It wasn't going to be hard to memorise this list.

'The others are just names, a few details. She's been seeing a Middle Eastern guy called Amir. He takes the penthouse at the Grosvenor and pays her twenty thousand for the weekend.' Sammy's face was a mask. 'For that price he likes to hurt her a little. Nothing that leaves evidence but she's always low for a couple of days afterwards. Tina keeps talking about giving him the boot but she still goes back.' She looked at me. 'They say money isn't everything but ten thousand a day is hard to walk away from. There's another client, the opposite type. A guy she's been seeing for a couple of years up in Buckinghamshire. Divorced. Very rich but no inclination to get attached. A real sweet guy, she says. I hear other names occasionally but they don't mean anything to me.'

'You ever hear of a guy called Slater?'

She looked blank.

'Lives in Hampstead. Married. A stockbroker.'

She shook her head. It had been a long shot. If the two of them talked it would be the bigger fish they hung up for show. Unlikely that Slater would warrant a mention in the circle that included MPs and captains of industry. I kept fishing.

'Did Tina mention a trip to Brighton? The Royal Trafalgar Hotel.'

That got Sammy's attention.

'Yes. She mentioned the Royal Trafalgar.'

'Any particular reason?'

Sammy nodded. 'She had to cancel a night out. My birthday bash. She got a late booking and called me to reschedule.'

'Was there anything special about that job? Anything about her client?'

She shook her head. 'She only told me about the hotel. They took the top-floor suite with a personal valet. Champagne and strawberries at breakfast. She didn't mention the client.'

'But travelling to Brighton would mean that she already knew him?'

'Yes.'

'Did she tell you anything else about that trip?'

She shook her head. 'The only special thing was cancelling my birthday thing. Otherwise she wouldn't have mentioned it at all.'

'Your birthday's in March,' I said. 'Am I right?'

It's these touches that impressed Watson.

Sammy stayed unimpressed. 'October,' she said. 'That's when Tina went to Brighton.'

Elementary, my dear Holmes. You can't beat birthdays as memory joggers. Another shot sliced into the bunker. Slater's Amex had him at the Royal Trafalgar in March. Sammy's date was five months too early.

'I'm looking at something more recent. Did Tina visit the hotel again?'

'She only mentioned that one time.'

'But she would tell you if she went away for the weekend?'

Sammy shrugged. 'Not every time. If we're both busy we may not mention it.'

I finished my coffee. Sammy's stood cold in front of her.

'I need Tina's mobile number,' I said.

She recited it from memory but I didn't write it down because I already recognised it from Slater's phone bill. The number confirmed the link between Slater and Tina, even if Slater's Brighton stay didn't line up with the date Sammy had Tina there.

'Who is this Slater?' Sammy asked.

'He's someone Tina may be involved with.'

'Is she with him now?'

'No.'

'Might he harm her?'

'I don't think so. But the two of them may be involved in something that's got her into trouble.'

'What sort of trouble?'

'That's what I'm trying to find out.'

'Sweet Jesus.' Sammy turned and looked beyond the walls of the café. A place of shadows. Something happening to Tina would certainly force a rethink of this woman's lifestyle. Maybe get her thinking of early retirement.

'Mr Flynn—'

'Eddie.'

'When will you know something?'

'Soon.'

'How soon?'

'A couple of days.'

'Two days.' Sammy retrieved my card from her purse and looked it over, paying more attention this time. Then she got up.

'Call me on Tuesday,' she said. 'If I've heard nothing by the end of the day I'm going to the police.'

She walked out. Heads turned.

I stayed to jot a few notes and a few more questions. The confirmation of Tina Brown's line of work opened up a wide range of possibilities as to why she'd go missing. And in normal circumstances, I'd put Slater's fixation on watching her apartment down to the action of an infatuated guy let down by his fantasy girl's elopement with another client. But his stalking her at the very time his stepdaughter had disappeared didn't constitute normal circumstances.

I called Gina Redding as I walked back to the car; filled her in on the fact that we now seemed to have two people missing. I warned her that I'd poked a stick into the Slater house. She should be ready for calls from the family. I also warned her that the next step might be costly and might lead only to dead ends. Gina wasn't deterred.

'Do what it takes, Eddie. I'll cover the bill. Just find Rebecca.'

My kind of client.

I told her I'd be in touch in a couple of days. By then we'd have the thing wrapped up. We'd need to. Two days was all we had before Sammy blew the whistle and things got complicated.

~~~~~

I headed back to Battersea and got busy in the kitchen. When Arabel arrived I had a leg of lamb roasting. We ate it with sweet potatoes and sour cream and roasted vegetables. Not even a nod towards healthy eating. The lamb disappeared, fat and all. Cooking unhealthy may be a cheat but it gets results. Arabel knew exactly what I was up to but my culinary shenanigans gave her an excuse to pig out once in a while.

She signalled her appreciation by grabbing me as I cleared the table and pushing me back onto the sofa with dirty suggestions, but both our stomachs protested simultaneously and threw the casting vote. So much for results. We got ready to go out.

While I was changing I caught Arabel in my loft, trying to sneak a look at her portrait. I drove her off with an old wives' tale that the picture would turn into an ogre if the sitter uncovered it prematurely. The real reason was that I didn't want her to spot imperfections before I worked them out. I liked her to think that painting came naturally to me, like cooking. My reputation for both would be shot if my techniques were known.

'When are you going to finish it, babe?' she said. 'At the rate you're going you'll need to add wrinkles.'

'Art determines its own time,' I said. 'Ask Picasso how long it took to create his masterpieces.'

'Picasso could finish stuff in three days,' she informed me. 'He did that Reclining Nude in one.'

Education can be a pain. I blamed myself for introducing Arabel to the Tate.

'The guy was all rush,' I said. 'Do you want to end up looking like his Weeping Woman?'

'Not if you want to live, Flynn.'

'Then keep your nose out. I'm not ready to die for my art.'

We went out and headed over to the Royal Festival Hall. I had tickets for the London Philharmonic performing Elgar. Next to jazz I went for classical composers. Next to soul, blues, reggae, hip hop and half a dozen other things so did Arabel. She would never admit to having an ear for the classics, but the only time I saw her listening to music with tears in her eyes was when I took her to a Dvorak symphony. Somewhere amongst those curves was a cultured soul, savouring what she'd denied herself in her youth.

The evening was almost balmy. I put the top down for the ten-minute trip.

'Have you been working all day?' Arabel asked.

'Justice never sleeps,' I said.

She laid her hand on my neck. 'Not even a nap at the weekend? This detective stuff draws you too tight, Flynn. You take the burden with the case.'

'That's how it is sometimes. Divorce, petty crime, that kind of thing you get the weekend off. But sometimes we're involved with something more serious.'

'Like when you worked for the police?'

'Not like that. With the Met there was no rush – my clients were all dead.'

'What about Rebecca? Is she dead?'

The question caught me.

Eventually I said: 'I don't think so. But she may be mixed up in something that's going bad. It's hard to take the weekend off when you might be someone's only hope.'

'Poor babe,' Arabel said. 'And who's going to save you?'

I grinned. Fought the wheel. We'd figure that one out later.

CHAPTER TWENTY-TWO
Tonka and the Gestapo

The Mitsubishi Warrior had been sat for an hour and a half on the meter without a penny going in, but the clock was ticking. The parking Gestapo was moving up on the far side of the junction and he'd reach them within two minutes. Sod's law said that the second they fed the meter their quarry would break, but it was the lesser of two evils – the possibility of wasting a few quid against the certainty of a fixed penalty notice. Roker went with the odds.

'Feed it,' he said.

Mitch broke off from feeding Pringles into his face and climbed out, rocking the vehicle on its springs, then stood on the pavement with the idea of psyching the warden out. Roker hissed through his teeth and leaned across to smack the dash. Mitch gave him a dirty look and slotted the coins home. When he climbed back in Roker was tempted to slug him, but he went with the odds again: Mitch could be unpredictable.

Mitch grabbed the wheel like he was about to wrench it off.

'I hate those uniformed gits,' he said.

'Stay focused,' Roker said.

They watched the warden walk up. He passed the Warrior without turning his head but a sideways evil eye said he'd spotted their game. Mitch turned to glare after him then attacked his Pringles again. 'When's this clown gonna move,' he said.

'Soon,' Roker said.

He was right. Their quarry came out exactly three minutes later and disappeared round the back of the building.

Mitch stashed the Pringles and started the engine. Roker watched the street.

'Go,' he said.

Mitch rolled as the quarry pulled out of an access road and headed across the junction up ahead.

'What the hell is that?' Mitch asked.

'Stay back,' Roker said.

Mitch growled. He didn't need Roker's advice. He could tail a guy all day and he'd not know it.

'It's a friggin' Tonka,' Mitch said. 'I had a bigger pedal car when I was two years old.'

Roker sneered. Mitch was shut in a room getting smacked round his head when he was two years old. Pedal cars didn't come into it.

'Is it a vintage?' Mitch asked.

'Yeah,' Roker said. 'Forty years. Probably ninety per cent rust.'

The car was the size of a shoebox. Racing green with a black soft top. The Warrior would run right over it if their brakes failed.

'No way you'd get me in something like that,' Mitch said, 'unless they were burying me.'

'Not even then,' Roker said. 'You'd need a Transit.'

Mitch held back then floored the pedal when the Tonka turned at the main road. They hit the junction five seconds behind but the traffic had closed up, blocking them. The Frogeye was disappearing towards Bayswater. If it got into the heavy flow they'd lose it. Mitch slammed his foot down and skidded out in front of a van. The van fishtailed and missed them by inches and the driver stayed on his horn long after he needed to. Any other time Mitch would have been happy to climb out and discuss the problem. It was White Van Man's lucky day.

Mitch accelerated and got to four cars back as the Tonka turned east towards Paddington Station then took a left and drove across the bridge and up the ramp. Mitch eased off and merged into the Westway traffic a hundred yards behind it. The Warrior's high vantage point gave them distance without risk of losing the quarry. Secure tails took a minimum of three vehicles but when you wanted the best single-vehicle job you put Mitch behind the wheel.

For the moment Mitch's skills were redundant. The Tonka stayed with the A40 and drifted towards the M25 in the mid-morning flow. At the junction the car took the slip and split left into the south link onto the Orbital. The variable limits were on and they cruised in the second lane at a stately fifty-five, holding well back. Heathrow came and went. The Tonka was in no hurry. They were past Reigate before it indicated and cut off onto the M23.

Mitch had substituted the Pringles with a ball of gum. He chewed furiously, focused on their quarry. Roker stayed silent, puzzling over where their target was heading. The M23 had opened up possibilities.

'Gatwick,' Mitch said.

Roker kept quiet.

'They saying this guy's a player?'

'Maybe,' Roker said. 'He'd just better know the rules.'

'What do they want us to do?'

'They want us to watch and learn,' Roker said. 'We're on a fishing trip, that's all.'

The M23 was nearly as busy as the Orbital. The Tonka's diminutive size demanded constant focus but Mitch was cool. After fifteen minutes they passed Gatwick and continued south. Roker stared ahead and felt something beginning to gnaw in his gut. When the M23 petered out the Tonka continued towards the coast and Roker knew they were headed for Brighton.

As they got onto the roundabout north of the town Mitch closed up the distance in case the Tonka made a sudden turn amongst the traffic, but the car kept to its southerly course and in a couple of minutes they were in the centre. The Frogeye swung round the park and continued towards the sea and a minute later they came out at the pier.

The Tonka crossed the roundabout three cars ahead and took a right along the seafront. Mitch jumped the queue and forced his way across, and they rolled west for sixty seconds between the hotels and the beach. Then the quarry indicated and turned across oncoming traffic into the walled-off parking lane fronting a five-star hotel. Mitch rolled a hundred yards past then swung the Warrior round to get back. He stopped short of the hotel and they watched the guy extract himself from the midget vehicle and go in through the entrance.

The hotel's name was marked in fifteen-foot letters across its white façade: ROYAL TRAFALGAR.

Mitch killed the engine and chewed. The place meant nothing to him. Roker's face told a different story.

'Shit,' he said.

Mitch turned.

'We got a problem?'

Roker's face stayed neutral but his eyes were locked on the hotel entrance.

'Yeah,' he concluded, 'we've got a problem.'

CHAPTER TWENTY-THREE
Fear and boggle-eyed greed

Revolving doors spat me out into a marble and glass foyer that echoed with the muted reverence of a cathedral. Five-star perfection gleamed in every polished surface, and the shine on the floor was enough to have you watching your balance.

The foyer was busy with big-hotel Brownian motion, people endlessly going somewhere. Reception held centre stage with the extravagance of a high altar. Baggage and Concierge stood back either side like lady chapels. Mahogany doors behind the reception led through to the admin area, which was where the people lived who'd have the information I needed – and who'd sooner have teeth pulled. I needed a way in.

A sweeping staircase encircled a roped-off bistro opposite the reception. I went over and flopped into a leather armchair. A waiter materialised. I ordered coffee. The coffee was excellent if you ignored the distraction of the bill which was presented in a saucer of its own. The bill was discreetly folded so you didn't have to see it till later. I'm the kind of guy who can't resist peeking. Spat out half my coffee. Holy hell! I'd have to work the drink into our expense sheet. Maybe claim it as an extravagant lunch.

Larry Slater had an impressive taste in playgrounds. If the lobby was any guide then the accommodation upstairs would be worth seeing. A stunning nest to spend a weekend with a stunning girl. A stunning bill at the end of it, too. Seemed Slater had cash to throw away. His Amex recorded him here twice, and my bet said that he had Tina Brown as company both times.

It took me twenty minutes to see the way in. I waited until the far end of the reception desk was clear then finished my coffee and slid a tenner into the folded bill. I signalled to the waiter and walked across to the desk.

The reception staff were bright and attentive in the way that big money demands, trained to the hotel's traditional standards, even if the tradition said that they should be paid a pittance.

The clerk at the end was different. When I approached the desk he was busy at his keyboard. Didn't notice I was there. I'd been watching him. He could do the bright and attentive stuff, but there was a phoniness he couldn't hide. His head had been up when I'd started my walk but was buried in his computer by the time I reached him. He knew I didn't fit here. Hotel staff have these instincts. I gave him thirty seconds then leaned over the counter to invade his space. He looked up and smiled and when he asked how he could help I recognised a fellow actor.

He was in his mid-forties with slicked-back hair and a badge that identified him as Gerald. Black frame spectacles hid the disappointment lines from two decades of missed promotions. He'd probably worked at another hotel in his youth before he realised that his prospects were nil. Joined the Royal Trafalgar on the strength of a gladly-given reference. He was the oldest of the check-in clerks by a decade. Seniority: the perk of never being promoted. I leaned closer. Lowered my voice.

'This will seem a little irregular...' I said.

The word cut him like I'd said something dirty. To Gerald, "irregular" was something that stayed outside the revolving doors, like a dog turd on the pavement. He worked up a frown but restrained himself with the thought that whatever I was after he was going to get the opportunity to trash me.

'I'm here in confidence,' I explained, 'on behalf of a lady.'

I looked into Gerald's eyes. His face remained pinched, the expression of someone expecting me to vomit over his counter. But he stayed cool. Let the rope play out.

'The lady suspects that her husband has visited the Royal Trafalgar under circumstances that were...' I searched for the word: '...unsalubrious.'

I had a feeling it should have been "insalubrious". So did Gerald, but he wasn't sure. And grammar wasn't the point. He was going to dish me whether I could speak English or not. I paused, worked the word in again for effect. 'The lady suspects that her husband may have visited this hotel for entirely unsalubrious purposes. She believes, in short, that he may have been unfaithful to her.'

Gerald's face was a mask of patience as he calculated the best moment to come in. He knew I was bowling him a spinner. The important thing was not to swing early.

'My client assumes that the Royal Trafalgar has a record of her husband's reservations...' I let the thought hang between us.

Gerald let it hang right there. The only sign he was listening was the glitter of the foyer spots in his spectacles.

'...and the lady would be deeply obliged for a little information.'

I gave Gerald my deeply obliged look. He gave me deeply patient.

'If necessary, my client would be happy to come to an arrangement...' I said.

Finally we had it. The spinner was angling towards Gerald's bat. Now I'd soiled myself with straight bribery it was time. Gerald leaned forward. The bat swung fast and true.

'Sir,' he whispered, 'I don't know what kind of establishment you take us for, but the Royal Trafalgar is not in the habit of divulging client information. If you'd like to leave your name and details,' – he was in agony, trying to keep his face straight – 'I'll pass your enquiry to the manager. Together with your offer of a financial arrangement.'

I held up my hand. 'Whoa! That won't be necessary. My client was thinking more about a private agreement.'

Gerald looked blank.

'She's willing to pay you,' I clarified.

Gerald smiled in the way of the devout when someone farts in the front pew.

'Perhaps,' he said, 'if you tried the Metropole. The lady's husband probably stayed there. It sounds more his kind of establishment. The Royal Trafalgar is not that kind of hotel, Mr...?'

'Marble,' I told him. 'Private investigator.'

'Mr Marble,' Gerald said, 'could I ask you to step away from the desk?'

He raised his hand to bring the concierge over. I shifted myself to block the view.

'Wait.'

He looked at me. I pulled an envelope from my jacket and opened it on the desk. Riffled a wad of notes inside.

'Five hundred. Yours.' I turned and nodded towards the bistro. 'I'll be waiting over there. Give me two minutes of your time when you take a break and you walk away with this envelope and no strings attached. You can throw me out on my backside. The cash is still yours. With my client's compliments.'

If I was expecting a shout of joy I was disappointed. The expression on Gerald's face had more pucker than a chimp chewing lemons. His contempt had racked up to the sublime at the sight of the dirties themselves. But I recognised something behind the look. Gerald was cranking the cogs. I slipped the envelope back into my jacket and went to order another coffee. I took a table at the back this time, well under the stairs.

I was sipping the dregs when Gerald slipped into the seat across from me. He tried to combine businesslike with stealth, the act of a schoolboy with his hand in the biscuit tin. He threw me a spiteful look as down payment for when this thing blew up in his face but to his credit he remained cool when I slipped the envelope across the table.

'My client's compliments,' I said. He didn't pick it up. He knew something was off. I nodded encouragement. 'Five hundred,' I said. 'It's yours.'

He worked a sneer onto his face while he waited for the flipside. Now it was my turn to stay poker-faced. Gerald broke first.

'What's the catch?' he said.

'None. The money's yours.'

That's when he realised what the catch was: more money. I saw the cogs mesh. Stretched my grin.

'If you help me, there's more of the same,' I said.

'What kind of help?'

I held my grin. Somewhere between the reception desk and our table we'd lost the Royal Trafalgar's high ideals. Gerald knew damn well what kind of help I wanted.

I slid a notepaper across the table with Larry Slater's name on it. 'I've listed the dates this was here. I want them confirmed along with any other dates he's been here in the last year. There's another five hundred waiting.'

'That's not so easy,' Gerald said. 'Searching the invoices takes time.' But he was just playing for more.

'Thirty minutes. I'll come to the desk. I want a printed sheet.'

I watched him doing the sums. My guess was that five hundred was a couple of week's net take-home. He gave the matter a little sour consideration for the sake of self-respect then snatched up the envelope and notepaper and headed back to the desk with as much dignity as he could muster.

I picked up a copy of *The Observer* and killed time until the waiter came and fingered my second saucer in a subtle hint to pay up. Places like this didn't do refills. At this rate it was going to be a race between Gerald and the bistro to get my money.

Spending Gina's cash like small change was a gamble. There was a risk that Slater's stay here was innocent, or at least unrelated to the missing girl. But I was going with the odds. Slater's Amex statement implied he was here with Tina in March. But Tina's friend Sammy remembered her being here the previous October. Maybe the couple had been here a few times. If my hunch panned out I'd have not only a clearer picture of what was going on between them but also something to wave under Slater's nose next time I visited him. Time was running. I needed the guy to let me in on what was happening to his stepdaughter. Maybe a little blackmail would lubricate his vocal chords.

Gerald was in the back office for twenty minutes. When he came out I wandered across.

We didn't need words. Just a fake smile and three sheets of paper pushed across the counter. It could have been any old guest checking his bill. I scanned the sheets. Database prints of three invoices showing the guest's charge details. Something was off though: the two March dates from Slater's Amex were there, plus one in January, but nothing for the previous October, which was when Tina's friend put her here. I raised my eyebrows.

'That's it,' Gerald said. 'Twelve months.'

So what happened to October?

I slid Gerald's second envelope across the counter, puzzling over the missing date. Was Tina here with another client? Maybe she'd been so impressed with the place that she'd talked Slater into bringing her back. But without Slater here in October I had no hard evidence putting him here with her at all. His calls to her number in March were interesting but nothing more. I'd needed the October date to tie the two.

Then something caught my eye. Gerald's paperwork said Slater's January visit was charged to someone called Alpha Security. The room was prepaid, with follow-up bar charges of two hundred and eighty-seven pounds, also settled by Alpha Security. More interestingly, the January booking was for three nights but Slater's name was registered for only the second. I flipped the paper round.

'What do you make of this?'

Gerald took a discreet glance. His voice stayed low.

'It's a company reservation for the three nights,' he said. 'Mr Slater was here just the one.'

So who were Alpha Security? And why were they throwing money away on unused reservations?

I scribbled the Alpha Security name on another piece of paper and pushed it across.

'I need all reservations and payments under this name,' I said.

Gerald was about to give me the no-no but my words stopped him.

'Two hundred for each one you find.'

Gerald's mouth opened wide.

I promised to return in thirty minutes and wandered back to my *Observer*. This time I resisted the coffee: the two-hundred-per-booking deal with Gerald might be affordable but more coffees were not. And if Alpha Security were regulars here I'd be bankrupted when I went back to the desk. I wouldn't actually be bankrupt, of course. My remaining cash only ran to five hundred, which limited my exposure. If Gerald turned up more than two bookings he was going to get shafted. But what's corruption without setbacks? What could Gerald do? Call consumer protection?

After ten minutes he reappeared, trying not to be obvious as he scanned the lobby for me. I ambled back over. More discretion and paper pushing and two more Alpha Security bookings were revealed. I folded four hundred into another envelope. A professional conjurer couldn't have slid the envelope out of my fingers with greater skill than Gerald.

I took a gander. The bookings were each for three nights in the Royal Trafalgar's outrageously expensive Millennium Suite.

One booking was in June, the other October, the date Tina was here. Seemed Tina was linked to Alpha Security.

On both occasions Alpha had a guest checking in for the middle night. The June guest was a David Hanlon with an address in Chevening, Surrey. The October booking was a guy named John McCabe. Address in Wimbledon.

I wondered how far back this pattern went. I scribbled again.

Pushed a note over the desk saying *Alpha Security. Last five years????* *£200 each*. Gerald's expression was a combination of fear and boggle-eyed greed. There might be dozens of bookings. He looked to see if I was serious. Were my pockets stuffed with cash? They weren't, but Gerald didn't know it. I left him hurdling towards the admin office and went back to my bistro. Adrenaline fired me up to order another coffee, and Gerald's last hundred took a hit.

He came out fifteen minutes later but was interrupted by the necessity of dealing with an arriving guest. I stayed seated and watched the fastest checking-in since Anne Boleyn arrived at the Tower. Gerald had the woman through in sixty seconds flat.

When I wandered across and leaned on the desk Gerald looked up at me with the expression of a rottweiler whose sausages have been snatched. A single shake of the head. June had been Alpha Security's first reservation. It was lucky, in a way. The sausage string wasn't as long as the rottweiler thought.

I thanked Gerald and touched my forelock in a manner way out of line with Royal Trafalgar behaviour and headed for the door.

The coffee had been expensive but I'd got something that was going to jump-start this case.

I just had to figure what it meant.

CHAPTER TWENTY-FOUR
Next thing you're swimming

'About time!'

Mitch watched the guy come down the steps. He'd been sitting in the Warrior for two hours and his backside was numb.

As the Tonka drove off Roker came out of the hotel and jogged up. Mitch had the engine running before he was halfway over.

'Go!'

Mitch hit the gas and made up distance, followed the Tonka back through the town. 'Thought you'd checked in for the night,' he said. 'How much longer are we tailing this joker?'

Roker kept his eyes on the target. 'As long as it takes,' he said.

Mitch said nothing but his belly was talking loud. They'd been on the guy since eight thirty this morning and they might have all afternoon to run. Apart from the Pringles Mitch had gone without. The guy had probably eaten in the hotel. Roker too. Mitch was almost minded to ask. Snarled at the road instead as they headed north, back out of town.

'He meet someone?' Mitch asked.

'He talked to a receptionist. Greasy little guy. Had him running errands.'

'He get anything?'

Roker watched their quarry manoeuvring in the traffic. 'Yeah,' he said. 'Two hours tête-à-tête with Grease Jockey tells me he got something.'

'He spot you?'

'Jesus,' Roker said. 'Watch the road. Don't lose the bastard.'

The moves the guy was making had sandpapered Roker's nerves. The moves said they were looking at a leak. And leaks grow. First a little drip; next thing you're swimming. Whatever the guy was up to, his digging around at the Royal Trafalgar didn't smell good. Roker's instinct said that they were going to have to do some plumbing. Soon.

Eddie Flynn. Private Investigator. Ex-cop. That was all Roker knew but it was enough. The "ex-cop" he didn't like. It meant the guy was no amateur. Flynn had been putting something together there at the Trafalgar. What Roker couldn't figure was who Flynn was working for. He held it all ways to the light but nothing came through. There was no one could have sent Flynn to Brighton. Unknowns scraped Roker's nerves.

They stayed with the Tonka as it picked up the motorway, holding the inside lane, occasionally skipping trucks. They passed Gatwick and it was beginning to look good when the Tonka turned east instead of west at the Orbital.

Roker and Mitch both cursed. The frigging mystery tour was not over.

They tracked east on the M25 until the Tonka took the Sevenoaks slip road. Mitch kicked in turbo and closed the distance with a brief sprint to a hundred and ten, braking late enough on the slip to have Roker hissing. The speed was needed. Mitch was barely in time to spot the quarry disappearing into traffic on the A21. He cut across a car and got out after it. Half a mile on the Tonka overtook an artic and was out of sight in front of it. Mitch changed down and pulled out to pass just as Roker spotted the quarry swinging off onto a slip. He yelled out. Mitch killed the manoeuvre and swerved back behind the truck to get the Warrior onto the turnoff. Roker gripped the door handle and gritted his teeth again as the Warrior leaned on its springs and skidded round the curve, but they got straight and the Tonka was right there ahead of them, heading west. The road narrowed and they hit traffic lights and the target turned just as the amber came on, four cars ahead. Mitch floored the pedal and passed the line, turned across traffic on red onto a road north, cutting towards Chevening. They got into the village and held back while the Tonka pulled up for directions then followed it on out into the country. A couple of minutes later it slowed alongside an estate wall and turned between brick gateposts. Mitch pulled them onto the verge fifty yards back.

'What's the bastard doing now?' he asked.

Roker jabbed his thumb towards a track that ran off behind them.

'Pull us in. He may come back this way.'

Mitch backed the Warrior against a five-bar gate twenty yards down the track and Roker jumped out and walked up to find cover opposite the estate entrance.

What the hell was this place? Had to be significant, judging by

Flynn's beeline from Brighton. The more Roker was seeing the less he liked. He sensed the leak expanding fast.

The way things were shaping up, they were going to have to sort this.

Urgently.

CHAPTER TWENTY-FIVE
The butler was deaf

I passed a stone gatehouse and followed the driveway which curved between twelve-foot rhododendrons to a wrought iron inner gate.

The Royal Trafalgar had recorded David Hanlon's address as a property called Sedgeworth Park. I'd anticipated a detached house with a pretentious nameplate back in the village but this wasn't the kind of driveway that depended on nameplates. Hanlon, whoever he was, was another wealthy party.

The gates were closed. I hopped out and pressed the button on a call panel high on the metalwork. Nothing. Seemed David Hanlon and his butler were both out.

You win some, you lose some. The diversion had been a spur of the moment thing. It would have been good to catch Hanlon cold, watch his reaction when I dropped names. I gave the bell a last push, held it for ten seconds. Maybe the butler was deaf. Maybe the sound didn't carry to the pool.

Nothing.

One for tomorrow. I backed the Frogeye out and turned at the gatehouse where an old guy was digging the front garden. He looked up and checked the car as I coasted up and braked.

'Long time since I saw one of those,' he said.

The Frogeye is a great conversation opener if you meet anyone over sixty. The younger generation think I'm driving a kit car.

I let the engine tick while I spieled a few facts and figures, waxed lyrical on how sweet she ran. Didn't tell him about the defective heater or the oil change every three thousand miles. I asked whether he knew when David Hanlon was expected back.

He apologised. 'Considering I live right here you'd think I'd know when they're in and out. But I don't really notice. I just see them coming and going from time to time.'

I clicked my tongue and looked at my watch like I was deciding whether to hang around.

'Any chance you'll be speaking to him today?' I said.

The guy shook his head again. 'I don't know them past nodding.

We've not been here long. I've met Faye a couple of times when she's been out with the dogs but I've never spoken to David.'

I thanked the guy. Worked the gears.

'Obliged anyway,' I said. 'I'll call back.'

'If I do see them who should I say was here?' he asked.

I smiled my gratitude. 'Coffee. Gerald Coffee.'

I threw a wave and rolled out onto the road. If the old guy did talk to the Hanlons he was going to get some funny looks.

I headed back to town. I'd return tomorrow. The Hanlons might be peripheral to whatever was happening to Rebecca but my bet said otherwise. David Hanlon's involvement with Alpha Security and the Royal Trafalgar linked him squarely to Larry Slater.

Brighton had been a fishing trip. I'd half expected nothing but I'd picked up a hefty bite – and more than just the names in the Royal Trafalgar records. The line had taken a tug today like a marlin wanted to play.

Time to start reeling in.

CHAPTER TWENTY-SIX

When you've been through the mangler...

They followed the Tonka towards Heathrow. The traffic congealed.

'Stay on him,' Roker growled. 'I want to know where this joker's going.'

'He's headed back to town.'

Mitch worked the lanes, adjusted distance. Roker needed to chill. There was nil chance he'd lose the guy in this jam. Then the Tonka veered into the Lodge Clacket services and they damn near did lose him. Mitch wrestled the wheel and forced gaps to make the slip road. He got clear and drove in, searching for the target. Spotted him on the pumps. He rolled the Warrior into a slot opposite and killed the engine. Tonka-Man was out and filling up, oblivious.

'How are we for diesel?' Roker said.

'Half a tank. We're okay.'

Roker was unconvinced. 'We are until the half tank runs out. After that we lose him, unless you push.'

Mitch shook his head. 'We've got the range,' he said. 'No way that pedal car holds more than a couple of gallons.'

Roker looked at him. 'You ever see how far a motorbike goes on a couple of gallons?'

'Then it's our unlucky day,' Mitch said. "Unlucky" would barely cover it if they were still following this joker by the time they ran dry. Mitch's stomach had been running on empty for hours.

'How about I grab a sandwich?' he said.

Roker thought about it. 'Make it quick,' he said.

Mitch skipped out and hurried across to the shop. He was in ahead of the guy but he needed to take a leak, which cost time. By the time he'd grabbed his sandwiches Tonka-Man had paid and gone. Back outside, Roker was gesturing. Mitch spotted their quarry accelerating towards the exit. He cursed and scrambled back into the Warrior.

He worked hard, bullying his way across lanes until he got the car back in his sight. Once he did he stayed close. Two near-misses were enough.

At the next junction the Frogeye took the filter for the A22 and

Mitch's hopes lifted. The guy was headed back into town, just like he said.

Inbound traffic was moving freely. Mitch drove one-handed, savaging his sandwich as they tailed the Frogeye up through Croydon and Streatham. They got clear of the Common and headed towards the river, then the car cut off and turned towards Battersea Park and pulled into a residential street, looking for a parking spot. Mitch let the Warrior idle at the junction as the Tonka backed into a space. Hallelujah! The bastard was through.

'Pull over,' Roker said. Mitch took them clear of the junction and Roker leapt out to jog back round the corner and nearly bumped into Flynn coming the other way. It was one of those moments, but Flynn went past without noticing. Roker turned and watched him disappear into one of the buildings.

Probably the guy's pad. Home for the night. Roker gave it fifteen minutes then made a call and walked back to the Warrior.

~~~~~

He had Mitch stop off at the office. The firm lived above a bookmaker's on Fulham Road. A door plate advertised them as Alpha Security, which covered a range of services. Roker went up. The place was empty, just Vicky tidying up, ready to go. She'd nothing for him so he went back out and had Mitch take him a couple of hundred yards to a club entrance just off Fulham Palace Road. He told Mitch to wait again and went in. The dim lighting illuminated half a dozen punters in for what the club jokingly termed happy hour. At most places happy hour meant half price. At this place you got a normal-price drink and a discount token for your next. And happy hour finished at six on the dot when the floor show started and your tokens were good for shit. Roker spotted his man leaning on the bar. He walked across. The man turned.

'Tell me,' he said.

Roker had learned to play it straight with the guy. Say his stuff and get out. The dim lighting did nothing for the man's appearance, which was grim in any light, though the guy seemed happy with it. When you've been through the mangler it's good for people to see it. Saves misunderstandings.

Roker signalled and ordered a scotch.

'He's on to something,' he said.

'What's he onto?'

'Brighton.'

'How?'

'I don't know.'

Roker detailed Flynn's head-to-head with the Royal Trafalgar's reception clerk.

'Why would reception tell him anything?'

'Cash. He was feeding it across and stuff was coming back.'

'So he's on to us?'

Roker's drink arrived. He slid a tenner across the bar, lifted the glass.

'I think he knows Slater was there. Maybe picked up the other names.' He thought of something. 'How did you know this guy was chasing around?'

The man studied the display behind the bar. 'Little bird,' he said.

'Yeah,' Roker said. He sipped the scotch and picked up the change from his tenner which was bugger all, plastic token to boot. Happy hour! There were more important things on his mind, though. 'I think this guy's going to be a problem,' he said.

'Yes,' the man agreed. 'He's going to be a problem.'

They stayed quiet. Roker drained his glass in a couple of sips. The fastest tenner he'd lost since he put his money on Frenchman's Creek in the National.

'Who's Flynn working for?' he said.

'That's the question,' the man said.

'Slater?'

'No.'

'One of the others?'

'That's what I'm thinking. Did Flynn poke his nose anywhere else?'

'Chevening.'

The man's eyebrows lifted. 'Chevening?'

'Big place. Estate. High walls. He was only in five minutes. Is there a connection?'

The other man swirled his drink. Sighed.

'That's bad,' he said.

'I thought it might be,' Roker said.

The man pushed his glass across the bar and the girl refilled it. A double. No tokens needed. One rule for some, etc.

'You want me to stay on him?' Roker asked.

'I'll let you know tomorrow,' the man said.

'And if he's onto us?'

'Then we'll stop him.'

~~~~~

'What's the man say?' Mitch asked back in the Warrior.

'He's not happy.'

Mitch grinned. 'Is Tonka messing in one of Mac's little schemes?'

Roker didn't smile back. 'The bastard has no idea,' he said.

He got Mitch to U-turn and drop him back at the office. Waved him off and went in to shut up shop.

Upstairs the lights were still on and Roker was surprised to find Vicky still behind her desk looking like she'd lost a fiver. It was way past five thirty.

'What's up?' he asked.

Then he saw that his office door was open and the lights were on. He looked at Vicky.

'Jesus, Jimmy,' she hissed. 'There's some guy waiting for you. Said you'd want to talk to him. I didn't know what to do.'

'You let him in my friggin' office?'

Vicky fluttered her hands. 'What the hell could I do? Jesus, I've been peeing myself. Why don't you keep your phone on?'

Roker did keep his phone on but the battery had quit after his last call.

The firm got visits from time to time. Went with the territory. But the stupid bitch knew better than to let people through his office door. He glared at her.

'Okay, Vicky,' Roker said. 'Get lost.'

Vicky didn't need a second invitation. She grabbed her stuff and ran out and Roker strode into his office. He'd had a hard day. Whoever had barged in had picked the wrong time.

When he got inside the day got worse. The visitor slid his feet off Roker's desk and waved him through.

'Glad you're back, Jimmy,' said Flynn. 'How was Brighton?'

CHAPTER TWENTY-SEVEN
Dead ends are never dead

The nearest I'd got to Roker at the Royal Trafalgar was when I'd sat down for my second coffee. He was three tables away reading a newspaper that he thought made him invisible. Maybe it would have but I'd been keen to see who'd been following me down the M23. I only managed a peripheral glimpse but it was enough. A face as ugly as Roker's doesn't need photographic memory. Up close was the same but worse.

'When you tail someone use a smaller car,' I said. 'Look for cover when you change lanes. Move easy. Don't bounce around.'

I could have gone on. Blah-di-blah. Shop talk to me and Roker. When I paused for breath Roker joined in.

'You!' He jabbed a thumb. 'Get the fuck out of my office.'

Moi? I folded my arms. Looked round the place. Roker had all the right computers and telephones and combination cabinets but that was it. When it came to style Alpha Security was an empty shell. Style is something we did have at Eagle Eye. Style is what tells you about the outfit you're hiring – or in this case about the outfit that's been hired to follow you. And Roker's office said it all. I turned my attention back to the guy.

'Three questions,' I said.

Roker strode across, came up close. 'Walk out while you can, Flynn,' he said.

'Number one: who are you working for?'

He leaned closer. His ugly beak hovered over me like a constipated hawk's. His fists were bunched.

'Two: what's your connection with Rebecca Townsend?'

Roker moved fast but not fast enough. He made a grab for my shirt collar but I snatched the wrist before he got half way and his knuckles hit the top of his desk with a crack, by which time I'd a good grip on his own collar. I pulled and squeezed. Roker clawed with his free hand but I kept the pressure on until we understood each other. Eased him away.

'Sit down, Jimmy,' I said.

He didn't. Too much nervous energy. And he stayed close enough to make *me* nervous.

'Flynn, you've just made the biggest mistake of your private-dick life,' he said.

This was untrue. The biggest mistake was when I'd helped un-hijack a truckload of Welsh sheep on the M4 and accidentally dropped the tailboard at the Leigh Delamere services. That's when I found out that rounding up fifty-seven sheep is not as easy as those border collies make out. The Leigh Delamere thing was by far the worst blooper but I guess Roker hadn't heard about that one.

'Three,' I said. 'What's the connection between Alpha Security, Larry Slater and the Royal Trafalgar?'

'Last chance,' Roker said. 'Walk out while you're breathing.'

Funny, from the guy who was red in the face.

'For a man who's been on my tail all day,' I said, 'I thought you'd be glad we'd finally got together.'

'No. I'm not happy. And you're wasting time you don't have, Flynn.'

I thought about it. 'Today hasn't felt wasted,' I said. 'Look what I've got. I've confirmed that Alpha Security is up to something with Rebecca Townsend's family. And I've learned that you're working for a goon who hangs out at the Club Algarve. Tell me, Jimmy, what else is going to pop out before I stir my cocoa?'

'Whatever you heard, you heard wrong,' Roker said. 'Go bark up another tree, Sherlock.'

I grinned. 'I think I'll give this tree a few more shakes. See what falls out.'

'Shake *this* tree any more and you're not going to like the result.'

'Occupational hazard. So what *is* going to come out, Jimmy?'

Roker leaned back into collar-grabbing territory. I sat back.

'Your guts will come out, Flynn, if you poke your nose in any further.'

'All this from a guy who knows nothing. I think you're stalling me, Jimmy.'

'Sue me.'

I sighed. Lifted my feet back onto his desk. Opened my arms. 'Correct me,' I said, 'but I think you know what's happened to the Slaters' daughter.'

'You're digging in piss, Flynn. I don't know any such girl.'

I looked at him.

'Well somebody does. Maybe I need to go chat with your chums at the Algarve.'

'Go ahead. See where that gets you.'

'What about the Royal Trafalgar thing? You're in on that, at least. Those suite bookings must have cost Alpha Security a bob or two.'

'Hospitality. Business clients.'

'What sort of business?'

'You're shitting me!'

'No, Jimmy,' I said, 'I really want to know what sort of business involves hiring a high-class hooker and the best suite at a five star hotel and sets you back three grand before you've even opened the minibar.'

'Confidential business,' Roker said, 'which means you've just hit a dead end.'

'Detective one-oh-one,' I said. 'Dead ends are never dead. You just look at what's blocking the road and you learn.'

'Not this time. Because if you carry on with this you're going to find yourself in a very dead end.'

'Is that a threat, Jimmy?'

'Take it how you want.'

I thought some more.

'What's the deal with Tina Brown? Was she just bait to hook Larry Slater? Are we looking at blackmail?'

'Time's up, Flynn.'

'And where is Tina? She's hell to track down right now.'

But Roker was through. He pulled his phone out.

'It's dead,' I reminded him. 'You should keep it charged. Your receptionist was pretty clear on that point.'

Roker cursed and grabbed the desk phone, which wasn't dead. I looked round his office again while he made his call. The place got worse the longer you looked. It was the sort of office that would make a VAT accountant turn up his nose. Maybe it was just brilliant cover. Roker finished the call and jabbed a finger.

'Hang around, pal,' he said. 'We can have your little chat.'

Any chinwag organised by Roker I could do without. I pulled my feet off his desk. Paperwork fell.

'The guy I want to chat to is the one who had you chasing me to Brighton,' I said. 'He'll know all about the Royal Trafalgar. And about Rebecca.' I stood and straightened my jacket.

'That's tough,' Roker said. 'Because I won't be making any introductions.'

I gave him a grin. Headed for the door.

'You already did,' I said.

CHAPTER TWENTY-EIGHT
Maybe you didn't hear me

I crossed the street, dodging evening traffic, musing on how the Brighton trip had turned from a long shot into a jackpot. Suddenly I was pushing a loaded trolley through checkout.

My phone rang. Arabel's voice above the traffic din.

'Where you at, babe? You said you'd be home.'

I kicked myself. When I'd set off for Brighton I'd had no idea the thing would snowball. Arabel was cooking at my place before we headed out.

'Bel,' I said, 'I'm a disgrace. Got carried with the flow. But I'll be there. Promise.'

'Sometime tonight? Or do you want your dinner in the freezer?' Sounded like dinner wouldn't be the only thing in there.

'Give me an hour, then I'm all yours.'

'Whenever you've got a minute.'

'Hey, I've always got a minute for you. I just got tied up with this thing. I should have called.'

'You out looking for the girl?'

'Yes. And things are creeping out of the woodwork.'

'Things that couldn't have crept tomorrow?'

'I'm worried about this girl,' I said. I was playing the sympathy vote. I could have turned up for dinner on time as long as Arabel didn't mind about a poor girl huddled in a dark cellar. The sympathy line used to work but Arabel had grown wiser.

'Flynn,' she cut in, 'I'd walk out right now if the casserole hadn't got me drooling. One hour then I'm eating. And I'm gonna be planning some suffering while I'm waiting.'

'Are we talking dirty?'

The phone cut.

Not dirty.

I turned down a narrow street and stopped outside a door topped by defective neon letters that said CLUB ALGARVE. The street windows were bricked up and the door was steel with a one-way glass. I pressed a button and it opened.

Behind the door a muscled guy in a tux stood beside a pay-kiosk. Admission was a tenner, which was cheek for Fulham, but a private investigator's life is nothing if not a charitable enterprise. I handed over the cash and went through. The rhythmic thump of dirty music beckoned.

Bad lighting played across teak veneer and fake red leather and lit twenty or so mostly-empty tables surrounding a postage-stamp stage where spots picked out the gymnastics of a lithe blonde whose skimpy clothing was dissolving by the second.

The place was a monument to wannabe respectability. The teak and leather couldn't disguise the fact that the place was a strip joint. The broom closets the girls changed in would have flaking plaster and mesh over the windows just like any in Soho. I sensed an investor with ideas of running a classy bar but unable to resist putting the girls in; the distorted looking-glass of the criminal trying to build a respectable image on dirty cash. When my eyes adjusted I spotted a shady character sitting in the shadows with two glasses on his table. One glass was half empty and looked like carbonated water. The other was full and looked like beer. I went over and sat down.

'You're just in time,' Shaughnessy said. 'The urge to filch your drink was growing.' He was studying the gymnastics of the blonde with either fascination or despair.

I took a sip of the beer. Put it down sharp.

'You weren't in danger,' I said. 'This stuff would stifle the alcoholic urge like wimples check fornication in a nunnery.'

'I've never been in a nunnery. How was your chat with Alpha?'

'Tense. I spoke to a guy named James Roker. He knows nothing about nothing.'

'Figures.'

'But apparently he knows someone who does.'

Shaughnessy indicated a table at the end of the bar where two men were talking. The first of them was so huge he was popping the shoulder seams on his sports jacket. The bar spots lit a face like a granite sculpture after the chiseller's drinking has taken a turn. His close-shaved head left him ageless. He could have been thirty or sixty. The second guy was late fifties with a taste for expensive suits, shirts with ties. He was a leaner build but with a heavy charisma. His deep-lined face sported bushy brows and girlish lips that hung in a natural sneer, and the light reflected off golden hair falling to his collar. He was the kind of guy who'd still have his mane at ninety. Half dandy, all thug.

Shaughnessy gestured at Granite. 'Roker chatted to him for a while. Looked like he was passing on bad news. Goldilocks showed up ten minutes ago. He's getting the replay.'

'Brighton news.'

Shaughnessy had picked us up at the Lodge Clacket services and stayed with the Warrior after I bailed out at Battersea. He'd watched the SUV stop off at the Alpha Security offices then move on to the club where he'd walked in right behind Roker and given me a call. By the time Roker had finished his report and headed back out I was already riding his office chair.

'Who's Goldilocks?' I asked.

'The boss, is my guess. And he's not a happy guy.'

Maybe he'd drunk the beer.

A waitress in a skimpy outfit passed by, giving Shaughnessy the look that girls on commission reserve for teetotals. I flagged her over. She was eighteen or nineteen. Nice-looking. Would probably graduate to the tiny stage at some point.

I gave her harmless charmer and got a smile in return. When she smiled she was beautiful, though the smile faded a little when she realised I was asking questions instead of ordering drinks.

'I know that guy,' I said. I nodded at the Granite-Goldilocks table. 'Can't recall his name. He one of your regulars?'

'You could say that.' She held her smile, even if it was a little forced. 'That's Paul McAllister. He owns the club.'

Club owner. That must be Goldilocks. Granite wasn't the business type.

I extemporised. Laughed. 'Not Paul. Hell, everyone knows him.'

'You mean Ray? He's in all the time.'

'Ray!' I tapped my forehead. 'Where did I see him...?'

'Ray Child,' she prompted.

'Got him!' I upped my smile to full wattage and pulled a tenner from my pocket. Ordered a whisky and told her to keep the change. Her smile broadened but not by much. Seemed the change wasn't going to make her rich. Still, commission was the name of the game. She walked off to the bar.

Paul McAllister and Ray Child. Goldilocks and Granite.

The names didn't ring any bells but then London's a big town.

'So where are we at?' Shaughnessy asked.

I filled him in on what I'd found in Brighton. Larry Slater's connection to Alpha Security through his stays at the Royal Trafalgar. Alpha Security's other hospitality bookings: guests Hanlon and McCabe. Maybe just business, like Roker insisted. Funny business, was my guess.

And we were looking at the guys who'd set Roker on my tail. The question was, who'd tipped them off?

'Slater,' Shaughnessy said.

I concurred. One visit to Slater's house and suddenly there's a posse on our tail. So who were these guys and why had Slater tipped them off? I watched the show. The girl writhed and gyrated. Lights danced across her limbs.

'He's either in with them or scared of them,' said Shaughnessy. 'You think they've got Rebecca?'

That was the question. If we were looking for kidnappers this pair would fit. And the two of them would have no trouble intimidating a family into keeping quiet. But had they frightened Larry enough to have him tip them off when I came on the scene?

My guess was that Larry's first weekend in Brighton was funded by these two. We just had to figure what their game was, and why Slater was chasing Tina Brown, and whether any of it was related to Rebecca. The jigsaw pieces were piling up. We just didn't know how many jigsaws we had. Our waitress came back with my Scotch and a smile. Maybe there was more left from the tenner than I'd estimated. Shaughnessy handed his glass back and waved off the refill.

'Gotta go, Eddie. Promises to keep. You hanging on?'

'Just as long as my Scotch.' I had thirty minutes to make good on my promise to Arabel. She was an easy-going girl but she liked her promises kept. That's why I rarely made any. 'We need to look at these guys,' I said.

Shaughnessy nodded. 'Tomorrow,' he promised. He slid out of the seat.

I sipped whisky and thought about it. We needed to close this thing before Tina Brown's friend Sammy blew the whistle. If the authorities got involved the waters would get well and truly muddied.

And I couldn't help wondering if Tina might not want the water muddying. I was seeing her as a part of this.

The stick in the hornet's nest. Why ditch a good idea? I caught our waitress' eye again and signalled her over. Pulled out a twenty this time. Turned Harmless Charmer right up. 'Keep the change,' I said. I nodded towards the table by the bar. 'A drink each for Paul and Ray. Ask them if they've been to Brighton lately.'

Her smile was genuine this time. We were establishing a pattern. With people like Shaughnessy you could give up hostessing as a bad job. Party Animal Flynn was a different story. Flynn meant tips and commission.

She went back to the bar and a couple of minutes later delivered the drinks and the men's heads turned in unison. I raised my glass. The music came on again. A new girl was warming up. I sat back to watch but she'd barely time to limber up before she was hidden behind two silhouettes. The silhouettes stopped at my table and sat down. Granite up close was worse than Granite far away. Close up I could see that someone had taken a knife to Ray Child's face one time. A scar ran from his left ear right down to the jaw line and he still seemed pissed off about it. Paul McAllister — Goldilocks — didn't have a scar but he wasn't happy either. He was looking at me as if he'd spilled his Smarties on the toilet floor. He leaned forward.

'You get this once,' he said. 'Pull your nose out and keep it out. If you don't, I'll cut it off.' His brows lifted to see if I'd got the message. Child watched me from the other side. His eyebrows didn't move but they didn't need to. Child had the kind of stare that had been intimidating people since the school playground. Myself, I'd been to a better class of school. I answered McAllister.

'Hello Paul. Sorry your boys had such a long trip. If I'd known they were going to Brighton we could have shared the ride.'

McAllister's face stayed expressionless.

'One comment,' I said. 'You're hiring cheap. There are firms who charge through the nose but they'll tail someone all day without being spotted. But I guess you get what you pay for.'

Child leaned across but McAllister's hand came up.

'Stop!' he said. His eyes hadn't left me.

I stopped.

'Maybe you didn't hear me,' he said.

Blame the music. It was kind of loud.

'Either that or you're stupid.'

He waited to see which it was.

'If you interfere any further in our business,' he said, 'I will bury you. You hear this once only.'

I'd heard it twice now but who was counting?

McAllister's stare was locked onto my eyes and his soft lips were turned down with the assurance of a hanging judge. I sat forward.

'I'm looking for Rebecca Townsend,' I said. 'And I'm finding connections – the Slaters; Roker; Brighton; Tina Brown; Hanlon; McCabe; and you guys at the centre. It's coming apart, McAllister. And I'm going to sledgehammer away until I get the girl back.'

I held up my own finger before McAllister could reply. 'Here's the message for you. If anything happens to the girl I'm going to hand so many threads to the police that they're going to form a knitting circle. They'll unravel your whole operation inside twenty-four hours. And you'll go down for anything that happens to her.'

I was exaggerating with the twenty-four hours. It would take even the agency longer than that. But McAllister got my drift. The two of them stayed quiet for a moment. Then Ray Child came in.

'You're a dead man, Flynn,' he said. He raised his fist and snapped his fingers in my face. 'Dead! Easy as that.' He turned to McAllister. 'I think this joker's too stupid to back off.'

But not stupid enough to keep buying their drinks.

I stood and squeezed past them, stopped to lower my mouth to McAllister's ear.

'Go for a makeover. Real leather. Neutral colours. Discreet lighting. Hire some classy girls. Lose the Costa del Crime atmosphere. And put less water in the beer. You'll make a killing.'

Not in Fulham, he wouldn't.

I walked out.

CHAPTER TWENTY-NINE
Expendable might be a problem

I got to Battersea with nothing to spare on Arabel's deadline. She'd held off on eating but it was a close call. Sweet talking and apologies only go so far.

'You're not sorry, Flynn,' she said. 'You're like a boy with his tadpole jar. The rest of the world is forgotten. Are you telling me I can't depend on you any more?'

I hadn't realised I'd ever been dependable. Maybe Arabel just hadn't noticed at one time.

'Bel, you can always depend on me,' I assured her. 'But sometimes things just happen in this business. They tie me.'

'Letting me know would have helped.'

'I'm distractible,' I admitted. 'But that's different from undependable.'

'Different how? Both of them mean you don't turn up.'

Argumentative, this one.

'A guy who's not dependable doesn't care,' I said. 'A guy who just gets distracted always cares. He hates himself for forgetting.'

'You hate yourself?'

'Whenever I let you down.'

'Oh, babe!'

Oh boy!

My shame would have been hard to swallow if I thought Arabel believed this stuff. But that's what I loved about her: she could go along with the fantasy that she had a sincere guy instead of a smooth-talking rogue. Maybe deep down she did understand that I was sincere. Maybe she was just a saint.

I got busy and uncorked a white wine and pushed a few things around on the table as the aroma of casserole filled the room and Arabel served the meal up in a steaming pot with creamed potatoes and vegetables. My diet so far that day had comprised a single sandwich at the motorway services. The casserole tripped a switch.

Arabel let me gorge for twenty minutes before interrupting to ask about the girl.

The thought cut through my hog heaven. Funny how easily I'd forgotten. But a man has to take a break. Sometimes you've got to stop saving the world. I told Arabel about the characters we'd unearthed. Didn't tell her about the risk to my nose or the death-threat stuff. The thought that I might not turn up at all one day wasn't going to convince Arabel she was investing in the right guy. Distractible or undependable she could deal with. Expendable might be a problem. And it was clear that *expendable* was the category Paul McAllister had assigned me. I was going to have to watch my back.

'Will you find Rebecca?' Arabel asked.

I quit thinking about myself. Thought it through.

'Sure,' I said, 'we'll get to her.'

We just needed to do so before someone got to me.

CHAPTER THIRTY
Selling a Porsche to a blind man

Eight a.m. Winter was fighting a rearguard action as I drove to Paddington. Heavy rain, batting gusts, a forecast of gales.

The lights were on in the front room and Shaughnessy was busy at his PC. I fired up the filter machine and spooned in Buckaroo from home. If the machine worked we'd get caffeine enough to fly to the moon. I went through and dropped into one of Shaughnessy's chairs.

'The entertainment warm up last night?' he asked.

'The full cabaret.' I described my chat with McAllister and Child.

'They sound serious. Better watch your back.'

I concurred. Listened to the silence in the outer office. Got up and went back out. Confirmed that the water was still cold in the reservoir, the coffee still dry in the filter. I flipped the switch, pulled the plug out and banged it back in. Got a flash and a spark. Something was connecting. Then the outer door opened and Lucy appeared in an explosion of red. She feigned shock.

'Do you guys never sleep?'

'The forces of law and order are ever vigilant,' I told her.

'What's law and order got to do with it?'

'It's an analogy,' I said. 'The forces of private investigation are a little like the forces of law and order. Private investigators don't get much sleep either.'

Lucy gave me smarmy. 'So how is Arabel?'

'Arabel is fine,' I told her. 'It's me you should worry about.'

'No longer,' she said. 'What's with Rebecca Townsend?'

'We're moving. If you can voodoo up some coffee I'll fill you in.'

I went into my office. The wind had chilled the back of the building and the place was like a bank holiday morgue. I switched on the two-bar and moved it under my desk then picked up the phone and called Philippa Scott.

Philippa was the sales director of a media firm that ran a half-dozen regional newspapers and two south-east society magazines. She'd once hired us to locate her estranged husband who'd done a disappearing act. Turned out the guy was lying low, avoiding people who wanted to discuss gambling debts. Just as we got to him they moved on to the stage of threatening Philippa and her kids. Small time but nasty with it. We helped sort things out.

Philippa's gratitude ran to offering help with research in her social files, a card I played without shame. A good investigator values shamelessness right up there with godliness and cleanliness.

'Long time no hear, Eddie,' Philippa said. 'Are things quiet or have you been on holiday?'

'A little of both.'

'Looking for some digging?'

'You know me, Philippa. Just tell me when we're out of credit. You paid your dues.'

'I could never pay the dues, Eddie. You gave me my family back.'

'I still feel guilty dining out on the result.'

Lucy had come in with the coffee. She didn't know whom I was talking to but the word *guilty* told her I was shining them on. I gestured for her to drop the coffee off. She made no move to leave. I hit the speaker.

'What's happening?' Philippa asked.

'Something you might relate to. We've a family in trouble. A girl missing. Suspected involvement of professional criminals.'

The speaker amplified an intake of breath.

'It never ends, does it?' she said. 'This stuff sells my papers – kids missing, assaulted, killed – it's what we feed people with their cornflakes. Other people's nightmares. But you don't know anything until it happens to you.'

'Yeah. We see plenty of nightmares in this game, though I'm not much of a newspaper reader myself.'

She chuckled. 'I can't see our rags cluttering your coffee table, Eddie. Luckily everyone isn't like you. I'd be out of business.'

'So would I,' I said.

'You still seeing that cute girl?'

The last time I'd bumped into Philippa I'd had a new girlfriend on my arm, just off shift and all starched up in her nurse's uniform.

'Yeah. We're still together. Looks promising.'

'She's a good girl. Hang on to her.'

'I do.'

'So what do you need?'

'Background on a couple of well-to-do families. Maybe they're in your area.'

'London?'

'One's Wimbledon, the other's a little out of town.'

I described the McCabe and Hanlon families. If they were in Philippa's territory they'd be in her society pages for sure.

'How soon do you need it?' Philippa asked.

'The soonest. We're worried about this girl.'

'I've got a meeting,' Philippa said, 'but I'll kick something off. Let's say an hour or two.'

'Appreciated.'

I killed the line. Reached for my coffee. The cup came complete with saucer and spoon and Lucy's backside now perched on my roll-top. I keep my desk cluttered to discourage perching but Lucy always seemed to find parking space. Private investigation runs on discretion. We operated on a need-to-know basis. Lucy needed to know everything. Maybe she had a vested interest this time since she'd kicked this mess off by setting Sadie Bannister onto me.

I brought her up to date. Described the Brighton hotel and the link to the McCabe and Hanlon families. Replayed McAllister's threat to my nose. Lucy shrugged that off. Asked if I had anything for her.

I told her to call me with whatever Philippa phoned through. Meantime she could do some of her own digging, see what turned up on the two families. And she could call Sadie Bannister to prod her for anything new she might have remembered or picked up in the last few days, including any snippets on Russell Cohen.

'You still think the guy's involved?'

'Gut feeling says no. This is between the Slaters and McAllister. But we need to cover all possibilities. I'm not ruling Cohen out.'

Lucy slid off my desk and went out.

I wasn't ruling Cohen out but you've got to follow the main smell, and it wasn't perfume that assaulted my nostrils in the Algarve. My guess said McAllister had Rebecca, leverage against the Slaters even if it wasn't a simple ransom scheme. Nothing was in focus yet, but yesterday had given me a hunch. I adjusted the angle on my Herman Miller and sipped scalding coffee and chased the hunch. Tapped a Poole number into my phone.

'DK Marine.' A man's voice.

'I understand you're agents for pre-owned boats,' I said.

'Indeed we are. Mr...?'

'Bligh.'

'Mr Bligh. We've an extensive portfolio. Would you like our listings or do you have something specific in mind?'

'I'm looking at a motor cruiser. Six berths. Good level of equipment. My wife and I mostly stay inshore. South and west coast. But we do Jersey too.' I wasn't sure if the cruising fraternity "did" Jersey or anywhere else. In fact I wasn't sure if there was such a thing as a cruising fraternity outside of Soho. But my amateur spiel passed muster with the DK guy. Salesmen handle the gamut of competencies. They'll sell a Porsche to a blind man.

'We've a range of cruisers in our listing,' said DK. 'Any particular specification?'

'We're still weighing things up,' I stalled. 'I was at the marina yesterday and someone told me the *Lode Star* was on your list.'

'My goodness, news travels fast. We haven't put it up yet.'

'But she's on your books?'

'Just this week. And you might be lucky. The owner wants a fast sale so we've financed it ourselves. We're ready to offer a knockdown price.'

'Financed? You mean you own the vessel?'

'It's a little unusual but the owner made us an offer we couldn't refuse. We completed yesterday. Effectively the *Lode Star* is on sale now and I think you'd be very happy with the asking price.'

'She's a nice-looking vessel,' I concurred. 'But I suspect she'd stretch us, even at a knockdown price. We're selling a fifteen metre, a few years older.'

'Mr Bligh... may I ask your first name?'

'Bill.'

'Bill: you might find that the *Lode Star* doesn't stretch you as far as you assume. We'll be asking only seventy-five per cent of market.'

'Seventy-five?' I put lust into my voice. 'Did I hear you right?'

'Seventy-five percent of market, Bill. And the survey's thrown in for free. You'd see everything before you spent a penny.'

'Well that's interesting. Might almost bring it within reach. What figure were you thinking?'

'I'd prefer to discuss that here,' DK said. 'Maybe we can take a look at your own vessel. But this is a once-in-a-lifetime. You'll never see a discount like this again.'

'You've certainly got me tempted,' I said. 'Hard to see what's in it for you.'

A chuckle. Old business buddies. 'We're quite happy with the margin, Bill. The owner needed a fast sale. He gave us a deal that was right on the rocks.'

'I bumped into the chap a while ago,' I said. 'Larry Something. Don't recall his last name. He never mentioned selling.'

'We never discuss client details,' DK said, 'but I gather that the need to sell came up suddenly.'

'Wow. The way you describe it...'

'Could I trouble you for your details Bill?'

'How about I call in? I'll give you everything.'

'Fine. Look forward to seeing you.'

I killed the line.

Aye-aye.

I sat back and lifted my heels onto the desk. So Slater was the *Lode Star*'s seller. If DK Marine were making a profit selling at seventy-five per cent of market price then Slater must have offloaded the boat somewhere around the fifty percent mark. What would the *Lode Star* pull in? Seven or eight hundred K? Boats weren't my thing but I knew a guy who'd splashed out half a million on a smaller boat a couple of years back. It sounded like Slater had just thrown away three or four hundred grand to get his hands on instant cash. Which brought us right back to the kidnap-for-ransom scenario. It just didn't explain what the hell was going on.

I slid my feet off the desk and went through to Shaughnessy's office. He'd just put his phone down and was working his computer.

'Anything on our Club Algarve people?'

Shaughnessy looked up. 'It's coming in,' he said. 'I'm waiting for a call back. Then we'll have the picture.'

I left him to it and headed out.

CHAPTER THIRTY-ONE
Blame the messenger

Rain started to hit the windscreen as I crossed Putney Bridge and a minute later came on like nobody's business as a hands-free came in from Lucy. She had Philippa's information on the McCabe family.

'The guy's a builder turned property developer,' she reported. 'Made his first million at thirty-two. Took an award for a restored Georgian on the top end of Blackheath. The house has been in *Ideal Home* twice. He has a wife and two kids. The family are in the society pages a couple of times a year. Philippa has a whole library on them.'

I struggled to catch the words over the din of rain on the soft-top.

'Tell me about the wife and kids,' I yelled.

'Wendy's forty-five, the same age as John. She's a housewife. Supports local causes. They've two girls, fourteen and seven. Both at the Mayfield School on the Common.'

Interesting. I swung right at the top of the Common and headed towards the McCabe's address. Asked about the other family.

'The Hanlons are out of Philippa's area. But she promised to keep trying. I'm checking around, too.'

'Anything you can get,' I said. 'The picture's coming into focus. If the families fit what I'm looking for we're nearly there.'

I killed the line and focused on the road. The rain had reduced visibility to a wall of spray. I leaned forward and spotted a turning. A tree-lined lane at the south end of the Park. The McCabe house stood behind brick walls that sported a gateway that was a smaller version of the one that had blocked me at the Hanlons' with the difference being that this was open. The driveway was a smaller version, too, barely thirty yards long. I drove up and parked on a forecourt in front of a red-brick Victorian mansion that promised *Ideal Home* perfection behind its ten-foot sash windows. A single car was parked in front of the house. A Fiat Panda. They'd need to shift that before the photographers arrived.

I sprinted to the porch and pressed the bell. Heard a hoover quit. A woman in her middle fifties wearing green work overalls came out. I asked if Wendy was in.

She invited me through to the back of the house where a too-thin woman emerged from a sun lounge to meet us. The lounge would be idyllic on a warm summer's day. Today the rain was like machine-gun fire and the place was cold. Wendy McCabe was pretty in a mousy kind of way. Glittery eyes and pointed nose. Kind of cute. But her smile was doubtful. After I'd left she'd remind her maid that strangers waited at the door.

I gave her an agency card. Apologised for calling out of the blue. Explained that there was an urgent matter she and her husband might help me with.

She didn't rise to the bait and tell me that her husband wasn't home. Smart.

'You're a private investigator?'

'Security and research services.' I left the job description at that. No need to mention of what kind of research we usually did. 'We're acting for a family who've been targeted by criminals. We suspect other families are at risk.'

Wendy McCabe's look switched to concern.

'You mean *our* family? What kind of risk?'

'Nothing specific. Maybe nothing at all. But I want to talk to anyone who might have been in contact with these people. Just precautionary.'

'Precautionary? You're frightening me more every minute, Mr Flynn.'

'Why don't we sit down?'

Wendy shook her head. No pushover, this one. 'Explain yourself,' she said.

I gave he a reassuring smile. Back-pedalled.

'We may be off-track, Mrs McCabe. But my clients felt an obligation to pass on the information we have.'

There's a limit to how many times you can circle the wagons. At some point you've got to move in. I pulled Sadie's photo from my wallet. Pointed to Rebecca. I didn't see the McCabes knowing the Slaters so the picture should mean nothing. If it did, we'd have a new situation.

Sure enough, Wendy McCabe's face stayed blank.

'Who is she?'

'I've been asked not to reveal names. But this girl's family have been threatened.'

'What kind of threat?'

'We're talking about abduction.'

Wendy's expression turned to stark fear. 'Are you saying our children are at risk?'

'We're just covering the possibilities. The people behind this are targeting wealthy families with kids. One of the conspirators may be involved in the London property market. Hence the possible connection with your husband. '

'Do the police know about it?'

'We're still trying to understand the threat. Right now we've nothing the police could act on. And your own family have only the faintest probability of being involved.'

Say, fifty-fifty. Don't ask me for racing tips.

'So what do you want from us?'

'I need to know whether you or your husband know the people involved.'

So far, Wendy McCabe was coming up blank. She'd shown no reaction to my talk of abduction beyond the obvious fear, nothing to suggest that one of her own children had already been taken. My theory about Rebecca Townsend said that the McCabes had gone through the same thing six months earlier. So either Wendy McCabe was an impeccable actress or my hunch was wrong.

'Has your family ever been threatened?' I asked.

'Absolutely not.' No hesitation. Just annoyance. The thought of her children in danger had Wendy McCabe ready to blame the messenger.

'Do you know a guy named Paul McAllister?'

She looked blank.

'James Roker?'

Nothing.

'Maybe your husband might know them through his business contacts?'

'Why not ask him?' Wendy walked over and picked up the phone. Hit speed dial and passed a curt message. A few seconds later her husband came on the line. She told him what was happening and asked if he knew what it was about. Repeated my name twice.

McCabe's voice crackled on the other end and it didn't sound like endearments. His wife turned to me: 'Can you go to Kingston?'

I said I could be there in thirty minutes. She passed on the information and handed me a business card with McCabe's address, a location in the centre of the town. I thanked her and repeated my assurances that all was well, but she kept her face set as she walked me to the door. Messenger or not, Wendy McCabe didn't want to see me again. Mothers are like that when their families are threatened. I'd begun to wonder if her shredded peace of mind had been worth it.

Maybe her husband would tell me.

CHAPTER THIRTY-TWO
Not exactly a bullseye

John McCabe was a surprise. Partly because his refined manner didn't shout ex-builder. But mostly because he didn't leap from his desk to get his hands round my throat.

He ran his business from a modest office in a three-storey block a stone's throw from the river. McCabe Enterprises comprised a reception and office space on the top floor. His own office was unpretentious. The only thing it boasted was a view of the Thames if you looked at an angle. I guess McCabe concentrated on the nuts and bolts rather than prestige side of the property development industry.

He shook my hand and I gave him a card and sat down. Repeated my spiel about threatened clients, bad guys and wealthy families. Got no sign of recognition. McCabe heard me out then spoke.

'You may be acting with the best intentions,' he said, 'but you scared the hell out of my wife.'

'Yeah. I regret that. But we suspect that our clients are not the only ones these people are targeting.'

'Is that not for the police to decide?'

'Ultimately. When we've enough evidence to take to them.'

'And what evidence do you expect to get from my family?'

'Any information you may have about these people. Any suspicious approaches by them.'

'Do you think my family have been targeted?'

'Has it?'

McCabe's eyes locked onto mine. 'No,' he said. 'We'd have informed the police.'

'These guys exert pressure to keep the police out.'

'What kind of pressure?'

'If they're snatching kids that should be pretty clear.'

McCabe continued to look at me.

'Well, there's been no abduction. We've had no contact with any criminals. So we're not involved – unless you're keeping something back.'

I answered in the negative, still watching for signs.

McCabe sat forward and planted his hands on his desk.

'I don't know what to believe here,' he said. 'You walk into my house and suggests that we may be under threat from a criminal group, ask if any of my kids have been abducted, then remain vague about what's behind this. I see why my wife was scared. Maybe I should call the police myself.' He held up my business card. 'Do you mind if I keep this?'

'Go ahead,' I said. 'We're a legitimate agency. The Metropolitan Police know us.'

They knew us, all right.

'Have you anything else?' He was looking at his watch.

'The men involved,' I said. 'Maybe you've come across them.'

I gave him their names but McCabe's stare didn't waver. Just a curt shake of the head. Either he and his wife were good enough to be on the stage or they'd never come across McAllister, Child or Roker.

'How about the Royal Trafalgar Hotel in Brighton?'

That got a hit but not exactly a bullseye. McCabe looked surprised and pursed his lips but just gave me a noncommittal nod. He knew the place but when I asked about the hotel's relevance he shrugged it off as business and refused to say more.

I persisted: 'Who did you meet in Brighton?'

McCabe shook his head and said sorry. Business. I pulled out a photo.

'Was this woman one of them?'

Another hit. A little nearer centre. McCabe's eyebrows raised sharply and he looked at me. But it was puzzlement rather than guilt or fear. He pushed the photo back over.

'What's this all about?'

'So you recognise the woman?'

'Really, that's not your business. Answer my question.'

I thought for a moment. Decided that answering McCabe's questions would be counterproductive. I'd got the spark of recognition for both the hotel and the woman but there was something off. I'd expected a firecracker. Got a damp squib, another piece of the jigsaw that refused to connect. If I told McCabe that Tina Brown was linked to my criminals it might push him the last step towards the police, a complication I could do without.

I tucked the photo away and thanked McCabe for his time. Stood to leave.

McCabe stood too and started to ask something but I gave him a cheery nod and was already out of his door.

~~~~~

I'd just taken another soaking sprinting back to the Frogeye when my mobile rang.

'Tell me what's happening.' Samantha Vincent's voice. 'I've called Tina ten times since we spoke. I sent her a text saying you were looking for her. She's still not answered.'

'Just hang in there,' I said. 'I think we're close to finding what's happening.'

'You told me you'd find her in two days. What have you got?'

'Nothing I can give you. But trust me, Sammy: just hold off a while longer. I'll call you the moment there's news.'

'Cut the bullshit, Mr Flynn. I'm going to the police right now unless you give me something.'

'Sammy,' I said, 'I won't lie to you. We've not reached Tina yet.' I considered how to phrase my next words: 'But there's a chance that Tina might not want the police involved.'

It took a moment.

'What do you mean?' she asked, but I knew she'd got it.

'She could be involved in something that requires her to stay low for a while. Something she might not want the police to know about.'

'Something criminal? I don't believe it.'

'Sorry, Sammy, it's a possibility. And we need a little more time to understand things.'

'I'm more worried about Tina's safety than the risk that she's mixed up in something.'

'I understand. But we're the fastest way to get answers. Give us another day. We'll talk to Tina within twenty-four hours. That's a promise.'

Sammy turned it over then made up her mind. 'Tomorrow,' she said. The phone went dead.

CHAPTER THIRTY-THREE
His speciality is disappearing tricks

I drove back to Paddington with the rain trying to punch holes in the soft top. The wipers were working but I couldn't see them. Springtime in London.

I parked on a meter and sprinted inside. I was risking a ticket but what kind of warden would be out in this storm? The dedicated kind, that's what. If I parked round the back of the building I'd get soaked. If I paid Westminster's parking rates I'd be bled dry. Life's choices.

Shaughnessy was at his desk lunching on a smoked salmon baguette. Lucy was sat atop Harry's side of the desk, fighting something less low-calorie. I flopped into a chair and dripped water.

They looked at me.

'The McCabes know nothing,' I said.

Shaughnessy's eyebrows lifted. He'd been backing the same horse as me: whatever was going on with the Slaters had already happened to the McCabes.

'Nothing,' I repeated. 'No threats, no funny goings-on, no missing kids.'

I detailed McCabe's lacklustre responses on both the Royal Trafalgar and Tina Brown. The guy had stayed at the hotel and he recognised Tina but none of it seemed to mean anything. And he'd never heard of McAllister. I asked Shaughnessy what he'd picked up on the Algarve people.

'Plenty.' Shaughnessy swigged water. 'We're looking at career criminals. McAllister's record goes back to his eighteenth birthday. He celebrated the occasion by getting nicked for robbing a convenience store. Sent down for eighteen months. Should have done it the day before and avoided the adult record. He was fingered again a few years later for armed robbery but the case fell through when witnesses changed their stories. Nothing since, but the Met have him pegged for capers ranging from robbery and extortion to horse doping.'

'The sport of kings,' I said. 'Should be an Olympic event.'

'McAllister learned his lesson and got smart. The Met haven't got near him in thirty years. He runs a body shop in Brixton but the shop would have to be the busiest on the planet to make the dough he flashes.'

'The guy's a big spender?'

'He lives in a house in Bayswater valued at six-point-five mill. Owns a three hundred acre farm in Kent. Rumoured to have commercial properties on the Costa del Sol. Then there's his hobby-horse.'

'The Club Algarve. The way he dilutes the drinks must be costing him a fortune in water rates.'

'My drinks were fine,' Shaughnessy said. 'Hard to water down water.'

I grinned. 'Where do you think the Algarve sourced your Buxton Mineral Water at four-fifty a shot?'

'The tap,' Shaughnessy said. 'Where else?'

Shaughnessy had talked to Zach Finch, my old sergeant at the Met. Zach and I went back. Zach had come within a whisker of taking early retirement himself when I got the boot but I talked him out of it. Painted a picture of him sat at home under the wife's whip. He reconsidered and put the retirement on hold. We stayed in touch and helped each other out now and then.

Zach's ears had pricked up when Shaughnessy dropped McAllister's name. He knew the guy well: McAllister had been one of the top dogs on his ground back in his uniform days and he'd stayed on the Met's untouchable list since then. Anything we could do to throw a banana skin under his feet, Zach was happy to assist. Zach also had info on Ray Child.

'A.k.a. Merlin the Magician,' Shaughnessy said. 'But his act isn't the kind you'd want at your kid's party. Child's speciality is disappearing tricks. He's McAllister's sanitation man, the reason McAllister's stayed out of jail. When the Met get halfway close to anything that could take McAllister down, informants or witnesses clam up or disappear.'

'So we're looking at career professionals. They sound perfect for a kidnapping racket.'

Shaughnessy slanted his lips. 'They've got Rebecca,' he said.

My feeling too. It didn't explain why McAllister had put Larry Slater up in five-star luxury though. The golden rule in kidnap-for-ransom is minimum contact. Strike fast, stay hidden, grab the dosh, get out. The family never sees you. No trail to lead back to you. The thing with the Slater family was all off-kilter. I thought it through but nothing came into focus. 'Anything on Alpha?' I asked Lucy.

'I checked the grapevine,' she reported. 'Roker's the kind of private investigator that gives the profession a bad smell.'

'A rarity.'

'He runs Alpha,' Shaughnessy added. 'Covers the full spectrum: investigation, notice serving, debt collecting, minders. Specialises in the latter two. High turnover, low skill stuff. They've a reputation for operating on the wrong side of the law. Basically they're hired hands for anyone who doesn't want his own fingers dirtied.'

'So Alpha Security organise the Brighton hotel and McAllister puts the hooker in. The question is, what kind of business deal needs that sort of sweetener?'

'A dirty deal,' Lucy speculated. The last of her baguette had disappeared.

'What we're missing is the tie in with Rebecca,' I said. 'This thing's going round and round. Let's go with the certs and work outwards: Rebecca is missing. Her stepfather is raising money fast and he's involved with McAllister. Putting two and two together the money is going to McAllister.'

'So why is Larry Slater chasing Tina Brown?' Lucy asked. 'Where's the connection between his dirty weekends and his stepdaughter's abduction?'

'Tina's the oddity,' I agreed. 'But Slater's fixation with her right now says there is a connection. She's involved somehow. Slater sees her as his route to Rebecca.'

'Except that the lady's AWOL,' Shaughnessy said.

'Just like Rebecca.'

'Maybe even with Rebecca.'

I nodded. 'That's where I'm finishing up. If they've got Rebecca hidden away then someone is with her. We know where McAllister and Child were last night. So who was with the girl?'

'And where are they holding her?' Shaughnessy looked at me.

'McAllister's farm,' I said. 'You want to take a gander?'

'I'm on it.'

'I'll take another drive out to Chevening,' I said. 'See if I can catch the Hanlons this time. The McCabe blank might be the exception.' I looked at Lucy. 'Anything else?'

Lucy patted coleslaw off her lips and gave me a smirk.

'Thought you'd never ask, Eddie,' she said. 'Do I get a bonus for detective work?'

'What are we paying you nowadays?'

'Nothing, usually.'

'Double it. But if you're a detective you'll have to come on stakeouts. Those long nights parked outside some guy's love nest get kinda lonely.'

'It wouldn't work out,' Lucy said. 'There'd be detectives staking *you* out if Arabel heard we were night-shifting together.'

'So what did your detective skills dig up?'

'The Hanlons fit what you're looking for. David Hanlon owns a computer wholesale firm. His wife's an interior designer with a practice in Sevenoaks. The family's worth around twenty million. Two kids: a daughter, sixteen and a son, six. Hanlon's active on the local council. Once ran for Parliament for the Conservatives. He has a seat on the CBI executive. The family's well to do. They fit the pattern.'

'Perfectly.'

'I made your other calls,' Lucy continued. 'Gina Redding's confident you're about to find Rebecca. Sadie's less positive. She thinks Rebecca's dead. She's coming to see you.'

'Well that saves some legwork. When's she due?'

'She didn't say. Wants to surprise you.'

'The girl's a fox,' I said. 'She should be working for us.'

'Then you'd have to pay her.'

'If she turns up,' I said, 'I'll be under the desk.'

'She'd track you down wherever you hid,' said Lucy.

'Yeah,' I agreed. 'Maybe I should just shoot myself now. Be on the safe side.'

CHAPTER THIRTY-FOUR
Evil genie

I made Chevening by two thirty and drove up the driveway to the Hanlons' inner gate. It was still shut and the bell still went unanswered. I pushed an envelope into a post box beside it and reversed back to the gatehouse.

A woman in her late sixties answered the door. Ginger hair hinted at former flame and her still-girlish face echoed youth. She'd turned heads in her time. I told her I'd spoken to her husband yesterday and she invited me in.

The cottage was furnished in dark oak with a museum's worth of bric-a-brac covering every surface and wall. The woman introduced herself as Lottie and called through to her husband. While we waited she launched into the story of how they'd spent their working life abroad. Her husband William had worked in the diplomatic service, toured four South American countries and Malaysia. They travelled the rest of the world in their vacation time. Then two years back William had retired and they'd not set foot outside the UK since.

William came through and nodded a greeting.

'Mr Coffee! Still no-one home?'

'They're out most days,' his wife said. 'Did you try telephoning?'

'I thought I'd surprise them,' I said. 'It's so rare I'm here.'

'Welcome to the club,' William said. 'We went eight years once without setting foot in Blighty. But now we've settled for good it's hard to believe we ever lived anywhere else.'

'I guess it's quite an adjustment. It's funny we didn't meet last time I was here.'

'Not if it's more than seven months ago. That's when we moved in.'

Seven months. Interesting.

'It's kind of a surprise,' I said. 'David and Faye were never keen to part with the cottage.' A believable spiel if the Hanlons had actually owned the property seven months back. But my guesswork was on target. William laughed. 'Lucky for us they changed their minds,' he said. 'We'd anticipated spending a year finding somewhere to live.

Spotted this cottage in an agents in Sevenoaks after two weeks. Fresh on the market and at a crazy price.'

'They sold it cheap?'

Lottie chuckled. 'William and I had a blazing row. The agent assured us that the property was a bargain but the price was so low that William was convinced there was something wrong. He didn't want to waste money on a survey.'

'The price was too low by far,' her husband declared. 'It pays to be cautious.'

'Cautious?' his wife said. 'We nearly walked away from a bargain! Good job I managed to squeeze the survey fee out of you. The report came up clean and we got a once-in-a-lifetime deal.'

'Sounds like David was in a hurry,' I said.

'They'd had their eye on a place in France,' William said. 'Got an offer they couldn't refuse and needed to raise capital right away. The cottage was the simplest thing to offload.'

'I've never thought of selling property as a fast way to get cash.'

'That's why the low price. The agent took the house off their hands overnight for a knockdown price. Expedited the whole thing. Must have made a killing when he sold it on to us a couple of weeks later.'

I shook my head. 'That's a nice bank account the agent must have, with enough free capital to pick up a house.'

William batted it away. 'These agents can get hold of millions if they need to,' he said. 'But my guess is they took the place off the Hanlons for around four hundred thousand.'

Four hundred thousand, seven months back. That put the cottage sale shortly after Hanlon's date with Paul McAllister in Brighton. This was Larry Slater all over again: first you're feted as McAllister's guest, then a couple of months later you're rushing to get instant cash. My chat with David Hanlon was going to be interesting.

Lottie offered me tea but I made excuses. Said I'd be back tomorrow to see the Hanlons.

'If you can catch them,' William said.

I grinned. 'I will,' I said. 'David and Faye will be home tomorrow.'

On this I was confident. Wild horses wouldn't drag the Hanlons out of their house once they'd opened their post box.

~~~~~

162

I called Shaughnessy. He was out at McAllister's farm. I asked if he needed backup. He didn't. The farm was deserted. Appeared to be a weekend home. No one living or working there. No sign of recent occupancy. Empty rubbish bins, bare larder. No one in the attic or cellar. He'd checked the house and walked the land. Found no suspicious outbuildings where you might stash a girl. Just a couple of barns and stored machinery.

You win some, you lose some. The farm had been an obvious place to look. I'd given it one in four. In the investigation business those are usually the best odds you get.

Shaughnessy said he'd give it another hour, let me know if anything turned up. Otherwise we'd talk tomorrow.

Tomorrow was D-Day. Time to end this, as I'd promised Sammy, although I wasn't sure it was going to end the way her friend Tina would want. I needed my chat with the Hanlons then we'd go to the Slaters with whatever we had. As a minimum we had the circumstantial triangle between a missing girl, McAllister and fast cash. Those links were clear enough to interest the Met if Slater refused to talk. We also had the paperwork that pointed to another kind of triangle, the one involving Slater and Tina Brown. Either Slater talked to us tomorrow or the police would be in his house by teatime and the divorce lawyers by supper.

I drove to Fulham. The Algarve was already open. Another tenner chalked to the agency's expenses and I was in. I took a table in the back and looked round. Three other customers and a dark stage. When a girl came over I ordered more weak lager and asked if my hostess from last night was in.

My girl came out two minutes later and grinned down at me. I toasted her and she grinned some more. No Shaughnessy and his mineral waters today. I passed her a tenner and turned Harmless Charmer to full strength.

'I've got a question,' I said. The girl's smile wavered but she kept a game face. I handed her the photograph of Tina Brown.

'You know her?'

She nodded. 'She comes in sometimes.'

'Recently?'

She thought about it. 'Maybe not for a couple of weeks,' she said.

'Why do you ask?'

'Tina's an old friend,' I said. 'Thought I'd catch up with her.'

Her face relaxed. She shrugged. 'I'm not sure she'll be in anytime soon,' she said.

'Does she usually come in with anyone special?'

She glanced round. A little nervous. Seems people didn't ask too many questions at the Algarve.

'Mostly with Paul,' she said.

'Paul McAllister?'

'Yeah. I think they have something going. She's only in when he's in.'

'Is Tina a friend of yours?'

She shook her head. 'I've never spoken to her. I only remember her because of her looks. I see her and think, "If only...'''

'Does she ever perform here?' I nodded at the stage.

She gave me a sad smile. 'Not her scene.' She looked round again. 'The Algarve is a little low-class for someone like Tina,' she said. 'I wish I was somewhere else, too.'

'I know what you mean,' I said.

'Can I get you another drink? I really should be working.'

'I'm fine,' I said. 'Just get one yourself.'

She smiled and turned away with her tenner. I abandoned my drink and walked out.

~~~~~

Tuesday night. A bare larder. Arabel out with her girlfriends. I put it all together and came up with only one solution. I freshened up and drove to Paddington. Parked behind the building and hit a Chinese down on the main road. Pigged out on Crispy Duck and three bottles of Chinese beer.

The weather was still foul. I walked the quarter-mile to the Podium in gusting winds and intermittent drizzle. Settled down in the warmth near the stage. Jack brought over a London Pride, no added water, as an ensemble called Black and Blue warmed up. I relaxed and let the discord wash over me. Half recognised a face in the shadows across the stage and wondered whether to go over, but I couldn't quite say if we'd met. Decided on isolation. Jack brought another beer and when the lead started up with a squeal of trumpet I was floating. D-Day tomorrow. Tonight my brain could pickle.

The jazz was mellow, post-fusion. Not my kind of stuff but the music soothed, and two more Prides did the pickling. The Podium filled. A couple of punks came and sat at my table and I raised my glass but didn't talk. A five-piece came on for the late-night set. They were fronted by a black singer in her late teens with a voice that took you back to Eartha Kitt. I succumbed to the hypnotic lullabies and drifted through the haze. When Barney came to roust me at two thirty the stage was dark and the Podium was emptying. Time to hit the office couch.

The wind had turned the rain to needles. I moved fast to get to the building before my clothes were too soaked to sleep in. The office couch was not conducive to the best night's rest even in dry kit. I could have stashed a sleeping bag in my cupboard but that would have been admitting that I used the place as a crash. My sense of style rejected the notion. I was averaging a night a week but it was always unplanned so it didn't count.

Two forty-five. I covered the empty streets in five minutes.

I turned into Chase Street and saw blue lights by the access road to the rear of the buildings. Spotted two fire engines and a patrol car. Somewhere in the shadows behind the building a light was dancing. Something burning. I walked past the police vehicle. A uniformed cop hopped out and yelled at me but I was way ahead. Jogged to where the fire hoses snaked into the alley. When I got to the corner I saw the Frogeye burning merrily, lighting up the back of the buildings. The copper caught up and grabbed my shoulder.

'Are you frigging deaf, mate?' he said. I shook him off but didn't go further in. Watched the firemen playing their hoses over the skeleton of my car.

'You think this is a bleeding show?' the cop said. Being pulled out into the rain had drained his manners. He grabbed my shoulder again. 'Come out now before I get annoyed.'

'It's mine,' I said. I nodded at the Frogeye.

He let go of my shoulder. Looked at the burning car. The flames were dying and white smoke was rising through the dark like an evil genie.

'Well, I hope your insurance is up to date. I don't think you'll be driving those wheels out of there.'

The last flames died. The show was over. I talked to the firemen while they damped down the wreck, then the cop sat me in his car to answer questions. His partner watched through his rear-view, bored by the action. I narrated my details as the firemen reeled in their hoses. When we were through the cop snapped his notebook and pushed it into his pocket.

'What's a Frogeye Sprite anyway?' his buddy asked. 'You get it at Hamleys?' I saw his grin in the rear-view.

I grinned back. Then I got out and walked up the street and let myself into the building.

The office was colder than usual and my clothes were soaked. I pulled off the outer stuff and carried the two-bar electric fire through to reception. Set it a foot from the couch. I lay down and told myself that tomorrow would be better. Maybe I'd wake and find that the whole thing was a dream. Maybe the Frogeye would be out there, green and shining. That's what I told myself. More realistically, the two-bar would burn the building down while I snored.

I looked on the bright side. A dead Frogeye was better than my nose.

I pushed my nose into the back of the couch and let the electric fire toast my back. Tried to sleep.

CHAPTER THIRTY-FIVE
Parking in Beirut

'We've some unhappy people downstairs,' Shaughnessy said.

I'd migrated to my office via the washroom and was sorting out a plan for the day which now included organising a set of wheels. The stink of burnt rubber seeping through the window gave the place a truly special aroma. Shaughnessy's nose twitched.

We shared the rear parking with Rook and Lye, and the fire had damaged Gerry Lye's spot and left a blackened skeleton and smell of burnt rubber to greet them when they parked their Mercs this morning. I'd never figured a firm of ambulance-chasers for sensitivity but I guess their perception of company image didn't involve parking in Beirut.

'Have you taken up smoking while you drive or is the Frogeye just due for a wash and polish?' Shaughnessy asked.

'It got all the wash it needed last night,' I said, 'but I won't bother with the polish. My street cred would be shot anyway, riding on wheel rims.'

'Lye wants to know when we're going to clear it. It's only the second time he's ever talked to me.'

'A glimmer of good from every misfortune.'

'Not entirely good: Gerry wants a response today. They're in conference now, figuring a strategy to sue us off the street.'

'Sue us for what? Is the parking area part of their company image? Maybe I'll charge for keeping the wreck there.'

'I guess they're thinking more of the financial impact.'

Shaughnessy had a point. Gerry's Merc, parked on a meter while we kept him off his slot, would run at fifteen quid a day. Add administration charges and they'd be billing us at a couple of hundred a week.

'Let them sue,' I said. 'We'll counter with a claim for access rights. How many times a week does Bob block the stairs?'

'That's not the same.'

'Not the same?'

'They're solicitors,' Shaughnessy explained. 'We're private

investigators. They do what they want.'

'Not everything. We're still here.'

Shaughnessy grinned. 'The crazy relatives in the attic. We've got that over them.' He stayed put in the door. 'So, was your car struck by lightning? Or is someone trying to tell you something?'

'The thing was torched. Seems someone was reaching out.'

'Let's hear it for the modern car,' Shaughnessy said. 'Locking petrol caps.'

'If the cap was locked they'd have smashed the window and started the fire inside.'

Shaughnessy shrugged. 'You make too many enemies, Eddie.'

'That's business,' I said. 'Only I've got a pretty good idea whose business we're talking about.'

'McAllister's. He must think you didn't hear him the other day.'

'That's what I'm sensing.'

I went through to make coffee; fed the filter machine and threw the switch. The light stayed off but that didn't mean anything. Sometimes you got lucky.

Shaughnessy unlocked his office, sorted stuff then came back out and dropped himself onto the sofa. The coffee machine coughed and spat hot water into the filter, and the aroma of Buckaroo filled the place. The day was picking up.

'Are we moving as planned?' Shaughnessy said.

'Yeah. I want to hear what the Hanlons have to say then we hit the Slaters.'

'It's all still circumstantial,' Shaughnessy said. 'The Slaters will stick to their story.'

'Sure. But this time we spook Larry with his Blueglades and Royal Trafalgar affairs. That should loosen his tongue.'

'So what do we know for certain?'

'What we know for certain is that there are too many connections.'

I found mugs. Opened the Marvel.

'Three families,' I said, 'three husbands linked to Alpha Security and a classy hooker in Brighton. Alpha Security, operating on behalf of a known criminal, Paul McAllister. The hooker a crony of his, currently lying low. Two of the three families known to have freed up substantial capital recently. One of those families currently missing a daughter.'

168

'The question is what it all means,' Shaughnessy said. 'It looks like we've got two things going. A photo-blackmail scam and a kidnap-extortion racket.'

'Only they're part of the same thing,' I said.

'How about the Hanlons for simple blackmail? Maybe the Slaters too, but for some reason the stakes were upped and they took the girl.'

I shook my head. 'Hanlon raised too much cash. Compromising photos are good for twenty grand not half a million. I want to know why they sold their gate cottage.'

'You think they'll tell you?'

I poured coffee. 'Something's kept them quiet up till now. But if I get a sense that something did happen to one of their kids then we'll know we're on track.'

I handed Shaughnessy his coffee. Treacle-thick. Black. His first and last of the day. I spooned Marvel and three sugars into mine.

'That's my plan,' I said.

Shaughnessy smiled.

'It sounds like a good one,' he said. 'It sounds like the only one.'

~~~~~

My motor insurance didn't run to courtesy cars so it was either rent cheap or walk. I looked up the local rent a wreck in Yellow Pages and they confirmed that they had something within my tenner-a-day budget. I was mobile again.

I found ValuDrive in a Portacabin behind a body shop off Camden High Street. I reached them by squeezing between a couple of cars that were going to be a challenge to even the most skilled of the body shop's mechanics. The Portacabin's office was the size of a broom closet, floored in cracked linoleum and smelling of Calor gas and mould. A woman wrapped in an anorak fit for Annapurna stood behind a counter littered with grease-stained contracts. She asked for my licence and card. I waited whilst she transcribed the details onto a contract form with a biro that kept smearing. Then she filled out a million details in triplicate and mashed my card twice through her machine. Once for the rental. Once for the deposit. Wrote the charges and asked me to sign. The rental was cheap but the deposit stung. If I totalled their vehicle my card was going to finance a new head office for the company.

I signed a contract that had text too small to read but would have significance if something went wrong. The woman gave me my copy with a scribbled telephone number for the breakdown service. The number was also unreadable. She lifted the flap and came out. The whole time she'd said nothing other than the essential. Rent-a-wreck, with service to match.

Outside, she took me to check a damage sheet against a lime green Citroen ZX that was one of the cars I'd pushed past on the way in. The checks went over my head while I made an adjustment to my understanding of the term *rent-a-wreck*. The wreck might actually be wrecked. Valu's offerings were everything you could ask for in this respect. The Citroen looked like the runner-up in a kindergarten drawing competition. It had an engine barely bigger than the Frogeye's to haul a car twice the weight, and the bodywork had enough things bent or hanging off to make the damage report sheet an insane doodle. The rear suspension was so far down it looked like the car was parked on a hill. All this for seven ninety-nine a day. Maybe I got air miles. I was suddenly regretting not getting the woman to write the breakdown number more clearly.

I signed the damage report on the basis that it covered the car so comprehensively that if I had a smash they'd never be able to prove it. Then the woman handed me the keys and walked away. The Citroen started on the fourth attempt, and either the petrol gauge wasn't working or they'd run it so low that even the vapour wasn't registering. A more talkative clerk might have told me to push the thing to the nearest filling station. Zero style, zero fuel. The private investigator back on the road.

I coasted on fumes to a BP station, keeping my foot light to conserve petrol and minimise the racket of the blowing exhaust. I pumped fifty-six litres of lead replacement but the needle stayed on empty. The car was telling me something. Then I fired up and headed across the river and out to Chevening.

The Hanlons' driveway was still barred by the electric gates but when I pressed the bell this time the metalwork swung open.

I drove a hundred yards onto an oval forecourt fronting a three-storey Queen Anne. Converted stables to one side provided garage space for a fleet of vehicles, but two cars were parked in the open, up against the steps. One was a silver Bentley Continental Coupe and the other a Merc sports. And the guy in the expensive suit waiting at the top of the steps was David Hanlon.

He watched as I swung the Citroen round to park by his Bentley, said nothing as I climbed the steps. When I held out my hand he held his own up to stop me.

Hanlon was a fit fifty-something. Lean, with streaked silver hair and bespoke wool suit and the no-nonsense stance of a company director. He asked for ID.

I gave him an agency card and my driver's licence. He scrutinised them. Held on to the card.

'You've got five minutes,' he said.

We went in. I heard dogs barking in the back. Hanlon directed me into a lounge overlooking the forecourt. No sign of his wife but my senses told me that she was close by. Seemed both of them had taken the morning off.

'If I get the gist of your note then I conclude that you're interfering in our private affairs,' Hanlon said. 'What's this about?'

I looked round at walls covered in more expensive artwork than the Tate.

'We're investigating a professional criminal,' I said. 'And we've picked up a connection to your family. I mentioned the guy's name.' It was in the note I'd dropped into their post box yesterday. Either it was third time lucky or the note had produced the desired effect. Hanlon might be playing uppity but he and his wife had both stayed home to see me.

Hanlon shook his head.

'The name means nothing to either of us. You said you had information related to the safety of our family. Is this some kind of game?'

I quit checking the artwork. 'No game,' I said. 'We're looking at a serious criminal operation. And the link's clear.'

Hanlon shook his head again. 'You're mistaken. I don't know this person.'

Maybe he really didn't know McAllister's name. The McCabes hadn't. So it must have been the mention of the Royal Trafalgar in my note that had given the guy the incentive to stay home. I asked him about the hotel.

'I stay in hotels all over the country.'

I lifted my eyebrows. 'Your business demands eight-hundred-a-night hospitality? I must be in the wrong job.'

Hanlon looked out of the window at the Citroen.

'You are,' he said.

Good point. If the shit-heap was sold it wouldn't buy a set of wiper blades for Hanlon's Bentley. But I wasn't swallowing his line about eight-hundred-quid suites being normal business in the IT trade. When you see that kind of extravagance proffered for free you know that business is not normal.

'You've some very generous business associates,' I said.

'None of your business.'

I smiled at him. 'Well, it's become my business. Maybe you didn't know it but your Brighton break was financed by a professional criminal. These people do things for reasons.'

'I've already told you – I don't know the man.'

'So bear with me. What business took you to Brighton?'

'Nothing I'm sharing with you. I've stayed home to find out what your note was about, not to be interrogated.' He looked at his watch. 'Your five minutes is almost up.'

'A couple more questions. Correct me, but you'd not be concerned if the Brighton thing came under the scrutiny of the authorities? You'd stick to your line about normal business?'

'Whatever I did would be none of your affair.'

'And you sold the gatehouse last year. How much did you lose on the deal? Half a million? What I've been asking myself is why a wealthy guy has to rush into a loss-making deal when he can raise money economically if he waits a week or two, sell some stock, cash in a few bonds. Unless he's looking to raise the cash double quick with minimum visibility. Did you sell anything else? Is your garage emptier than it was?'

'This is utter nonsense,' Hanlon said.

'I'd say it's a puzzle. Why does someone need to raise cash so fast? I can't help thinking of dodgy business deals. Payoffs. Is your company into something it shouldn't be?'

Hanlon shook his head like a mastiff shaking fleas. 'Let's stop messing around. If you have something then spit it out. Otherwise

I'm going to end our discussion here.'

'Okay,' I said. 'The theory I'm looking at is that someone was threatening your family. You've got a girl and a boy. Was one of them a target? Was either of them taken?'

Hanlon forced a laugh. 'So that's it. Wild guesses. Illegal business deals. Kidnappings! I don't know what the hell your McAllister is up to but you're barking up the wrong tree. The man has never had any connection with my family. And now we're through.'

'Why do you think one of our children was taken?'

Faye Hanlon had walked into the room behind her husband. He turned, quick.

'The man has nothing,' he said. 'He's on a fishing trip. I've told him we've never been involved with any criminal racket.'

Faye was in her early forties but worry lines added a decade. Maybe the lines came with her job. Like her husband, she didn't look like she took nonsense from anyone.

'Why do you ask about our children being taken?' she repeated. She tried to back up her husband's bluster but there was a shakiness in her voice.

'We're investigating a family who've been targeted by the same people,' I told her.

Faye Hanlon's eyes widened.

'Has someone been abducted?'

'A young girl's missing right now,' I said.

Faye paled. David Hanlon moved to her side and spoke softly.

'The man's scaring us gratuitously,' he said. 'He's absolutely no proof for anything he's saying. Our children are under no threat.' He gripped his wife's shoulder. 'Remember that!'

He turned to me.

'We're through, Flynn.'

I smiled. Scaring people gratuitously. We should add it to our Yellow Pages listing. But Hanlon was right: I was through.

'Who did they take?' I asked Faye. 'Clarissa or Harry? Am I right: it was your daughter?'

Faye opened her mouth but Hanlon moved fast. His own face wasn't pale.

'That's it!' he said. 'I want you off my property.'

I let him manhandle me to the door. I had what I'd come for. The

McCabes' denials yesterday had been puzzling because they smacked of truth and threatened to demolish my theory. But the Hanlons' denials smacked of desperation. They said I was on the mark. It was time to take this thing to the Slaters.

Hanlon opened the front door but I stopped and got off a final shot. Held up a photo.

Bingo.

The picture poleaxed Hanlon like garlic bread on Dracula's dinner plate. His jaw dropped before he could control it. He knew Tina Brown.

'I guess you don't know her real name but you remember her face. We have her at the Royal Trafalgar with you. She's missing too. Any ideas?'

Hanlon got himself back under control. Apart from his too-straight face you'd never know he was coming up for air.

'Stir up trouble,' he said, 'and I'll sue you for everything you've got.'

I nodded: 'Sure. But if there's something I should know you have my card.'

Hanlon said nothing. I trotted down the steps. Flicked him a salute and climbed into the car. I jabbed the key into the ignition and turned the engine. It clanked over but didn't start. I tried again, cranked it for twenty seconds while the battery drained to a dying chunter. I watched Hanlon through the chipped windscreen and kept my face neutral. Released the key and pressed my foot delicately all the way to the floor. If the carb flooded that was it. I waited ten seconds then turned the key again. One last shot. The engine chuntered as woefully as before but then it caught and spluttered to life on three cylinders and the vehicle shook like a spin dryer with a brick. I found reverse and tried to look cool as I backed out, careful not to damage the Citroen's bodywork on Hanlon's Bentley.

As I drove away I saw Hanlon in my rear-view crumpling my card.

~~~~~

Back in Paddington I parked in Gerry Lye's vacated spot beside the Frogeye. The tarmac had bubbled and the broken glass didn't feel too good under the ZX's wheels. Shaughnessy's Yamaha stood on the far side, clear of the debris.

Lucy gave me a sympathetic look when I went in. I'd had the Sprite when the two of us were together. The car had memories for her. I poured coffee. Stirred sugar.

'I nearly *died* when I saw it,' Lucy said. 'You've gone and upset the wrong people again, Eddie.'

'All part of the job.'

'That was a good car.'

'Yeah. But you should see the replacement.' I sipped the coffee. The hot-plate light was on but the coffee was cold. Everything normal.

'You've new wheels already?' Lucy asked.

'Wait till you see, Luce. You'll be begging for a ride.'

'You know I'm a girl who likes fancy wheels.' Lucy grinned her heartbreaker. Flirting already. Was she serious? Wait till she saw the colour.

'Anything new?' I said.

'Utilities-final-demand stuff or detective stuff?'

'Detective. I'll save the tough business till next week.'

'Next week we'll have no electricity.'

'Is that what they say?'

'And there's a reconnection charge.'

'Bloodsuckers! Pay them.'

'What with?'

'Don't get technical, Luce.'

'That's what you always say.'

'And you always find a way.'

'I don't know how you guys would stay in business if I wasn't here.'

'We wouldn't, Luce. You're invaluable.'

'So are you going to give me an invaluable salary to match?'

'One day, Luce, I'll dress you in diamonds.'

'Wow, Eddie! You sure know how to treat a girl!'

I gave her my sly uncle. 'I'll even take you for a ride in my new car. Just don't touch anything.'

'I won't. But don't expect any funny business.'

Not in the ZX I wouldn't.

Shaughnessy came out and I brought him up to date. David Hanlon recognised Tina Brown. And they'd had a child taken.

Time to give the Slaters a choice. Bring us in, let us help, or have the police in the house within the day. We had enough to convince the Met that a major felony was under way, and the only way the Slaters could keep a lid on this was to co-operate. And if we decided that the police were needed we'd call them in, with or without the Slaters' permission. Simply blocking us out was no longer an option.

'I'll call Slater,' Shaughnessy said.

I sat on Lucy's desk to make another call and let Gina Redding know what was happening, but before I could hit the keys my phone rang.

I looked at the screen. Sadie Bannister. I almost let it go. Changed my mind. Better to know what she was up to than have her jump me. I picked up.

I'd expected frantic. Heard it.

'Eddie,' she screamed, 'is that you? Did you hear?'

Did I hear? My blood frosted. We'd been chasing in circles since yesterday, convinced that we were finally spiralling towards the girl. But there was also the chance we'd hear bad news at any moment.

'Calm down, Sadie,' I said. 'What happened?'

'She's back!'

'Rebecca?'

'Yeah! She's okay!' Sadie's volume hit my pain threshold. I held the phone away. 'I can't believe it,' she screamed.

Lucy watched me. Sadie's voice was loud enough for her to get the conversation even without her paranormal powers. 'Becky's okay!' Sadie yelled. 'She really was ill! All that time! Can you believe it?'

I looked at Lucy and switched on my shit-eater. Did I believe it? Sure. It was crazy but I believed it.

'When did you hear this?'

'Right now. I'm just off the phone.'

'Rebecca called you?'

'Yeah!'

'She said she's been ill?'

'I went, like, totally ballistic that she'd not been in touch, but she said her load had run out and she'd been too ill to top up. She only got out of bed yesterday.'

'At home?'

'At her aunt's. But not her Aunt Kathryn. I didn't know she had another.'

Neither did I.

'How did she sound?'

'Down. Like when you've been ill? But she's okay, I guess.'

'Well, that's great. Thanks for telling me, Sadie.'

Sadie's voice dropped. 'Maybe this just got out of hand, Eddie. It seems kind of stupid now. Becky was gobsmacked that I'd had private detectives after her.'

'Don't worry about that,' I said. 'You weren't the only one fooled. The family didn't help anyone.'

'Are they going to be mad at me?'

I thought about it.

'We'll talk to them. They've no reason to be mad.'

'Thank God it's over,' Sadie said.

'All's well that ends well,' I said. Original to the last. I told Sadie we'd speak soon and cut the line.

Shaughnessy had come back out.

'Slater's not answering,' he said. He looked at me. 'Was I hearing right?'

I nodded. 'The girl's back. Apparently she was never missing.'

Shaughnessy raised an eyebrow. Looked at me.

I flipped the Citroen's keys and he followed me out. The guy had always hated the Frogeye. Today he was in for a treat.

CHAPTER THIRTY-SIX
If that call goes out I'll break your fingers

Shaughnessy made out like he was cool with the ride but he slid himself into the Citroen like he might catch something. I went through the start-up ritual and we pulled out onto the street.

The weather had switched again, and the sun shone hot in a blue sky. I wound the window down. The blowing exhaust hurt my ears. I wound the window back up and turned on the fan; got a wash of hot air from somewhere under the dashboard. I killed the control and we rode along like a cheap fairground ride, jounced by the engine's three cylinder act. Shaughnessy finished checking his seat and got back to subject.

'What do we say?' he said.

'I'm more interested in what the Slaters have to say.'

'I don't see them rushing to talk to us.'

Me neither. Our plan had been flawless. March in through their front door and hit them with what we had. Their choice: talk to us or have a spanner in the works. It had been a great plan whilst their daughter was missing, not so attractive with the girl there to tell us we'd been dreaming the whole thing. We'd just got warmed up and the final whistle had blown. Game over. Another case solves itself under the threat of the agency's attention. We could feel good if we knew what had happened. The real question was what to put in Gina Redding's billing report.

'I want to see evidence that the girl actually is safe,' I said. 'I want to know if there's still a threat to other families. And I want to know who torched my car, why we're riding round in this shit-heap. If this is a kidnap–ransom thing and McAllister was sending Rebecca home then why stir things up by attacking me?'

Shaughnessy shrugged. 'It's the kind of guy he is. He assumed you wouldn't follow up. It was only a car.'

Shaughnessy was sitting ramrod straight to keep his clothes off the upholstery. Maybe the Sprite didn't seem so bad any more.

'The Frogeye means nothing,' I said. 'I'm going to bring the house down over whatever's happened to Rebecca. And to the Hanlons.

Over whatever McAllister's got lined up for some other family. Not to mention the dent this has made in Gina Redding's bank balance.'

'You think she'll pay us?'

'Maybe not. We might have to kidnap the girl again.'

We reached the Slater house. Larry's Lexus was there, parked askew as if he'd arrived in a hurry.

I steered the Citroen off to the side where it might go unnoticed but the heap had other ideas. When I killed the engine it backfired twice and jetted black smoke to announce our arrival. The fanfare worked. The Slaters' front door opened and Larry Slater appeared. We walked across. I had a nice opening ready but Slater got in first.

'Holy shit,' he said, 'you guys take the biscuit.'

We stopped on his step. 'Larry, meet my partner Sean Shaughnessy,' I said.

'You've got ten seconds to get off my property,' Slater replied. 'Or I'm calling the police.'

Ten seconds is short. A ten second pitch needs to be good.

'Larry,' I said, 'if we leave here without answers I'm going to come back tomorrow and see if your wife can help us. Maybe she'll know why your Lexus spends half its time parked in Holland Park. Maybe she'll even know your friend Tina.'

Slater shook his head like he was hearing something too stupid for a response.

'Go right ahead,' he said. 'Tell her about Holland Park.' He sounded confident. Like he might bluff his way through.

'And while I'm at it,' I said, 'I'll bring along your Amex account – the sheets with the Blueglades payments and the Royal Trafalgar bills. Shall I go ahead on those, too?'

Cheap but to the point.

The phoney indignation dropped off Slater's face. 'You've been through my Amex bills? Holy Christ, I'll have your balls!' He pulled a mobile out. 'I'm phoning the police right now.'

Disappointing, but at least we were through the ten second barrier. We just needed to find a way past Slater's defensiveness so we could chat a little more calmly. We needed to talk him out of making the call.

'If that call goes out,' Shaughnessy said, 'I'll break your fingers.'

Slater stopped. Gave Shaughnessy the goldfish look.

I looked too. Sean should have been a union negotiator.

I switched back to reason.

'Let us help, Larry. If not your family then others.'

'Are there *other* families?'

The voice was a whisper from the doorway. Slater turned and made shooing motions. 'Stay out of this,' he said.

She came forward into the light. A slender teenager with her mother's face. The same high cheeks and pretty eyes but pale, her hair a mess. Right then the illness story looked credible. But there was something in the girl's face that wasn't caused by the flu. This wasn't someone bouncing back. Rebecca Townsend just looked sad.

Slater made to shoo her again but she swiped his hand away. Stared out at me. Her face softened into a grin.

'You're the gumshoes,' she said.

I grinned back. 'Yeah,' I said. 'We're the detectives. I guess Sadie told you she had us out looking?'

Slater moved to get back in control. He grabbed Rebecca's arm and tugged and tried to close the door but the door wouldn't close on account of Shaughnessy's foot, and all the while Rebecca was saying some unladylike things. Slater started to snarl back then something snapped. He yanked the door open and was out. His finger jabbed in my face.

'Stay there, Flynn. The cops are on their way.' He keyed his phone, broken fingers forgotten. Shaughnessy sighed and took the phone from him and shouldered him out of the way, and we followed the girl into the house. Slater came after us, cursing, but Rebecca was yelling right back, and finally the girl's anger got through. Rebecca stopped and turned and Slater faltered. He faced her, wordless, a puppet with its strings cut.

'Let them talk to me,' Rebecca said, 'or I'll go right out and tell them everything.'

Before Slater could reply Jean appeared. She put her arm round Rebecca's shoulder and pulled her gently away. Her voice was weary. 'No, Rebecca,' she said, 'we don't want you to talk to anyone.' She looked at me and Shaughnessy. 'Why don't we sit down?'

Larry Slater swore again but no one was listening. We followed Jean through to the lounge. Jean sat down with Rebecca beside her. Shaughnessy, Slater and I all stood.

'Whatever you're looking for,' Slater said, 'there's nothing here. Whatever misinformation has had you stalking us the last week has been a waste of your time and somebody money.'

'Gina's,' Rebecca said. 'She hired them.' She looked at me. I shrugged and raised my eyebrows to take some of the tension out of the moment. 'Your friend Sadie was kind of insistent,' I said. 'And Mrs Redding was kind enough to retain our services.'

'And all for nothing,' Larry said. 'We explained that Rebecca was ill, that she needed time to recuperate. Why don't you people listen?'

But a quiet smile was playing on the girl's face. The smile was for Sadie and Gina. It must feel good to know that someone cared.

Jean Slater broke in to back up her husband. 'Mr Flynn, this has all been mix-up. Crossed wires. Rebecca has already explained everything to Sadie.'

Talked to her. Explained nothing.

'Mix-up or not,' Larry Slater said, 'this harassment needs to end. As you see, Rebecca's safe. Tell Mrs Redding to stop wasting her money.' He glared at me. 'End of investigation.'

'The investigation ends,' I said, 'when we decide.'

Slater's mouth set hard. 'Then you're fools. And I won't hesitate to call the police in.'

I turned to Rebecca.

'You okay?' I said.

She looked at me but said nothing. Jean answered for her. 'She's tired,' she said, 'but she's fine.'

I kept watching Rebecca.

'We know who took you,' I said. 'You don't need to lie.'

'Stop!' Slater said. He stepped between me and the girl. Jean's eyes closed.

'How many times must I repeat myself? Get off our backs.'

He would have said more but his words were broken by Rebecca. She stood and called him a *Fucker*. Slater turned to face her and the two of them locked stares. Then Jean stood. Clenched her fists.

'Stop it!' she commanded. 'You're tearing us apart.'

I didn't know if she was speaking to Rebecca or Larry or to me. I watched Rebecca. She unlocked stares with Larry and turned to us and the half smile came back.

'Private detectives,' she said. She shook her head. 'That Sadie is one crazy bitch.' The smile stayed on her face as she walked out.

'Okay,' Larry Slater said. 'Show over. Pass the message to Gina Redding.'

'First we've got a report to write,' I said. 'It would help if we knew what happened.'

'Report?' Slater said. 'What the hell will you report? There is nothing *to* report.'

'Sure there is, Larry. But it's all loose ends.'

'Jesus.' Slater turned to his wife, but she returned a look to cut steel.

'Your daughter was kidnapped by a guy named Paul McAllister,' I said. 'Now she's back. Which means you've paid him off.'

Slater shook his head.

'And it was you who tipped Paul McAllister off after I came to see you.'

Another shake. 'You're flying blind, Flynn. No one has kidnapped our daughter. I don't know anyone called Paul McAllister.'

McAllister was a guy a lot of people didn't know.

Shaughnessy had strolled across the room and was inspecting a Rothko print.

'Don't lie, Larry,' he said. 'We've evidence that you've been in contact with the guy.'

'We've also got similarities between your family and another,' I said. 'A family who also paid McAllister off a few months back.'

'All nonsense,' Slater said.

I spoke to Jean. 'The other family has a teenage daughter too,' I said.

Jean's face fought to stay neutral. You could see the muscles holding fast.

'What were you raising the cash for?' Shaughnessy asked.

Slater's laugh broke even as he forced it out. 'Are you two never going to quit?' he said.

'The *Lode Star*,' I said. 'Why did you sell it?'

Slater shook his head.

'What I do with my money or belongings is none of your business. Is that all you've got?'

I thought about it.

'There's the Amex thing,' I said. 'We could discuss that in more detail.'

Jean looked at her husband.

Slater gave it his best shot. Gave her indignation enough for an Oscar. 'It's nothing,' he hissed. 'These idiots are chasing shadows. And now I really am calling the police. Or are you still going to break my fingers?'

He sneered at Shaughnessy. Shaughnessy said nothing.

Slater stalked out of the room and went for the hall phone. His mobile was on the coffee table but maybe he wasn't too sure of the answer to his question.

I turned for a last word with Jean.

'The people who took Rebecca – we're going to track them down,' I said.

Explaining the Amex charges wasn't necessary. We walked out and Shaughnessy took the phone out of Slater's hands as we passed by and set it back in its cradle. Slater stood silent

~~ ~~ ~~ ~~

Lucy was waiting back at the office. We gave her the state of play. Next step was a talk with Gina Redding so she knew her own commitment was over. The investigation would go on, though.

Shaughnessy and I had agreed that on the ride back. We had three certainties. One: a kidnap and ransom racket was in play, with at least two victims to date. Two: the racket was being run by McAllister. Three: McAllister had more victims lined up.

We also had a few unknowns, the main one being whether Tina Brown was part of the caper or a victim.

Our plan to coerce the Slaters into spilling the beans was shot. Plan B: go after McAllister directly. Dig up enough to bring the police in. It might not be enough to close McAllister down but police investigations would disrupt his games for a while, maybe persuade the guy that his caper had reached its sell-by date.

Lucy agreed with our conclusion

'You've almost got the guy,' she said. 'You just need a little more fertiliser then you can sow your oats.'

Shaughnessy and I looked at each other. When Lucy tosses metaphors you need to duck.

'Lucy, you're a poet,' said Shaughnessy.

I shook my head in wonderment. 'Lucy, we should pay you more.'

'You should pay me,' she said.

~~~~~

Shaughnessy headed out and Lucy started closing up. I had a couple of things to do then I was through myself. Had an evening arrangement with Arabel, though when she saw my new wheels she might recall a prior engagement.

The first job was to call Sammy. I wanted to know whether Tina had reappeared. If she hadn't I needed to buy more time.

It turned out to be open season for telepaths. My phone rang while I was scrolling for Sammy's number. I recognised her voice.

'I was about to call,' I said. 'See how you wanted to go with this.' I started to explain but she cut me off.

'Tina sent a text.' Her voice was scared.

'Tell me.'

'Someone's got her. She's been abducted. Jesus, Eddie, we need to go to the police.'

Abducted but sending texts? 'Did she give any details?' I said.

'Just a name. Addingford. I don't know what it means.'

But I did. It was the name of McAllister's farm.

CHAPTER THIRTY-SEVEN
Some you lose

I headed out into the rush hour traffic. The Citroen's three-cylinder act had the car bucking and jumping, and I had to work my feet to keep the engine alive at each stop. Either the distributor was shot or the HT leads were cracked through. Something that might get rapidly worse. The unreadable emergency number on my rental contract was playing on my mind but I consoled myself with the thought that even if the number had been embossed in gold it was unlikely anyone would turn out to tow me.

Sammy had agreed to hold off whilst I took a look at the farm. The place had been deserted when Shaughnessy checked it yesterday which suggested that the text was a ruse, but it was a ruse I couldn't ignore. Answers of some kind were waiting there.

It took an hour to reach the M25 at Swanley where I eased onto the motorway and pushed the car's envelope to fifty-five in the inside lane. The intermittent misfire settled into a regular beat that promised trouble soon. Traffic was heavy but it was all faster than me.

Shaughnessy had located McAllister's farm a mile off the A21 south of Lamberhurst. If I got a clear run I could be there by seven. I pulled into the middle lane to pass a battered Transit and crawled past it with an artic coming up fast in my rear-view and no indication that it was fitted with brakes. The truck's grille expanded until it filled my mirrors and the roar of its engine shook the Citroen enough to set the oil light flickering but not enough to move the petrol gauge out of red. I aced the Transit and regained the slow lane and the artic batted past with a horn blast. Tomorrow morning, just like every morning, the traffic reports would have an overturned lorry on the M25. With luck this would be the one. Then the vehicle got clear and I read the three foot tailgate lettering: HP LOGISTICS.

I felt a chill. Even with my new wheels the bastards had spotted me.

I hit the A21, passed Lamberhurst and found a shale track dropping to a cluster of buildings a hundred yards from the road.

Spring cereal was sprouting in the surrounding fields. They were either someone else's fields or McAllister rented them out. I didn't see him driving a John Deere.

I backed the Citroen into a stub road by a copse just beyond the lane. The engine stalled as I manoeuvred it in and I left the wreck where it died.

A field of spring barley separated the copse from the farm buildings. I climbed a gate and walked along the edge of the trees to a lower meadow. Struggled over barbed wire and walked back up under cover of a hedgerow towards the buildings, which were losing definition in the dusk along with the cowpats.

A gate opened into a farmyard. Concrete replaced mud. I cut between a rotting corrugated metal storage barn and a modern brick structure and reached the house. The windows were dark. No cars parked. If anyone was home they were hiding.

I checked out the barns first. The rust holes in the older building showed glimpses of farm machinery. I crossed to the new structure to check that there were no vehicles parked there before I went into the house. Maybe Tina Brown's text was genuine: maybe she was here and needed help; maybe her abductors had been considerate enough to leave her mobile phone in her hands. But maybe not. Someone was waiting here somewhere.

The barn was open at its far end. I walked in. Spotted two vehicles inside. One was a tractor. The other was a Merc S Class that was so out of place I knew immediately something was up. Then someone stepped from the shadows and he didn't look much like a farmer, though he was pointing a shotgun. When the light hit him I recognised Ray Child.

I barely had time to register my incompetence when a second figure emerged. Paul McAllister, also pointing a gun. I'd expected them to be inside the house but I guess hiding in the cowshed was more in character. I would have left but McAllister told me not to move and waved his gun at face level. It was a Mossberg 500. He literally waved it, like a smart alec with a blade. I'd never seen it done with a big gun. I wondered how heavy McAllister's trigger finger was.

The two came over. I didn't know who was more scary. Ray Child, who held his gun as casually as a kid with a stick, or McAllister who wanted me to know that this was all good fun.

'Mr Flynn,' he said, 'my advice failed.' He lifted his eyebrows to jog my memory. I tried to think of a smart reply. With a Mossie pointing at you the smart thing to say is nothing. I went for that option.

'The advice,' McAllister clarified, 'about keeping your nose out.'

I gave him the evil eye. It was the only weapon I had.

'I guess you didn't hear me either, Paul,' I said. 'It's coming undone. We've talked to the Hanlons and the Slaters. We've got your caper filed and indexed.'

McAllister made a mouth. 'I'm peeing my pants, Flynn. Truly I am.'

He didn't seem too scared but then the Mossberg wasn't pointing his way.

'Is Tina Brown here,' I said, 'or have you learned to text by yourself?'

McAllister's brows stayed high, maybe surprised that I was asking, more likely just signalling that I had more to worry about. But you can't keep a detective's curiosity down.

'Is she part of your operation or just a victim?'

McAllister gestured with his gun. Child came round to my side and suddenly his weapon swung and the stock hit me like a sledgehammer just in front of my ear. I didn't go down but I danced a little and the side of my face opened like a ripe tomato, trickling warm blood onto my collar. I swore and turned to face Child. Just a little nearer and he'd be in McAllister's field of fire. But Child wasn't so stupid. He stayed clear, angled his gun and pointed it at my head like he was considering things. He didn't have orders to open fire but I was on a tightrope.

'People know I'm here,' I said. 'It's going to be hard to clean up if your gorilla does something stupid.'

McAllister's eyes stayed on mine. 'I'll give you ten out of ten for bullshit,' he said, 'but only one for brains. You had the chance to walk away from this.'

'Call me persistent,' I said.

'I'll do that. Where's your car?'

'Behind the office,' I said. 'Standing in a pool of rubber.'

McAllister gave it some thought. Tried again.

'You came by car. Where is it?'

I described the stub-track. If it was the Citroen he wanted it was his. He should have said.

'Key.'

I reached into my jacket and flipped him the ZX's key. His Mossberg never lost track of my abdomen as he caught it.

He flicked his head in the Merc's direction.

'Pop her.'

Child pulled out a remote. The Merc flashed like a Christmas tree and the boot hissed open. McAllister tilted his head. 'Get in.'

I looked at the shadows inside the open boot and some bad outcomes flashed through my mind. I stayed put.

McAllister angled his gun to point at my feet. 'Walk over,' he said, 'or we'll carry you.'

I went over and climbed in. It wasn't actually bad after the Citroen. The two of them stood over me. I expected the lid to slam down but they waited. Child held out his hand.

'Mobile.'

Some you lose, etc. I handed it over.

'People know where I am,' I repeated. 'If you're thinking of doing something stupid it's not going to work.'

'Stow it,' McAllister said. 'You're off the books, Flynn. I can smell it. And we've a place where no one will come looking.'

The boot lid slammed down.

Blackness.

The Merc's engine whispered to life.

I'd known I wouldn't find Tina Brown.

CHAPTER THIRTY-EIGHT
Ray's going to be a while

I felt the Merc climb up onto the road and turn towards where I'd ditched the Citroen. Thirty seconds later we stopped and someone got out. Child, I guessed, taking the booby prize, driving the wreck. Then the Merc manoeuvred and we set off at speed.

I'd seen it in the movies but this was my first time in the boot of a car. The combination of suffocation and blackness plays hell with the senses. Whenever the car turns it feels like you're spinning through space and your stomach floats with every dip in the road. In a situation like that it's useful to have something to distract the mind. Fear seems to work. All kinds of things were dancing through my thoughts as we ate up the miles, uppermost being the realisation that I'd just disappeared from the world and that McAllister was of a mind to make the arrangement permanent. When we got where we were going I'd need as much luck as finesse.

The Merc cruised for twenty minutes then slowed and took a side road whose potholes had me bouncing off the metalwork. It felt like McAllister was trying to write the car off. Maybe it seemed worse in the dark: probably we were crawling. What was certain was that the blood dripping onto the carpet was mine. McAllister needed to sharpen up on the forensics side of his activities.

Then we stopped and McAllister got out, waited while the Citroen's exhaust sounded in the distance. The din got louder until it was like machine gun fire. The heap finally arrived and its engine died and the Merc's boot clicked open. I squinted up at McAllister's gun. He waggled it and I climbed out.

We were in a narrow lane outside a thatched cottage under trees. The lane dead-ended at a wire fence thirty yards on. We weren't going to be bothered by passing traffic.

Child opened a wooden gate and walked through the garden and round the back of the building. I watched McAllister but he'd read my mind.

'Go ahead, Flynn,' he said. 'I'll put you down right here. I pay Ray to clean up so it's no bother.' He jerked the gun provocatively like that would entice me. I didn't take the bait. But soon I'd have to. I didn't need mind-reading skills to know McAllister's plans.

Child came back out. He was carrying a spade, held casually alongside his shotgun. He had two flashlights. Handed one to McAllister. McAllister waggled the Mossberg and directed the light at a path that ran beside the cottage into the trees. Gestured. We set off, me first, McAllister three paces behind, Child further back. We got into the trees and I was looking for an opening in the undergrowth where I could do a head-dive, but a jab in my spine told me I wouldn't make it.

The path climbed steeply. A hundred yards up it branched and McAllister called a halt. I turned. McAllister pointed the gun and told me to turn back.

'Hands on the tree.'

I placed my palms on the bark of the tree in front of me. McAllister stayed back. Not even the hint of carelessness. We were only twenty miles from his farm but I hadn't a clue which direction we'd taken and these woods suddenly seemed lonely as hell.

Child moved forward and stepped off the path and picked out a shallow mound of earth with his flashlight, then propped his shotgun against a tree while I speculated on what might be under the mound.

Child put his foot to the spade and started digging at fresh undergrowth. Neither of them spoke. They didn't have to. I was putting two and two together and coming up with a bad sum. I sensed McAllister, focused like a snake behind me, heard him light up a cigarette. I opened the play.

'This isn't going to work,' I said. 'I left details of where I was going. Your farm will get a visit.'

McAllister didn't reply.

Child kept digging.

It was like I'd ceased to interest them.

'Two people missing, both connected to you,' I said. 'There's no way you're going to paper across that. And there's a file in my office a mile thick. When I don't turn up my partner is going to visit your farm with a posse, McAllister.'

'Keep talking, Flynn,' McAllister said. 'Ray's going to be a while.'

'When the file is handed over you'll be crawling with cops. Your caper will be dead.'

McAllister hissed smoke. 'So we'll clean out your office,' he said. 'Burn the file.'

'You'll be too late. My partner will be there tonight.'

'That would worry me,' McAllister said, 'if I thought your partner was working the night shift. But I think your sidekick's at home with his feet up or his leg over. I think you're full of shit, Flynn.'

'Check my phone,' I said.

'Why would I do that?'

'You'll see.'

Ray Child quit his spade work to take a breather. The undergrowth was tough. He'd barely taken the soil a couple of inches down over a six-by-three area. Not that I was complaining. He could take all night.

'Pull the trigger, Paul,' he said. 'We're not going to get any peace until Snoopy's out of it. Why isn't he doing the spade-work?'

Wouldn't work. I dig slow.

But I knew that McAllister couldn't care less whether they dropped me in an hour or right now. Suggestions like Child's I could do without.

McAllister was silent behind me but the dancing of his flashlight told me that he'd pulled out my mobile, was pressing buttons. Curiosity and all that. He didn't believe there was anything on there but he couldn't take the risk. When he checked my inbox I knew by the silence that he'd found it.

'What's this?' he said.

The inbox had a single message.

'It's from my partner. He'll be heading back to the office anytime now. And when he reads my note your file will be gone.'

'Problem?' Child said.

'Maybe. Looks like Snoopy's not bluffing. Okay Flynn, tell me.'

'It's like it says. That's my partner confirming that he got my message to call at the office if I don't contact him by ten. I've left a note there. When he reads it your file will be gone and there'll be some people at your farm tonight. Maybe you can just shoot them all.'

'They can look all they like. There's nothing to find.'

'Sure. You had the girl here at the cottage. But the farm is the last place they'll have me. If I go missing they'll know who to come looking for. You're not going to put out that fire.'

'So you want to see us burn, Flynn?' Child pulled the spade from the ground and moved towards me from the side. Just a few more feet and he'd be within McAllister's line of fire. When he swung the shovel I'd be ready.

'Stop,' said McAllister.

Child stopped.

McAllister thought it through.

'Back to the house,' he said. 'We need to put a lid on this.'

'Bury him first,' Child said. 'Save listening to any more shit.'

'No. I want you in their office before his partner gets there. Sanitise it. Bring out what they have.'

I grinned at the tree. I'd needed McAllister to buy that one. The intermission was more than a delay: it was my only opportunity.

Child cursed like a kid who's had his sweets stolen. He planted the spade and retrieved his shotgun and McAllister aimed the torch back down the track.

'Walk,' he said.

I left the tree and we walked back down to the lane and through the garden, into the cottage.

The parlour was old-fashioned but charmless. Cheap furniture and frayed carpets, no lived-in feel. Just an untraceable rental, somewhere for McAllister to hide his abductees.

An IKEA coffee table held an ash tray overflowing with butts, and an open doorway to the back kitchen gave a view of unwashed cups and takeaway cartons. My guess was that Rebecca Townsend had spent the last ten days here. Maybe Tina Brown too.

'Give me your jacket,' McAllister said.

I turned and gave him quizzical. McAllister's eyes stayed uninterested but his gun twitched and Child started to move towards me. I didn't fancy another tap in the face so I took off the jacket and tossed it onto the sofa. McAllister waggled the Mossberg some more.

'Pockets.'

'The office keys are in the jacket. Or are you looking for fivers?'

The gun dipped to point at my feet. I turned out my pockets. Empty. Ray Child rooted through my jacket and came out with a Swiss knife, a dry-cleaning ticket and a bunch of keys.

'These open the office?' McAllister asked.

'Yeah,' I said. 'Don't leave the lights on.'

His eyebrows raised.

'You're a funny man, Flynn. You should be on telly. Probably pays more than snooping. Better for your health, too.'

'I had a bad career advisor.'

'Tell me his name. I'll put a brick through his window.'

And he would. McAllister was the type to right little misdemeanours. I let his offer pass. He gestured to an armchair.

'Make yourself comfy,' he said. He handed the Merc keys to Child.

'Put your foot down,' he said. 'In and out before Snoopy's friend arrives. If he does show up shut him down.'

Child turned his ugly smile on me. 'Maybe we can put your whole firm out of business tonight, Flynn. If he turns up your partner is going to wish he'd never read your text. Stayed safe in front of his telly.'

Shaughnessy didn't watch TV but Child didn't know it.

Nor had he read any text message, but I didn't mention that either.

CHAPTER THIRTY-NINE

I'm still trying to figure why you buried her

Child went out and McAllister relaxed on the sofa with the gun across his lap. I did some calculations. An hour to Paddington. Twenty minutes at the office. An hour back. We had two and a half hours to kill.

'Have I got it right?' I said. 'You've just extorted half a mill. from the Slaters.'

McAllister lit a cigarette. Kept quiet. Most villains can't shut up. It's the criminal ego: the urge to air their personal philosophies, as if talking their delusions through makes them real. Villains never see their own uselessness. Tend to confuse respect with worth. If they are respected they must be important guys. They never figure that it just means everyone's scared of them.

McAllister wasn't the delusional type. He was the worse breed, the one who just enjoys doing bad things. It was the taking that drove him. McAllister wouldn't have earned his bread legitimately if he could have pulled in twice the dosh. Villains like McAllister didn't want your respect. They wanted the raw thing: fear.

To McAllister I was a fly in the ointment and he needed me out, and the reason he wasn't chatting to me was that he didn't give a damn.

'I'm guessing half to three quarters,' I persisted. 'That's a good take-home for a few days work.'

McAllister watched smoke eddying under the ceiling.

'We've got three families on file,' I said. 'And we've got Alpha Security and the blackmail thing and those ties to Tina Brown. It's all backed up on our online servers no matter what Child comes back with. He isn't going to wipe the slate clean, Paul.'

McAllister sucked on the cigarette. Finally opened up.

'You mistake me for an amateur, Flynn.' He was still watching the ceiling. 'Do you think your two-bit outfit frightens me? Let me explain.'

So even McAllister couldn't resist the yackity-yack. Boredom does that.

'I don't give a damn what's in your computers. I actually assume there's nothing. Everything you've got will be squirrelled away in a card-file on your desk which the hobgoblin will retrieve. When that's safely out of the way there won't be enough left for the filth even to send me a birthday card.'

Hobgoblin! I wondered how Ray would like that one. Maybe I could work it into the conversation when Child got back; stir up a fight whilst I dived through the window.

McAllister was still talking. 'You were rocking the boat, Flynn. Becoming a dangerous bastard. Our business depends on peace and quiet. When Ray gets back we'll resume that walk into the woods and then I'll have my peace and quiet.'

I thought about it.

'Let's see if I have it figured. You stake out wealthy families. Not so rich that they have minders but rich enough to get their hands on upwards of a million quid inside a week. Then you fete the man of the house at a five-star hotel with a five-star hooker thrown in. That's the bit that stumped me. Was that just a phoney business deal to feel the guys out before you went for the kids? It didn't make sense. You already knew that the families were sitting ducks. And you booked the suite for three nights when your guest was only staying one. The extra nights had to be so you could set things up. Cameras and sound. So we're looking at a honeytrap blackmail. But this thing's supposed to be about taking the kids.'

I watched McAllister. He blew a stream of smoke, watched it rise.

'Finally I got it. The thing with the hooker actually is blackmail. You set up a phoney business meeting and throw in a night on the town for your guest with your girl as an irresistible extra. If the guy falls into the trap then you've got your blackmail ammo. Only the blackmail's not for money. Sex-blackmail isn't going to bring in half a mill. Kidnapping the kids brings the jackpot. The blackmail kicks in afterwards.'

McAllister was still watching the ceiling. It was hard to tell if he was pleased that someone had worked out his caper or didn't give a damn. Probably the latter. I went on anyway. I talk when I'm nervous.

'The whole thing's about repeat business,' I said. 'The ideal kidnap and ransom scheme is one you can repeat: the one the cops never hear about. And your caper never gets out because you've got the father by the balls. The family pays the ransom and the kid is sent home with the usual threats that you'll come looking for them if they blow the whistle. The threats are enough to make them think twice, but not enough to keep them quiet for long. So that's where you enlist the help of the man of the house. You show him the movies of his weekend away and persuade him that it's his job to make sure his wife and kid clam up permanently. He's your Trojan horse. His wife is screaming for the cops but the husband stands his ground, persuades her that it's too dangerous. What he doesn't tell his wife is what he's really afraid of: those movies. The ones of him in bed with the villains' hooker. What's his wife going to say when she hears it was his bit of fun that gave the crooks the opportunity to target their kids in the first place?

'So you've got the ideal caper. You've got the family while you're holding their child, then when you release the kid you get the husband to lock the front door. And off you go to the next job.'

'For a two-bit private eye you're pretty smart,' McAllister said. 'The sooner we take that walk the better.'

'So how many have you done? Five? Ten? Or were you just warming up? Were the McCabe family next?'

McAllister quit watching the ceiling. Frowned across at me while his fingers played over the gun.

'The McCabes were our little failure,' he said. 'Tina had the guy drooling down his dinner jacket but the retentive bastard sent her packing at the last minute. You win some, you lose some. No dirty movies, no snatch. But yeah, we've others lined up.'

'Was Tina Brown part of your scheme? Did she baby-sit the kids? Or was she just the bait? I'm still trying to figure why you've buried her in the woods.'

McAllister raised the Mossberg and pointed it.

'Ask her yourself. You'll soon be friends.'

'I'm thinking she wasn't in on it. All she knew was that she was hired to supply a little corporate hospitality. You killed Tina because she found out.'

But McAllister just lit another cigarette and lapsed into silence.

'You had Tina's phone,' I deduced, 'and you picked up Sammy's message about me searching for her. That spooked you enough to entice me to your farm.'

McAllister sighed. 'To be honest,' he said, 'that text was a long shot. That was the goblin's brainwave. I told him that not even you would be stupid enough to walk into that trap. I stand duly corrected.'

'How long did you think you could run this thing?' I said. 'Once or twice I could buy. But if you keep going back, no matter how tight your operation is, it'll fall apart sooner or later. Maybe a family that isn't intimidated. A mother who won't stay quiet despite her husband's efforts. A father who's been caught before and doesn't see your dirty pictures as such a big threat.'

McAllister shook his head. 'We do our homework. Our husbands are all kosher. Clean peckers, the lot of them – at least as far as anyone knows, which is what counts. These are gentlemen of standing. They all have good reasons to avoid bad publicity. And Tina could tempt a saint. She was truly wonderful at her art.' He shook his head. 'I've got pictures that would shock you.'

'Alpha Security organised that side of it,' I said. 'A full-service operation.'

'Roker thinks we're just scamming the husbands for fifty thou.' McAllister smiled. 'The real game's just between me and Ray.'

But he still hadn't told me why they'd buried Tina.

'There's no foolproof caper,' I said. 'Sooner or later your racket's going to come unravelled.'

'No. I look after the detail. The thing isn't going to come out, ever.'

'Maybe it won't be the families. Maybe your scheme will be brought down from the outside. You're looking at proof of that right now.'

'I'm looking at bad luck. Not to recur. And now the Slater girl is back and telling her mates that nothing happened do you think anyone will keep stirring?'

'The agency will keep stirring,' I said, 'until you and the hobgoblin are hatching your schemes behind bars.'

'I tremble,' McAllister said. 'Truly I do.'

'Why keep going back? You've made your stash. Whatever you say about the thing being tight you know it must crack sooner or later. Are you just greedy, Paul?'

McAllister thought about it. Gazed into space then gave me his conclusion: 'The truth is,' he said, 'I enjoy it. I like to see those families climbing the walls. I like to see daddy's face when we show him the pictures.' He gestured round the room. 'I like having the kids here, spoiled brats facing the real world for the first time. The Hanlon girl was a treat. She got it into her head that we were sex fiends, out to rape and murder her. She actually wet her pants. It wasn't difficult to get her to put on a convincing tone when she called her parents. All wonderful stuff.'

I thought it through. Gave him my conclusion.

'McAllister,' I said, 'you're a piece of shit.'

But he didn't reply. Just lit another fag and blew clouds. Clammed up.

I quit nattering and time rolled on. The parlour got cold. Two and a half hours came and went and I was beginning to wonder where Child was. Maybe he'd had a crash or a stroke, or maybe he'd got religion and wasn't coming back. Wishful thinking: at twenty to eleven the Merc rolled up outside and Child came in with the Slater file. He hadn't needed to search. Picked it straight off my rolltop. It couldn't have taken him more than five seconds to spot it, five minutes to confirm there was nothing else lying around. I made a note to be less tidy in future. Hypothetically thinking.

Child cracked a beer and sat on the sofa arm whilst McAllister flicked through the paperwork – the telephone numbers, addresses and hotel bills. Not so much, really. Nothing that looked irreparable to him.

He closed the file.

'That was it? You were going to bust us with this?'

'It's more than enough,' I said.

McAllister turned to Ray Child.

'Any trouble?'

Child sneered.

'None. Snoopy's partner stayed home. His lucky day.'

McAllister tossed the file down and stood up. Arched his back.

'That's good,' he said. 'Better that way.'

He gestured to me with the gun. The wavy stuff again. Up and down. Very casual. Like he was inviting the dog out for a piss before bed.

'Second time lucky,' he said. 'I think we can finalise things this time.' He looked at me. His eyebrows floated like cumulus clouds.

'Unless you've any other little ruses.'

I didn't have.

'Good,' McAllister said. 'So let's take that walk. And one funny move and I'll pop you. You understand, Flynn?'

I understood.

'Go out, Ray. Cover us.'

Child looked at me. 'You're going to dig this time, Flynn,' he said. 'Exercise is good for you.' He laughed and headed through the door.

Everyone's a comedian when they've got a gun.

CHAPTER FORTY
Linen's hell to uncrease

Child went out first. McAllister took the rear, out of reach and clear of Child's line of fire in case I did something clever.

Nothing clever came to mind.

Outside, Child pointed his flashlight at the ground and walked across to the gate. McAllister prodded me with his gun and stepped out behind me and we set off back to the woods.

We didn't make it.

I'd got ten paces clear of the cottage when McAllister yelled fit to scare your granny's pants off. I turned and saw him going down as a silhouette pulled the shotgun from his hands and stepped sideways out of the doorway's light. The gun snapped up, pointing at me. I hit the deck. Child turned at the gate. The doorway voice yelled at him to drop his weapon.

His answer was to loose off two shots like bombs going off. Shot fizzed over my head and smacked into the side of the cottage. The parlour window exploded. Child pumped the weapon to refill the chambers but he never pulled the triggers. The shadow rose from its crouch by the door and two booms shattered the night so close to my head that they nearly took my hair off. Child went backwards and down. By the doorway McAllister was half up, ready to come back into the game, but whatever had hit him had struck hard. He moved too slowly. As he heaved himself up the Mossberg's stock came down on his neck with a force that nearly put him through the ground. He lay there face down, groaning. Out by the gate Child was face up and quiet.

I stood up, feeling to see which side my hair had parted. My ears were ringing like the bells at a vicarage orgy.

'Am I late for the show?'

Shaughnessy's voice was a faint echo as he walked past to check Child.

'Late? You nearly missed the finale.'

McAllister was struggling up again but his heart wasn't in it. I walked across and put my foot on his back. Pressed. It was unlikely he had another weapon but there was no point taking chances.

Shaughnessy finished checking Child and came back over. The way he ignored Child's gun saved me a question.

'Looks like your pals were about to cut up rough,' Shaughnessy said.

'They told me it was just a midnight hike.'

Shaughnessy leered.

'They've a spot,' I said. 'Up in the woods.'

McAllister was still squirming and I was still pressing, hard enough to cramp my damn leg, but I'm tough. The pressure held.

'Watch his jacket,' Shaughnessy said. 'Linen's hell to get the creases out.'

I lifted my foot and stooped to grab an arm. McAllister was growling threats but he let me haul him back into the cottage where Shaughnessy tossed a pair of cuffs over. Plastic. Strong as steel. The cuffs help occasionally with citizen's arrests, which is technically what we were doing. Our arrest technique was that I kicked McAllister's ankles out and Shaughnessy pressed on his head and the bastard went down. You've got those funny bones in your buttocks that hurt like hell if you ever land on them and the way the floorboards shook I figured McAllister was going to have difficulty sitting for a week. I got his wrists into the cuffs and looped them round a central heating pipe. The pipe wouldn't hold him for long, but I rooted round and cut the cable off the TV and used it to bind his arms and ankles. Electric cabling has many uses. By the time I'd finished McAllister wasn't going anywhere, with or without the central heating.

I relieved him of my mobile phone whilst Shaughnessy dialled emergency and informed the operator that we had a shooting incident. He had our location off pat when the operator asked. The advantage of not riding in a car boot.

I checked McAllister. Trussed and weaponless, but the whack from the gun was wearing off. He got chatty again.

'I'm going to kill you, Flynn,' he told me.

I guess he'd forgotten that that was what he was trying to do in the first place. I considered pointing it out. Decided against it. By the time McAllister got the chance to make good on his threat he'd have to come after me with a Zimmer frame. I'd have one too, but mine would have racing treads.

~~~~~

We looked round the cottage. Found an upstairs bedroom with a sleeping bag on a single bed, food wrappers littering the floor. A metal chain was padlocked to the bedstead. Its other end was probably round Rebecca's neck the last week. Scattered plastic fasteners told us they'd tied her hands when they left her. We moved on. Checked a second bedroom. Found nothing to show that anyone had been here babysitting. Probably Child called once a day to feed and water Rebecca.

'How many have they had here?' Shaughnessy asked.

'My guess: just Rebecca and the Hanlon girl. But McAllister had long-term plans. His scheme was good for a couple of capers a year. That's one to two mill. steady income.'

Shaughnessy pursed his lips. 'All revolving around the fact that none of the families would blow the whistle afterwards.'

'The bastard thought he could keep it going forever,' I said. 'Why are the smartest criminals always the stupidest?'

Shaughnessy shrugged. 'Did he say how they kept the families quiet?'

'It's what we figured. Threats backed up by photos of hubby misbehaving. Belt and braces.'

'Photos starring our girl Tina Brown.'

'But she wasn't in on the scheme. All she knew was that she was being hired to show business clients a good time. She knew nothing about the blackmail or kidnapping.'

We went down.

'Do we know where she is?'

'Let's take a walk,' I said.

I checked McAllister on the way out but he was going nowhere. I wasn't thrown out of the Boy Scouts for nothing.

We took a flashlight and went out through the garden, giving Child's body a wide berth. Crime scene contamination and all that. I took Shaughnessy into the woods and up the hill to where Child's spade was planted in the ground. Shone the light on the mound of earth beside it.

'Poor woman,' Shaughnessy said. 'What did she do to get in their way?'

'She found out. She was the thing McAllister's still denying – the flaw in his perfect scheme.'

'He denying his scheme's fallen apart?'

'He figures it's just bad luck. Maybe it was. First he had bad luck with Tina Brown then he had bad luck with us. McAllister thought he had the whole thing covered. Take the kid, take the money, then shackle the family by blackmailing the husband. A perfect tie-up. His only flaw was that he didn't keep Tina isolated. He wouldn't have made that mistake again.'

'The question is how she found out.'

'Larry's going to tell us that,' I said. 'The police will get it from him but I want to hear it from the bastard's own mouth. Maybe he'll not be so reticent when he realises that he got Tina killed.'

We looked at the grave, barely visible in the torch light.

The half-dug hole next to it was harder to look at. Shaughnessy didn't ask and I didn't say.

CHAPTER FORTY-ONE
Call it a character flaw

Blue lights strobed through the trees as we walked down. When we came out into the lane two East Sussex patrol cars and two vans had pulled up a hundred yards short of the cottage and an armed response unit was dispersing behind cover.

One of them yelled at us to identify ourselves. I yelled back that it was over. The bad guys were out of action. The cops were not in trusting mood. They brought me and Shaughnessy forward and patted us down under the muzzles of semi-automatics. Then they had us wait with our hands on a patrol car roof while four of them moved through the cottage garden and went inside. A couple of minutes later they called it clear and a guy who introduced himself as their squad sergeant told us to start talking.

We handed him our IDs. Told him about the body up in the woods. He wasn't interested in the woods. He was focussed on whether there was going to be any more shooting. I reassured him; asked what McAllister had said for himself.

'Nothing,' the sergeant said. 'He's clammed up.'

'Waiting for his lawyer,' I said. 'Sign of a guilty conscience.'

They radioed details and called for support but didn't relax. Two of them stayed in the house with McAllister and they gave me and Shaughnessy the back seat of a car each. I didn't know if we were arrested or not so I guess we weren't. It was nearly eleven thirty.

My phone showed three missed calls. I called back.

'Bel, I got caught up.'

'Caught up?' There was an edge to her voice. We hadn't spoken for nearly forty-eight hours and the night out we'd arranged was in the sink. Changes of plan were nothing new to Arabel but I should have called before I rushed off to Kent. I apologised and told her that things had blown up fast. She'd see how much they'd blown up when she saw my face – and my wheels.

'Another fun night with the detective,' she said. 'You going to make it at all tonight?'

'Guess not. I'm gonna be tied up,' I said. I promised to call tomorrow. We'd set something up. I threw in a sweetener: Rebecca Townsend was safe.

Arabel's voice lifted. 'You got her, Flynn?'

'She's safe at home right now.'

A pause. 'What about the bad guys?'

'We got the bad guys too. We're just tidying up.'

The news passed muster. Arabel's voice softened. 'Be careful, babe. I don't need you to get hurt.'

I was touched. Promised caution. Didn't mention my face.

I closed the line and cleared a single text from my inbox. The message had served its purpose. It was the one McAllister had read, suggesting that Shaughnessy would call back at the office to check the Slater file, the text that took Ray Child back to London and bought me the reprieve.

Shaughnessy and I don't text each other. I'd sent the message myself from Lucy's phone. Neither were we the types to chase off to a remote farm and a probable trap without backup. The backup is usually on-scene but tonight things had happened too fast and I took a risk. Briefed Shaughnessy on where I was going and had him wait for my call. If the call didn't come in by eight p.m. he'd ride out to the farm. If there was nothing there he'd wait at the office until one of the bad guys showed up. If the bad guys read the text they might do that.

The clever scheme didn't paper over the fact that I'd misjudged things. I'd expected trouble at the farm but didn't plan on walking straight into McAllister's gunsights. And if something did go wrong I expected the action to stay at the farm until Shaughnessy gatecrashed. The ruse to divert one of the bad guys back to the office looked more desperate the longer I sat in the patrol car.

After twenty minutes things started happening. More headlights approached. Two plainclothes men appeared and went into the property. They spent a while inside then came over and asked us to step out. The man in charge introduced himself as DCS Skinner of the East Sussex police. His buddy was DS Parch. Skinner asked for IDs. He was a stocky guy in his mid-fifties with a taut face halfway to fat. I recognised a lifestyle thing. His eyes were smart, though. He listened to a rerun of our story then went back into the house. McAllister's conversational skills mustn't have improved because they were back out in two minutes. Skinner was trying to figure which way to play this. We were going to be taken in. Private detectives don't go round shooting people no matter how the heat turns up, and Skinner had a mess that only a mountain of paperwork could salve. He nodded towards the woods.

'Show me.'

We picked up a couple of flashlights and set off back into the trees with two SOCOs carrying portable lighting. When we got to the spot Skinner looked at the mound of earth.

'This is the woman?'

'Name of Tina Brown. She was mixed up in this but we don't yet know how she became a liability.'

'Don't *yet* know?' Skinner was sharp. 'Are you two figuring on carrying on with this? Am I interrupting something?'

'We just want to close a few loose ends.'

Skinner looked at his sidekick then moved up close and his eyes weren't friendly.

'Consider the ends closed,' he said. 'If I believe your tale then you've done a nice job of digging out some nasty people. It would have been much nicer, of course, if the nasty people were all still alive. So if there are any loose ends we'll be taking care of them.'

'No problem. You'll get everything we have.'

'Technically, I need to arrest you both. You'll need to spend the night in our hospitality suite whilst we check out your story and decide how the shooting will be played.'

I grinned. 'You going to cuff us?'

'I'll think about it,' Skinner said. We walked back down.

Skinner went through the arrest formality and sat us in the back of separate cars again whilst he organised things outside. He didn't say anything more about cuffs. He went into the house and brought out McAllister. McAllister's hands were cuffed. He was pushed into the back of another car then Skinner and his partner stooged around for an hour with the SOCOs. At one point Skinner pulled me and Shaughnessy back out separately and had us go through the exact sequence of the shooting. Our descriptions seemed to tie in.

Skinner and his buddy finally put us in their backseat and drove us south in convoy with McAllister's squad car. Twenty minutes later we were in Brighton.

They took us up to the CID room. Skinner sat us in separate interrogation rooms but offered coffees. Shaughnessy asked for a glass of water. I asked for black, extra strong, plenty of sugar. McAllister was taken into another room. I didn't hear anything about coffee.

Skinner took my statement and asked me to sign it. Then he told me to sit tight whilst he had another chat with McAllister. Now that McAllister was arrested I guess there was a little more formality behind his refusals to talk. Skinner was in there fifteen minutes getting the *no comment* line. When he came back he threw a weary grin.

'The bastard wants his lawyer. That's fine by me. We'll have him here first thing tomorrow. My real problem is how to play it with you two.'

'Check us out. There are people who'll vouch for us.'

I gave him Karl Dewhurst's name. Karl was a commander in the Metropolitan Police. Skinner raised his eyebrows.

'You're ex-job?'

'A while back.'

'So why the move to the private sector?'

'There were complications,' I said. 'The job no longer fit.'

Skinner looked at his watch. 'So now some Metropolitan brass is going to jump out of bed at two in the morning to vouch for you?'

I grinned. The image of Karl being pulled from his bed had an appeal. Karl and I went back. He'd vouch for me all right. He'd just need a decade afterwards to bitch about it.

Skinner looked at his buddy and made a decision. He walked across to his office to pick up Karl's number. Five minutes later he came out. Looked at me in a new way.

'It looks like you've still got admirers on high, Flynn. So how come the best detective inspector they ever had – quote, un-frigging-quote – with high-up friends, is scratching around as a private investigator?'

I gave him my shit-eater. 'Not enough of the high-ups. They only spread so far.'

'A good detective doesn't need a truckload of friends to stay in the job,' Skinner said.

I held the grin. 'Call it a character flaw.'

'Commander Dewhurst tells me I should send you home to bed,'

Skinner said. 'Probably wants me to make your Horlicks and tuck you in. Whereas the standard procedure for a couple of guys who've just shot a man is to keep them behind bars where we can keep an eye on them.' He looked at me. 'Which should I do?'

'I don't know about my partner,' I said, 'but I find Horlicks a little sickly. Going home would work, though.'

Skinner nodded.

'I want to go right through this tomorrow,' he said.

'Just tell me when you want me in.'

'First thing.'

'We'll be here,' I promised.

Skinner and his buddy were going to be tied up at the station for the rest of the night but they got a patrol car to drop us back at the cottage. The garden was lit up with arcs. Ray Child's body was gone. A couple of SOCOs were tidying up and a uniformed man was unreeling crime tape across the path into the woods. The main action had moved up there.

It was two thirty.

I climbed back into the Citroen. Child had left the keys in the ignition and a wad of chewing gum on the dashboard. ValuDrive could keep the gum. Maybe they could increase the rental. Shaughnessy's Yamaha was hidden in the trees a hundred yards down. I gave him a lift and he hopped out as Citroen stalled by the bike.

'Give my apologies to Jasmine,' I said. 'I'm sorry I ruined her evening. You told her that this was an emergency, right?'

Shaughnessy shrugged. 'I mentioned that your life was in danger. Asked her advice.'

I looked at him. Sometimes a straight answer would do.

'Tell Jasmine we'll be seeing her,' I said. 'We'll have a day out.'

'I'll do that,' Shaughnessy said. 'I'll tell her you're alive, too.'

'Let her know it was you who saved my neck,' I suggested. 'That should be good for a few brownie points.'

Shaughnessy smacked the top of the Citroen. I fired up and rolled before he could do it again.

'I'll tell her,' he said. 'Yet again.'

But I knew he wouldn't.

Yet again.

CHAPTER FORTY-TWO
As you probably know, the car's not running very well

I hit the sack at four and stared at the ceiling for two hours. Whenever I dozed off I was snapped awake by images of trees and darkness. I quit trying. Got up and pulled on my running gear and headed out into a calm spring morning. Ran three laps of the park, snail slow. Added another to prove I still had willpower. Pushed the pace until I was overtaking the first of the morning runners and arrived at the Sun Gate gasping like a bulldog in a sauna.

I kept up a jog for appearances but back inside the door the act failed. I barely made it to the top of the stairs. I stood for twenty minutes under a lukewarm shower and let needles of water batter my head. My cheek had swelled up nicely and the water stung where it hit. The mirror told me that the thing needed a few stitches. I made do with Savlon and a plaster. Then I called Shaughnessy, drank orange juice and headed out into bright sunshine.

The Citroen went through its start-up act and clunked away south against the rush hour and I began to feel half human. Even the shit-heap's asthmatic progress was less depressing in the sunshine.

I was in Brighton by eight thirty. Found a café round the corner from the police station and gave Shaughnessy the location. Then I boosted my spirits and cholesterol with a full English. It was the first thing I'd eaten in twenty hours and it slid down as if bacon grease was the new super-lubricant. I was mopping up with the last slice of bread when Shaughnessy came in. He ordered fruit juice and watched me like a disapproving aunt. I called the police station. Confirmed that Skinner was waiting. We paid up and left.

A uniformed woman took us up to CID. As we went in I spotted a face through the open door of a holding room. On the far side of a metal table James Roker's expression betrayed the ugly mood of someone rousted at the crack of dawn. I'd given Skinner the details of Alpha Security's involvement and I guess he'd read our file. Roker had a few questions to answer. Skinner's buddy Parch was in the room. I stopped at the door. Our escort tried to keep me moving but I resisted until Roker saw me. He gave me a look.

It was going to take more than looks.

'How's it going, Jimmy?' I said.

'Fuck you, Flynn.'

Some you can never talk to.

'Have you told them how you set it up? They seen the dirty movies? Those guys with Tina?'

Roker raised a hand and gave me an emphatic bird.

Spirit.

I threw in something to dampen it.

'Have they told you they've dug Tina up?' I was making an assumption but I was on safe ground. 'It's a murder rap, Roker. I guess that's the chance you take when you work dirty jobs. Go for Queen's Evidence is my advice.'

Parch had jumped up and was slamming the door in my face. The last I saw of Roker he was giving me the bird again and the feeling he put into it suggested that he understood his situation perfectly. As we walked away the door opened again and Parch skipped out to escort us the rest of the way. He gave me a filthy look.

Skinner had us in for two hours, going over the details, and Parch came in for part of it. The two had been on the job since last night.

Skinner gave us a little info. in return. He was just in from the morgue, viewing the body they'd brought out of the woods. The body was Tina Brown's. I'd known it but it was still a blow. Somewhere along the way Tina had become our adopted client. I'd hoped to see her safe, and preferably innocent, back home along with Rebecca Townsend. Now I had to call Sammy.

I took them through the whole thing: McAllister's scheme and the part Alpha Security had played. When Skinner had everything he needed to go back and continue their chats with both McAllister and Roker he sat back and puffed his cheeks; exchanged a look with Parch.

'This could have gone on indefinitely,' he said. 'If you can keep the families quiet there's no reason a racket like this couldn't run on and on.'

'That's what McAllister thought,' Shaughnessy said. 'Another guy with the perfect crime.'

'McAllister probably thinks he was just unlucky,' Skinner said.

I nodded. 'He'd be right. You wouldn't expect some upstart college girl to blow the whistle when her friend's family are shutting her out. And McAllister didn't anticipate the Tina Brown problem. So maybe he *was* unlucky. But sooner or later something would have come apart because McAllister wasn't going to stop until it did. He didn't see that that was the flaw in his scheme.'

'What went wrong with Tina Brown?'

'Larry Slater knows that,' I said.

Skinner flipped his notepad shut. He was scheduling a trip to see the Slaters as soon as they'd cleared things up at this end. He turfed us out and we headed back to town. I was back at Chase Street just after midday.

I parked the ZX on Gerry Lye's spot and watched a little guy with a cord jacket and clipboard prodding the Frogeye's carcass. The insurance company, quick off the mark. I identified myself as the owner.

'Bit of a mess,' the guy said.

You can't fool these people.

'A write-off,' I agreed. 'Unless you know a good paint shop.'

The guy looked at me po-faced. He was the type who only recognises humour when it comes from his own lips. 'I'll put in the report,' he said. 'We'll see.'

'Sure, but you agree the car's a write-off?'

He stayed noncommittal. 'The company makes the decision. I just confirm the condition of the vehicle.'

I gave him aghast.

'You think they can resurrect this?'

'Not for me to say, Mr Flynn.'

I looked at the guy. I'd had assessors before. They're usually working mechanics from the body shops. It looked like this company had its own department dedicated to stupidity. *Stupid* was the only way you could categorise a guy being cagey about a heap of ashes. But what the hell? If the insurance company wanted to resurrect the Frogeye they were welcome. The guy knew and I knew that the car was dead. I turned and walked away.

~~~~~

The day had topped out at eighteen degrees. Spring had sprung. We drove up through Cricklewood onto the North Circular. The heat coerced me into braving the din of the Citroen's blowing exhaust to let fresh air in but when I tried to wind the window down this time it seized. If I forced it further the mechanism would snap and leave it permanently open. I wound it back up; tried the fan in the hope that it might have cured itself; got the same wash of warm air as yesterday. I killed the fan. Gripped the wheel. Sweated.

We quit the North Circular and drove along the HP Logistics fence. The barrier was up, just like last time. Unlike last time I didn't make the courtesy stop, and even the Citroen was fast enough to beat the pensioner.

We parked outside the maintenance entrance and went up.

Godmotherzilla was still manning the defences. She must have recognised me because she came up from behind her counter as if she'd been stung in her main target area.

Trouble is, when you're big you're not fast. We were past her and into Harold Palmer's office before she could tear off even one of my limbs. She came huffing behind but I slammed the door and put my back to it and after a few seconds rapping she got the message and backed off.

Palmer had jumped out of his own chair across the office and was standing like a bull in the arena, watching us with popping eyes. His panoramic window had been replaced. It looked much the same as the old one.

'What the hell is this?' Palmer said. 'I'm calling the cops!'

He reached for his phone.

'Better listen first,' I said.

He paused.

'That was a mistake,' I said.

'What the hell are you talking about?' Palmer said.

'You'd made your point,' I said, 'and I'd made mine. Better we'd left it at that.'

'You're not making sense. Get the hell out.'

'I'm talking about knowing when to stop. I was out of your life. No threat to your little scheme to get your haulage contract.' I grinned. 'A company called Fashion-Ex. We dug out their name.'

Palmer came over to go chest to chest with me.

'HP's business is nothing to do with you. You declined our

commission, Flynn.'

'Yeah. Your illegal scheme lacked appeal. That's why I walked away. Better if you'd left it at that.'

Palmer leaned forward. 'What are you saying?'

'I'm saying you shouldn't start fires you can't put out.'

That got him. The bastard couldn't hold back a sneer. 'So how's your toy car running?' he said. He was still leaning, trying to push me back. I stayed put.

'As you probably know, the car's not running very well at all.'

Palmer laughed. 'Pity. I heard it was vintage.'

I stared into his eyes. 'That was a stupid thing to do, Harold.'

His laugh finished in a smirk. 'Are you accusing me of something, pal?'

'You had to have the last shot,' I said. 'But I guess it's the kind of man you are. The trouble is, that kind of thing can rebound.'

'You're accusing me?' Palmer was amused.

'You burned my car out of spite because I wouldn't work your little scheme. Yeah, I'm accusing you.'

'Prove it! Prove there was any scheme with Fashion-Ex.' His eyes closed up suddenly. 'Are you taping this?' he said. 'Is that it? Are you trying to incriminate me? You take me for an idiot?'

I shook my head. 'This is just between us.'

'Then take this as just between us: you've got nothing that proves anything, Mr Mer-Reject. Nothing about Fashion-Ex and nothing about your poxy little car.'

'I assume you found another firm to steal your info?'

Palmer laughed again and stood back, shaking his head.

'You're a joke, Flynn. I'm not telling you anything. But yeah, we're ready with our bid. And yeah, we got the information we needed.'

I grinned. 'You're in trouble if you don't get that contract, Palmer? All those units idle?'

'We're going to get the contract. Believe me.'

'Unless your illegal spying game gets out.'

Palmer sneered. 'If you put one whisper onto the street, Flynn, I'll sue you for everything you have. How come it needs two of you to come threaten me?' He looked at my companion. 'You're a real talker, mate,' he said. 'The two of you make a good act.'

I turned to the guy at my side. 'Do you need to talk?' I said.

The guy looked at Palmer. Shook his head. 'No. I've heard enough,' he said.

Palmer looked from one of us to the other. 'What is this?' he said. He took a step back.

The guy handed Palmer a card. Palmer scanned it and his face froze.

The card wasn't Eagle Eye's. The card had the logo of Fashion-Ex and the name of Andrew O'Connor, Purchasing Director. O'Connor didn't need to say anything. Not even *Save the postage on the bid*, which in his shoes I would have said. But Palmer's pop-eyed look told us that he understood that his bid was dead in the water.

We left him to it and walked out.

Back at the Citroen O'Connor whistled.

'We owe you, Eddie,' he said. 'If they'd put in the rigged bid we'd have swallowed it. We'd have had Palmer running our logistics for the next two years. Working with criminals we can do without.'

'Just a little tit for tat. We were going to keep our nose out, but Harold tipped the scales.'

O'Connor shook his head. 'To think he burned your car. You'd think a firm would be above that.'

'An organisation stoops to the level of its highest officers,' I noted. 'In this case they had to stoop low.'

O'Connor smiled. 'How were you so sure it was Palmer who torched your car?'

'It would never have occurred to me,' I said. 'We've had far more likely suspects on our plate recently. It was just a face in the wrong place.'

We were back at the gatehouse. The same old guy came out and raised the exit barrier with a scowl on his face. HP were a company of scowlers.

Behind the guy, through the glass, I saw the face I'd seen at the Podium two nights back, just before the Frogeye went up. Palmer had set his security man a little out-of-hours assignment. The guy must have followed me that night and seen his chance to go for the car while I was at the club. It had taken a day or two for the image to click, but when it did I knew who'd burned the Frogeye. Not McAllister after all. The joke was that Harold Palmer had unwittingly turned up the heat on McAllister's operation. Maybe it made no difference. Events have a momentum of their own, but I like to think that Palmer helped us move faster on McAllister.

As the barrier lifted, the guy behind the glass looked up and spotted me. I saluted and he returned a look of surprise. Knowing HP Logistics' shaky financial condition the guy would probably be scanning the job ads next week.

Maybe he could try for insurance assessor.

~~~~~

I was back in the office by three.

Shaughnessy was catching up on stuff and Lucy was out. I was at a loose end, lacking the case files to close off the Rebecca Townsend job and in no mood to go back to my company-exec telephone trawling.

I'd already called Gina Redding and told her that her commission was closed. Explained that the agency couldn't take credit for Rebecca's reappearance. Gina didn't care. All that mattered was the girl. And we'd caught the bad guys. The family were free.

I angled my Herman Miller back and was reclining behind my desk in an indecisive daze when Shaughnessy came through. He flopped into a club chair.

'You going to talk to them, Eddie?'

I nodded. 'I want to close off the Tina Brown connection. I figure Larry will talk now. He already knows the police are on their way.'

We heard steps on the stairs. The outer door opened and Lucy came trotting through.

'Hey, you guys are heroes! You got the girl.'

'The Slaters paid the ransom and Rebecca was sent home,' I corrected her. 'We weren't involved.'

'But you got the villains. You've stopped this happening to anyone else.'

'That's what Gina Redding said. She seemed happy about it.'

'Happy enough to pay the bill?' Lucy's eye was on the bottom line.

'Send it out,' I said.

'Wilco. I'll pay the water people tomorrow. Maybe even me.'

'Sure. Clear your back-pay, Luce. Take a bonus.' I was throwing money around.

And maybe my insurance company would throw some cash my way so I could get some new wheels and save the ValuDrive rental.

The phone rang in the outer office and Lucy went to take it. She came back in a hurry.

'It's Jean Slater,' she said.

Life's surprises. Shaughnessy and I looked at each other.

I pushed myself out of my chair and went out to take the call.

If I was expecting to hear grateful on the other end I was disabused. What I heard was panic.

'Mr Flynn?' Jean's voice was desperate. 'Something's happened. We need to see you.'

CHAPTER FORTY-THREE
Pretend I'm OK

The Citroen stalled twice before I got to the street. I coaxed it back to life and progressed on three and a half cylinders towards Swiss Cottage. I tried to jump the crawling traffic on the main road but whenever I put my foot down I hit a flat spot. The Citroen bucked and lost power and the crawling traffic drove round me with horns blasting. Twenty-five minutes of white-knuckle got me to Hampstead.

The house door opened before I was out of the car. Jean Slater. Tears on her face. She urged me in to where Larry was sitting forlornly in the lounge. Yesterday's assertiveness was absent. Now Jean was the one making the play. She didn't wait for me to ask.

'Rebecca's gone,' she said.

She picked up a sheet of paper from the coffee table. It trembled in her hand. Larry stayed quiet, his face a mixture of disapproval and confusion. Two sentences were scripted in red felt-tip across the sheet:

Pretend I'm OK. That always works.

'We thought she was asleep but when I went into her room I found the note.'

'Have the police called yet?'

Jean shook her head. 'They said they'd be here early evening.'

'Did they say what they wanted to talk about?'

'They know about Rebecca's kidnapping. They've caught the people responsible.'

I nodded. 'They've got the main guy. Name of McAllister.' I looked at Slater. The name still produced no reaction.

'What you told me yesterday about Rebecca being ill...' I said. 'We're not pretending anymore?'

'We're not pretending anything any more,' Jean said.

'What's Rebecca been doing since yesterday?'

'She's just stayed in her room.'

'She come out for meals?'

'No. I've just taken a few snacks in. She only came down for half an hour this morning because my sister called.'

Kathy Pope.

'Does your sister know what's been going on?'

Jean shook her head. 'She was here before the police phoned. We were still trying to keep it quiet. She noticed that Rebecca was off-colour but we told her that she was recovering from flu.'

Still the lie.

'What else did Rebecca do today? Did she mention going out?'

'No. She was in her room sleeping and listening to music. She wouldn't talk to me. She didn't want lunch.'

'A reaction to what's happened?'

Jean looked away. 'I thought she was okay. She was emotional at first when they brought her back. Assumed we'd call the police right away. We had to explain how these people could still hurt us. Larry managed to persuade her that it was best to keep the police out.'

'Has Rebecca talked to anyone apart from Sadie?'

'She may have done. She had her phone. Now it's switched off.'

'Might she be with Sadie?'

'I've called her. Gina Redding too. They haven't seen her.'

'When exactly did *you* last see her?'

Jean Slater tried to pull her thoughts together; hit a dead end.

Larry Slater finally spoke: 'Jean went up at twelve. Rebecca spoke to her but wouldn't come out of her room. Then my wife went up about an hour later to break the news that the police were coming to see us. That's when she found the note.'

So she'd been gone three hours.

'She probably needs time alone,' I said. 'She may be on her way to Sadie's right now.'

'The note doesn't sound like that,' Jean said. 'I'm frightened to death she might do something foolish. If she was going to see Sadie she would have called her.'

'Has Rebecca ever tried to hurt herself?'

Jean shook her head. 'No. She's highly strung but she's sensible.'

But maybe sensible wasn't enough this time. Even the strongest person would find something lacking when they got home from their nightmare to face the Slaters' wall of denials. Before the police contacted them the Slaters had been fixated on hiding what happened. Maybe for Rebecca being in the house was worse than being alone. My guess was that she'd gone off to take a breather. Anywhere but this house. She probably just needed time to catch up. I didn't know the girl or how badly she was hurting so it was just guesswork. Mostly though, I didn't know why Jean Slater had called me. This was nothing to do with what went before. The agency wasn't in the social services business, like I'd told Sadie Bannister right at the start. But Jean was looking at me with a desperation in her face.

'Is there any way you can find her? I want her home.'

Needles in haystacks – Eagle Eye's speciality. One girl. The whole of London. And barely a hunch.

I looked at the misery in Jean Slater's face.

'I'll find her,' I said.

~~~~~

The whole of London. One girl. The thing might daunt some. But sometimes you get lucky. My hunch panned out: I found Rebecca inside twenty minutes.

I parked the Citroen on the Inner Circle of Regent's Park and walked across to the café. The place was just closing up but there was a scattering of customers still inside. Rebecca had a table by the window. She was nursing a cappuccino that had gone cold a couple of hours ago. She looked up and her face pulled up a tired smile.

'Eddie,' she said. There was no surprise in her voice. As if she'd taken it for granted that someone would find her. More likely it was just indifference. I sat down.

'How you doing, Rebecca?'

She took her time, continued watching the world outside. She'd fixed herself up. Her hair had lost yesterday's dull stringiness. It was washed and flowing over her shoulders in a gleaming black river. Her face was what her mother's would have been two decades earlier, skin so clear it was almost translucent. But the unhappiness in her eyes was plain to see. The last week had taken its toll.

We watched the trees.

There were a couple of grey squirrels darting round in the

branches. I recalled a day trip from Yorkshire when I was a kid, feeding the same squirrels one autumn afternoon in Hyde Park before heading back to King's Cross. Different time, different world.

'Did Sadie really go hiring a private eye?'

I pulled my attention back. Rebecca was watching me. The clouds had drawn back a little. This was the one thing she could hang on to. A world where you could depend on crazy friends.

I hid my grimace in a smile. 'Your friend had the idea that she could just walk into an agency and have half a dozen heavies on your tail in ten minutes. Sadie's an interesting girl.'

The clouds stayed parted. 'Yeah,' Rebecca conceded, 'She's okay. Just a little nutty.'

Nutty! Finally I could give Lucy exact instructions: keep the damn nuts out of my office.

'She was going to pay us out of her savings account,' I said. 'I didn't ask how much she'd got in there.'

Rebecca's eyebrows arched as she dug through her memory. 'A bit over three hundred,' she recalled.

Three hundred! So Sadie would have shafted us after all!

'Luckily,' I said, 'your friend Gina had a little more capital. And she went along with Sadie's idea that someone should find out what was going on.'

'Yeah. At least someone cared.'

'Your family cared, Rebecca. I think they've been through hell.'

She said nothing.

'Did those people hurt you?'

She shook her head. 'They just chained me up. Left me to rot. One guy really scared me, though.'

Ray Child. Not someone you'd leave your kids with. My guess was that the only thing that had reined him in from harming his charges was that McAllister's scheme depended on the kids staying safe. It would be difficult to keep the families quiet if their children were brought home hurt or raped. The problem was that Rebecca hadn't known about the scheme. Having Ray Child as a jailer for ten days was not an experience any young girl would appreciate.

'They feed you okay?'

Rebecca grimaced. 'Crap! Cold pizza. Sandwiches. Soft drinks. I got so I was nearly throwing up. They had soap and water but the water was cold. And I had to use one of those chamber pots. That was the worst thing. That and the way the guy kept looking at me. I never knew when he was going to do more than just look.'

Ten days with some very unpleasant people. That's a hard thing to put behind you. But the hardest bit had probably been when Rebecca got home and was told to bottle it.

'That must suck,' I said. 'Your parents wanting to keep it a secret.'

Rebecca stayed quiet; stared at her coffee. Her voice was tiny when she spoke again.

'That's all they're interested in. Pretending the whole thing didn't happen. Larry insists that the men will hurt us unless we keep quiet. So I'm supposed to lie to Sadie and Gina and everyone else.'

She looked at me. 'I guess eventually they'll even convince themselves that it never happened. I told Larry no way I was keeping it quiet but my mother got in such a state I felt like I'd be hurting her if I let it out. That's what it comes down to, their own fears. Like they'd got a stolen car back. No harm done. Just a few scratches. Don't call the insurance company. Keep the no-claims.'

The last of the customers had walked out and the staff were busy cleaning. We were alone.

'It's as if what happened didn't matter,' Rebecca said. 'When you came to the house yesterday we all just lied. Then the same thing when my aunt called this morning. She asked how I was and Larry started this whole thing about how I'd had the flu. It's a little play we have to perform over and over. The story of how nothing happened to me.'

A single tear expanded in the corner of one eye.

'It's over,' I said. 'The play won't be running any more.'

She looked at me.

'The men who took you have been caught. They'd taken another girl before you and were planning more kidnappings, but it's over. There's no threat against your family. No need to keep the secret.'

She said nothing. Her eyes flicked back to the world outside and dislodged the tear. It rolled down her cheek. She blinked and looked back.

'Are they really caught?'

'The police have arrested the people involved.'

'Was it you who caught them?'

'We were involved. It's police business now. They'll be calling at your house later and they'll need to talk to you all. And they aren't interested in lies.'

'But it was you who got them?'

We seemed to be stuck on this point.

'You can thank Sadie. She set us on their tail.'

The clouds drew back. The hint of a smile again, but there was still a shadow behind it.

'Will we really be safe? Maybe they can get back at us some time.'

I shook my head. Reached across and took her hand. 'Rebecca, your family are of no interest to these people. They only needed to threaten you so they were free to kidnap other kids. That's all changed. The men won't be abducting anyone else.'

'So they'll go to jail?'

I released her hand.

'One of them will. The big guy – the one who frightened you – had an accident last night. He didn't make it.'

She watched me.

'It's over, Rebecca,' I repeated.

We waited for a while longer. The light was fading. Staff circled us armed with mops.

'How did you know I was here?' Rebecca asked finally.

'I'm a detective. I analysed your note.'

Her mouth opened wide enough to drive a train through.

'Bull-*shit!*'

Kids!

The woman wiping the table next to us gave us a look.

'There was nothing *in* my note. I was just angry. I wrote the first thing that came into my head and ran out of the back door. I didn't know where I was going myself.'

'That's what the note told me. That's how I knew where to find you. You couldn't charge round to sob on Sadie's or Gina's shoulders because you thought it was all still a secret. Seeing them would have made things worse. You ran out with the secret bottled up inside you and nowhere to go.'

She was watching me like I was a mind-reader. One of the skills of the profession.

'I talked to your ex- last week,' I explained. Rebecca kept her face straight but her eyes gleamed a little. 'Marcus told me how you'd come here to sit and watch the world, think things through.'

A smile finally reached her eyes.

'He also told me to make sure you were safe. He seemed pretty emphatic on that point.'

She smiled some more.

'I guess this whole thing – getting kidnapped, held to ransom – was just icing on the cake. From what I hear it's been a bad couple of months.'

'Yeah. It's been a shitty year so far.'

'I got the impression that Marcus was having the same bad time. Maybe you should talk to him. You need his number?'

She laughed and rolled her eyes. 'You think I need a detective to give me my boyfriend's number? I'm not that stupid.'

The café woman finally pounced and snatched Rebecca's mug, started wiping the table. I sensed a hint.

'You need a lift?' I offered. 'I still need to talk to your father.'

'Yeah. That would be great. But he's not my father.'

I said nothing.

We stood up and she turned to me. 'Sadie said you had this cute little car,' she said.

I gave her my shit-eater. Held it wide.

'She told you that?' I said.

CHAPTER FORTY-FOUR
Surely they didn't...

Jean Slater raced out and smothered Rebecca in a bear hug. I saw the weight come off her shoulders as the girl pushed her face into her neck. No more secrets. When the two of them unclinched I followed them into the house.

Jean offered a drink. I declined.

'I just need a word with Larry,' I said.

Jean gestured to the lounge. She couldn't care less. She and Rebecca walked up the stairs.

Larry was sitting where he'd been two hours ago but had been joined by a half-empty bottle of scotch. Easing his own burden in his own way.

'Better go steady,' I said. 'You'll need your wits when CID arrives.'

He looked up at me.

'Where did you find her?'

'Where she often is. Alone.'

He thought about it. Concluded nothing. Switched topics. 'So: you chased these people down,' he said

'They chased us. It came to the same thing.'

He reached forward; poured another shot.

'I only wanted to protect Rebecca,' he said. 'The money was nothing.'

'Maybe protecting the family should have started the night you were offered a good time with Tina Brown.'

'Jesus,' Slater said. 'How was I to know what they were up to?'

'I spoke to another family. The guy was cast the same bait. Same place, same woman. He didn't bite. Their child didn't get taken.'

Slater cracked his glass down and jabbed a finger.

'Well fuck *you*, Flynn. You *and* your preaching.'

'Events are the best preachers,' I said. 'You reap what you sow, and all that. But if you'd kept your hands off Tina Brown then your stepdaughter wouldn't have been put through this.'

'We'll make sure she's all right,' said Slater. 'Whatever it takes. We're not monsters.'

224

A somewhat vacuous assurance from a guy showing the unhealthy interest recorded in his stepdaughter's diary.

'What about Tina?' I said. 'Will she be okay?'

'You tell me. I don't know what the hell's going on with Tina.'

So the police hadn't told him.

'I'm trying to square the details,' I said. 'Figure how Tina derailed McAllister's scheme.'

'Well you're talking to the wrong guy. I don't know what the hell she was up to. She said she knew nothing about Rebecca's kidnapping.'

'She didn't. All she knew was that she was being paid to entertain McAllister's business contacts.'

Slater looked up.

'She wasn't in on the blackmail?'

'No. That's why she became a liability.'

Slater swore; retrieved his glass.

'Fill me in,' I said. 'My guess is that it started that first night in Brighton. You liked what you tasted. Wanted more. Tina had strict orders – no follow-up contact – but you made her an offer she couldn't refuse.'

'She's a stunning woman,' Slater admitted. 'I was out of my mind. I persuaded her to see me again.'

'How many times?'

'Three. Once here in London. Twice back in Brighton.'

'The very thing McAllister needed to avoid,' I said. 'You got to know Tina. You found out who she was and where she lived.'

'I dropped her off at her place a couple of times. She didn't hide from me.'

'Then one day the bomb exploded. Rebecca went missing and you got a call from the bad guys.'

'The big one with the shaved head came here,' Slater said. 'Came right into the house. Right where you're standing. Jesus, he was a frightening bastard. You always know there's this underworld operating, but here it was right in my living room.'

'Ray Child. He told you the deal: no police, not during and not after. And he showed you the stuff they'd collected to help the "after" bit.'

Slater's shoulders dropped. 'He laid it all out. If we wanted Rebecca back we kept the police out and paid the ransom. Then my job was to keep Jean and Rebecca quiet afterwards. He showed me the movie stills. The stupid thing is that the blackmail should have convinced me that they were serious about returning Rebecca, but I wasn't thinking straight. I saw us handing over the cash and Rebecca staying missing. I assumed Tina was in on it. She denied everything but I didn't believe her.' He drained the scotch; planted the glass; rubbed his palms over his face. 'I tried to persuade Tina to help me. When she told me she knew nothing I kind of lost it with her. The next time I called her she was gone.'

'Unfortunately she was telling the truth. But my guess is that she didn't think it through after you confronted her. She just stormed in to see McAllister and threatened to blow the whistle. That's why she disappeared.'

Slater looked at me.

'Twenty-four hours after Tina threatened him McAllister had solved the problem.'

Slater stared. 'Sweet Jesus – surely they didn't...'

'The police identified her body this morning.'

That finished him. Slater put his head in his hands and shuddered.

'The bastards!' he said. 'And she knew nothing!'

'She knew nothing until you talked to her. The two of you were the flaw in McAllister's scheme. Tina was supposed to remain the anonymous girl in the blackmail pictures. See nothing, hear nothing. But when you talked her into seeing you again you started a crack in the caper that put her right into the firing line.'

Slater's head stayed down as I left.

~~~~~

As I got out of the house my phone rang.

'Babe! You coming to get me?'

Arabel.

'Where are you?'

'Work. My shift ends in thirty.'

'I'll be there,' I said. 'What are we doing?'

I heard a laugh with an undertone. 'You owe me for last night, Flynn. I've told the girls you're taking me somewhere swanky.'

'You're looking for a special night?'

'Got it in one.'

Something special. I looked at the Citroen. The suspension had dropped further. The exhaust was now dragging along the ground, the result of Child hammering it along that track last night. The thing was a zombie of the auto world. Not quite dead but only capable of moving in lurches.

'What time are you out?'

'Seven thirty.'

'Come out of the main entrance,' I said. 'Bring the girls. I'll drive by and sweep you away.'

There was a happy laugh from the other end.

'You're the best, babe,' Arabel said.

'Aye,' I said, 'ain't that the truth.'

I killed the line.

THE END

ACKNOWLEDGEMENTS

You're holding this book thanks to the vision of two organisations – New Writing North and Business Education Publishers. The people there saw an opening for a fresh imprint within the British crime writing scene dedicated to bringing new – and maybe different – writing to the market. Moth Publications is the result of that vision and I was lucky enough to be selected as one of their first authors.

For their determination to bring their venture to fruition, as well as for their faith in this book and their work to get it into the marketplace, I'd like to thank Andrea Murphy of Moth Publishing and Claire Malcolm and Olivia Chapman of New Writing North, together with their production teams.

Writing the book was fun. Polishing it into a form where a reader might also enjoy it felt a little more like work. Considerable help in that task was given by Sarah Porter at Moth, whose ear for what is right and what is wrong has kept out flaws that might otherwise have spoiled things. Imperfections that remain are all mine, and my technique for dealing with these is to ask you to overlook them. If you did enjoy the book, scuff marks and all, maybe we'll meet again...

THE DEVIL'S SNARE
Michael Donovan

They call them the "Killer Couple". Accused of slaying their daughter the
Barbers have been on the run from public opinion for two years.

But the Barbers are still fighting. And if their high profile campaign to
clear their name and get their baby back has made them rich that was
never their intention.

Meanwhile a failed prosecution hasn't dampened the media's hunger for
revelations. Their investigators are on the job, moving towards an
exposure that will spotlight the Barbers as the killers they are. And now a
dangerous vigilante has joined the fray: if the system can't bring justice
he'll mete out his own.

P.I. Eddie Flynn doesn't read the tabloids. Shuns limelight. Trusts only in
facts. But can't resist challenges. When the Barbers come to him for help
he pushes judgement aside and signs up. His mission: keep them safe and
find their child.

Sounds like nice, solid detective work. Until Flynn realises that his clients
are hiding something...

'A slick, dynamic mystery.'
Kirkus Reviews

'Escapism at its best'
Postcard Reviews

'... complicated ... wonderful ... brilliant. I recommend anyone ...
to try this book. [It] will haunt your days and nights.'
Georgia Cuthbertson, Cuckoo Review

www.michaeldonovancrime.com

COLD CALL
Michael Donovan

In the black of night the intruder breaks into a house armed with a knife and garrotte. A woman's body is found thirty hours later, a mass of stab wounds, a deadly laceration round her neck.

Is this the Diceman, killing again after seven years lying low? Or does London have a copycat killer?

P.I. Eddie Flynn has been out of that world since his failed hunt for the serial killer let him go free and cost him his job in the Metropolitan Police.

Now, with the new killer on the rampage a bizarre phone call from the grave drags Flynn right back to centre stage and a new hunt. But this killer – copycat or not – takes a P.I.'s interference personally.

So now he has a new focus for his madness.

'Chilling ... crafted with style...
wild nightmarish scenes.'
Bookpleasures

'Masterful... If you haven't been
introduced to Eddie Flynn yet, be prepared.'
Red City Review

www.michaeldonovancrime.com